PENGU

COUNT

Nicholas Royle was born in Sale in Cheshire in 1963. He is the author of over sixty short stories, which have been published in magazines such as *The Fred*, *aBeSea*, *Sunk Island Review* and *Interzone*, and in the anthologies *In Dreams* and *Sugar Sleep* (to name but two). He was the 1993 winner of the best short story prize in the British Fantasy Awards and edited the award-winning anthologies *Darklands* and *Darklands 2*. Nicholas Royle now lives in London, where he works as a journalist.

Counterparts is his first novel.

NICHOLAS ROYLE

COUNTERPARTS

PENGUIN BOOKS

PENGUIN BOOKS

Published by the Penguin Group
Penguin Books Ltd, 27 Wrights Lane, London W8 5TZ, England
Penguin Books USA Inc., 375 Hudson Street, New York, New York 10014, USA
Penguin Books Australia Ltd, Ringwood, Victoria, Australia
Penguin Books Canada Ltd, 10 Alcorn Avenue, Toronto, Ontario, Canada M4V 3B2
Penguin Books (NZ) Ltd, 182–190 Wairau Road, Auckland 10, New Zealand

Penguin Books Ltd, Registered Offices: Harmondsworth, Middlesex, England

First published by Barrington Books 1993
Published in Penguin Books 1995
1 3 5 7 9 10 8 6 4 2

Verse by Terri Walker

Counterparts is a work of fiction. Any character resemblance to people living or dead is purely coincidental. All the events taking place in this book are imaginary.

Printed in England by Clays Ltd, St Ives plc

Thanks and acknowledgements to the following: Professor Ashley Montagu for anthropological advice; Dr Adele Fielding for medical advice; *Piercing Fans International Quarterly* for inspiration; Bella and Berni for the squat; Zoran Petrovic for St George's Hospital; Andrea Wedekind, Fraser McIlwraith, Isabelle Poittevin for places to sleep; Bill Doherty for giving me the chance to work with Brad and Sean; Kim Stanley Robinson for shelter; Stuart Appleton and Russell Twisk for photocopying facilities.

And thanks for help, encouragement and support to Mum, Dad, Jools, Jo, Simon, Alice, Rada and Julie Akhurst, Clive Barker, JB Barzo-Reinke, Thomas Bauduret, Giuliana Becciu, Jean-Daniel Brèque, Chloë Bryan-Brown, Heather Budge-Reid, Alison Campbell, Ramsey Campbell, Peter Craze, Ian Cunningham, Ellen Datlow, Camillo Di Biase, Dennis Etchison, Vicky Faul, Chris Fowler, John Gilbert, Susannah Hickling, Judy Hines, Brian Howell, Wendy Howitt, Steve Jones, Graham Joyce, Roz Kaveney, Nigel Kendall, Chris Kenworthy, Par Kumaraswami, Julian Kurer, Joel Lane, Ken McDonald, Dominic Midgley, Mark Morris, Kim Newman, Caroline North, Phil Nutman, David Pringle, Brian Radcliffe, Dill Roberts, Jim Rowntree, Clarissa Rushdie, Mike Smith, Jenny Snowdon, Nick Summers, Dave Sutton, Karl Edward Wagner, Terri Walker, Di Wathen, Mike Wathen, Nel Whatmore, Conrad Williams, Doug Winter, Liz Young.

For Mum and Dad
and to the memory of Robert Ground

Contents

Part I—The Wire

Part II—The Rail

The Wire

First Cut

Asleep, he lies there for hours, then rises from the bed and walks to the kitchen. The newspapers are piled high in a cupboard under the sink. He takes an armful and returns to the bedroom. He spreads them out and they cover the floor, several sheets thick, in a semi-circle around him as he perches on the edge of the mattress. He sits there without moving for some time as if deep in thought. But he's still fast asleep and not thinking at all.

The razor blade hovers like a guillotine. The fingers holding it tremble slightly, as if reluctant to begin. Sweat causes the blade to slip. It dips and turns, flashing, before landing with a little crash on the paper. He wipes his fingers, picks up the blade and slices into the flesh.

The blood comes first, followed by the pain, which he blocks in his sleep. Now he carefully inserts a double thickness of paper tissue into the cut to stop it knitting.

Then he blacks out.

An hour later he rises from the floor, his forearms and thighs stained with blood and newsprint.

He collects the newspaper into a single pile and buries it in the dustbin. Back in the bedroom he straightens a small table and picks up the paperback thriller which had fallen off it. He gets into bed.

When the sun wakes him a few hours later he recollects nothing.

The Archway

He chose Hungerford Bridge and Waterloo Bridge, attracted by the curve in the river. Drawing a straight line between them would create a geometry which might stimulate his performance.

Gargan disembarked at Temple and walked by the river, down Victoria Embankment and on to Waterloo Bridge. He looked across at Hungerford and watched a train scuttling through the mesh of iron. Not yet ready to walk it, he sized it up. How far was it? Three hundred yards, maybe, from centre to centre.

It had surely been further in East Berlin slanting diagonally over the River Spree. The walk had gone well, the wire behaving perfectly, the wind a mere breath sufficient to dry his sweat. Crowds had gathered on the banks. The appearance of the police had spurred him on to walk faster, but they failed to see the joke and arrested him. Dissatisfied with his statement, they decided to contact his embassy, but when Gargan explained he was of dual nationality they seemed to lose heart and simply ordered him out of Berlin.

The restaurant was just filling up. Its mix of features – European menu, informal atmosphere, West End location, low prices – had endeared the restaurant to an interesting cross-section: students, American tourists, provincial families, fashionable young people, and a steady trickle of commuters. Gargan shared his table with two women with lacquered hair and *Daily Expresses*; and three expensively dressed Italian boys, groomed, smoking and talking loudly in Roman accents.

Gargan ordered. His food arrived within minutes and the Italians, upwind, lit up fresh cigarettes. The two women followed their example and the stuffed aubergine became smoked aubergine, making him wish he'd ordered fish.

Born in Czechoslovakia to an Irish mother, Gargan never knew his father, thought to be an Australian – possibly with Aboriginal blood – from a touring theatre group on the last leg of a ground-breaking tour of Eastern Europe.

His early years were spent on the move from city to city in the East. He vaguely recalled the frequent presence of a man, though not necessarily the same one from week to week. While their backdrop shifted from Prague to Budapest, to Sófia and Bucharest, his mother's activities remained lively but mysterious. There was usually a separate room for him, often with a washbasin and a window to piss out of. When there was no window he would climb on a chair and piss in the washbasin. Occasionally he shared with his mother, in which case he often found himself having to go out and play in a rear courtyard. Growing tired of his own devices he would wait at the door to his mother's room until the man left and his mother brought him in, making a fuss and drawing him into her bed for the night. Sometimes the man stayed and the boy was given blankets and a corner. He always used one of the blankets to cover his ears, indeed his whole head, one night resulting in near asphyxiation, coitus interruptus and a week of abstention for his mother.

He was thirteen when they went to London and lived in a small flat near the Archway, a steel bridge arched over the A1 which the boy came to regard with almost religious awe. Gargan would spend hours, with the patience of an old man, standing in different places on or under or alongside the Archway. A solitary figure, he rarely sought company, and his only contact with people his own age came on the few occasions when crowds of youths would pass under the Archway and shout abuse at him to impress themselves and the girls who walked behind them. He felt nothing: no anger, no fear, no wish to be like them. He just let them mouth off and pass on under the Archway like particles of grit carried in a river.

His mother was now working ostensibly as a dancer, though he didn't see her perform. She had regular engagements at a theatre in the West End, which was never named when spoken of. One evening he followed her to work, feeling like a private detective, always fifty yards behind on the street, one carriage down on the tube, several steps lower going up the escalator. He trailed through the dirty, gaudy streets of Soho and watched with dismay as his mother disappeared through a doorway hung with plastic strips. DANCING GIRLS DANCING GIRLS DANCING GIRLS, the sign outside announced.

He supposed that was the evening he became a man, at fourteen. His mother's familiar back swallowed by the mucky swish of clinging plastic, he stood in the middle of the pavement not knowing where to go, how to feel or what to do with his hands. He walked back to the tube, looking over his shoulder and up side streets. In the train everyone stared at him. They all knew where he'd been and what his mother did for a living. Half of them got off at his station and followed him up the escalator. He dodged through the barrier and sprinted out to the street, taking a circuitous route home.

He never told his mother what he had learnt that evening, so that she took his sullenness to be a symptom of adolescence and did nothing to alter it. Instead, she began to stay out some nights, coming home drawn in the morning, taking her make-up off at the time when she used to put it on.

One afternoon she sat him down at a table in the kitchen and, seating herself opposite, talked in a serious voice. 'Have you got a girlfriend?' she asked him. 'No,' was the honest answer. 'I think you should find one,' she said.

He didn't, and instead he spent more and more time at the Archway, usually standing in its shadow, occasionally on top, on its back, looking down at the cars rushing beneath up and down the A1. It swooped in a graceful arc from one steep bank to the other. A rise and a fall, from whichever side you approached. Instinct drew him back time and time again, to share the security of the architecture, the certainty that once begun the arch would finish, symmetrically. A pattern, a representation of order. Looking at it, standing under it, walking over it.

He recalled one occasion in his mother's room in Bucharest. Perhaps believing the boy to be asleep his mother had submitted herself to a great passion with a Romanian man (who lasted two weeks, just before mother and son went to Britain, by which time Gargan had begun dimly to understand the nature of his mother's activities) and it seemed that her reward for once was not purely financial. The Romanian heaved and pushed and his mother responded, flinging her back into an arch. The man arched the other way, stretching upwards. They held the position for a long time, the stillness interrupted only by rivulets of sweat running down his mother's body. Her face cooled to a calm the boy had not seen before and the archway began to ease down. The man shifted to one side; the arch melted and with a final quiver was gone.

The boy silently buried his head in the blanket and slept with the image behind his lids of his mother at peace. It didn't leave him, not even the following morning when he was woken by the Romanian fleeing from the room.

He still had that peaceful image of his mother when he watched her walk into the DANCING GIRLS place and it compounded his distress.

Smoked or not, Gargan finished his aubergine and Rada came to take his plate away, asking, 'Something else for you?' He'd spoken very few words to the Yugoslavian waitress beyond those on the menu, but he was obsessed by her. In moments of abandonment he thought he was in love with her.

As he chewed on the lumps in his custard he thought about another woman, the one he had seen the day before: her face had seemed unsettlingly familiar.

He had set up a practice walk, preparing for the river, between two large trees in one of the Royal parks. People gathered as soon as he began fixing the wire and Gargan exchanged casual remarks with them, even enlisting help with a leg-up to the wire. He set off, joking at first, then becoming serious as he passed over a path where people were walking. He was just coming to the end of the wire when a face detached itself from the crowd watching him. There was a niggling familiarity about her but he couldn't make an identification.

Who was she, where had he seen her before, and would he see her again?

Without knowing why, he felt sure that he would.

He didn't remember all of the dream he had in the early hours of the next morning. He was woken by a bottle being smashed in the street below his window and then became aware of a need to evacuate his bladder. The dream was left behind in his bed like a sloughed skin, destroyed and lost at the point of tearing.

Once fully awake he was no longer tempted by his damp sheets and so found a jumper and a pair of trousers. Stepping into his Chinese slippers he left the house and returned five minutes later with a pint of milk, a roll and a newspaper. After the quick crossword, the roll and a coffee, he sat down with a second coffee to try to reassemble those fragments of his dream he could remember.

He was walking along the top of the Berlin Wall. Although much thicker than a wire it felt like one. He was either drunk or half asleep and would have benefited from having a pole. On his right was West Berlin, on his left no-man's-land and beyond that the East German Wall. He couldn't remember how he'd got up on the Wall. It felt as if he'd always been there. People on his right watched with admiration. Perhaps it looked more difficult than it was. Scattered applause reached his ears. On the Eastern side nervous border guards followed his progress with automatic rifles. Beyond them, knots of East Berliners were tightening on the streets.

Warning shots were fired and he kept on walking careless of the danger. The people in the East had raised their voices in a chant. Gargan could not make out the words but their message was clear. From a concrete watch tower rifles were pointed in their direction and the volume of their protest swelled in response. Gargan speeded up. Within a few yards the numbers of people on both sides of the Wall had increased tenfold. He felt an inexplicable rush of joy, then a shot was heard and he felt himself falling.

As he fell a jumble of images and sounds passed before his eyes. Huge crowds of people pressed towards the Wall from both sides. A line of tiny cars stood waiting on a congested road. Jets of water played on happy revellers. Night fell but arc lights maintained a permanent glare. Flashguns strobed tear-streaked faces.

He'd fallen, it seemed, into no-man's-land.

Rue du Pôle-Nord

In Paris there are many rivers.

The hilly areas of the city run with rivers and streams and rivulets. Strength and breadth of flow depend as in nature on the volume of water, the gradient of the slope and the dimensions of the channel. Supply is not determined by climate and the flow is interrupted daily, preventing erosion.

The rivers are released by men from hydrants into gutters. They roll, kick and tumble downhill carrying rubbish which has been swept into the stream. At crossroads they turn away into new streets, hugging the kerb. Since the streets are mostly cobbled the streams bubble and break in shallow turbulence. Flat angled planes inside the flow capture the early light and throw it back then shatter. At any given moment a thousand twisting mirrors snap into life then are gone in the streams running down from the Parc des Buttes Chaumont.

The men who open the hydrants wear drab green suits. Most of them are immigrants or their sons, having left places that gave them little apart from dreams of emigration. Their new home welcomes them with open legs, clamping her thighs around their heads. It can take a long time to asphyxiate, breathing such a mixture of scents, the acrid and the ambrosial.

They use iron rods to twist open the hydrants, then move on, following the contour line, to unlock others. Without looking down to see where their waters fall they move across, swinging their rods like diviners.

They didn't see the water which crashed into the side of my face, breaking on my cheek and splashing over my greasy hair. They didn't see the way it urged my eyes both to open and remain tightly shut at the same time. I didn't want any trouble with my lenses.

But then I shouldn't have had my head in the gutter anyway.

Nor should I have been lying with my legs in the road, but what can you do? I don't know how much I'd had to drink the night before, but it felt like a lot that morning. I started to shiver, my teeth chattering, as the water seeped through my hair and drained down my back. I tried to move but couldn't: my joints had seized up. Maybe the brain just wasn't working sufficiently well to make my body move. It had taken a beating and the blows were still falling.

Parisian winters vary in harshness but generally the range is not great. The winter which followed almost immediately upon the final squeezed-out days of October, the month I arrived in the city, however, was a striking exception. The cold applied itself to the body in the manner of a close-fitting garment and tightened its grip straitjacket-style. I had chosen unwisely this particular evening to drink beyond my capacity. Temperatures, I learned later, were heading down towards double minus figures, so it was maybe as warm as −2 at sunrise when the green-suited men fulfilled their duties.

Dawn was no great improvement on the night, though, from where I was lying. The water didn't help either. I remember waking up precisely at the moment when a green three-wheeled van belonging to the city cleansing department hurtled down the narrow street and almost ran over my legs, which were sprawled in the road. Some prescient sense, alert when I was asleep, drew my legs in just in time and I became fully conscious when I felt the van's wheel nudge the sole of my shoe.

I vowed never to drink again, heaving my frozen body on to the pavement. Not just not to drink too much in the evening and spend another night like that one, but not to drink at all.

How many times had I made that promise to myself?

Ten or fifteen times since I'd arrived in the city, and I'd only been there a month. I didn't think I had a drink problem. Or, at least, I didn't before I arrived. It was more of a loneliness problem: I knew nobody, or hardly anybody, and I felt sorry for myself.

It occurs to me that if there's no one around to feel sorry for you, you might as well get on with it yourself. But that's the ultimate in self-pity, believing you're all alone in the world. I did find it hard to meet people and turned to drink. At first I went to cafés and ordered wine. Soon I could no longer afford to do this, so I bought cheap stuff in bulk from supermarkets and drank at home, in the park, even on the métro. This didn't help me to meet people, but some would say I had already given up trying when I began feeling sorry for myself. I was ordered out of cafés; the seat next to mine on the métro remained empty. Money was low, which didn't help. I could have got work teaching English, but I was too busy wallowing.

I'd gone to Paris for acting work, which without a card had been difficult to come by in London. I had heard things were more relaxed in France. However, once I'd exhausted the obvious small theatres I scouted round the British Council and the American Church, but the only offers I came across were for apartment-shares and language lessons.

I arrived on a dreary rainy day no different from those which followed. A taxi took me rattling from the Gare du Nord to the Rue du Pôle-Nord, where a German acquaintance was expecting me. Birgit was a friend of friends several times removed and my only contact in Paris. We didn't know which of the three obvious languages to speak with each other and ended up using all three to the detriment of effective communication.

I went out almost as soon as my bags hit the floor, on the pretext of looking for an apartment. I felt a bit awkward with Birgit: her nose was long and her teeth rather yellow and she seemed overly conscious of these facts. I didn't know where to look. 'It's raining,' she said, 'you can't go out.' She looked around for a less obtrusive place to address me from. I assured her I would go directly underground and stay there till I got to where I was going.

Birgit's apartment was on the sixth floor. The stairwell was dark and the lights clicked off when I was only two flights down. Halfway across the street, looking for the métro and avoiding the puddles, I realised I didn't have a key to get in if she wasn't there when I got back.

This was my first time in Paris and a childish instinct made me head for the centre. Noting the concentration of métro lines at Châtelet-Les Halles I got off there and wandered around. Unimpressed I blamed the rain which was falling with a light insistence. Retreating underground I went a couple of stations west and walked across the Place de la Concorde. The river was misted over, the Eiffel Tower just a sketch. Shoulders hunched I walked down the Rue de Rivoli to Les Halles where I drifted into a cinema to watch a film I didn't really want to see, an adaptation of a Contemporary American Novel.

When I came out of the cinema I was disorientated, having lost that precocious degree of familiarity the afternoon had given me. Groups of people passed in both directions smiling because they all had somewhere to go and knew how to get there. I turned confidently and slunk off towards the métro.

At the apartment in the Rue du Pôle-Nord, where the door had been thoughtfully left on the latch, I washed up the dirty pots littering the kitchen and sat down to read a book until Birgit returned. I didn't have to wait long. She had trouble opening the door and I rose to go and help just as the door flew open, slamming into a flimsy cabinet, and Birgit stumbled into the apartment. She looked distressed: red, swollen eyes and tear tracks down her powdered cheeks. I asked her if she was all right and could I help? She dropped a friendly hand on my arm and tried to smile. Wiping away fresh tears she crossed the sitting room with heavy steps and shut herself in the bedroom. A couple of minutes later the snuffles abated and I heard a muffled cry. If it was a plea for help I didn't consider myself suitably qualified.

Twisting and creaking in the wickerwork armchair, which was preferable to the wooden floor, I fell asleep within minutes and wasn't aware of my discomfort until I awoke, freezing, the thin blanket trailing on the floor, an early-hours stillness settled like a black dust-sheet over forgotten furniture. Although in pain, I just shifted in the chair instead of moving to the floor. I would lose too much heat uncurling my body and the bare floorboards would replace none of it.

I kept waking and turning in the uncomfortable chair, trying to get back to my dreams, until the room succumbed to wintry daylight. I went out for croissants. Birgit broke hers with drunken fingers and scattered crumbs over her bed. Through the hotel where she worked she knew of a man who was willing to let an apartment near the Opéra to a trustworthy tenant.

I went to see this man, Monsieur Lefarb, in his office. I never gathered what he did but his job was one of those that come with a brass nameplate on the wall. There was a lift but I didn't call it in case it already contained a passenger, who might exit and pass too close to me or stay in the lift and make me nervous. The stairs wound round a central drop back down to ground level. The banisters framed a hole with coffin-shaped dimensions. I don't know why I was so morbid that day.

A secretary raised her eyebrows from something secreted in her lap only to point with them towards a door with brass fittings. No one answered my knock. I looked round but a long fringe obscured the secretary's view. I knocked again briefly and eased open the door.

The room was long. At the far end four tall thin windows blinded me, then shapes emerged but they were all black. The room in fact was quite dingy and it took me a moment to spot the silhouette of a man sitting at a desk. At first I thought he had two heads but one was revealed to be a globular lampshade which remained still while he leant to one side to peer at me. I pictured myself from his point of view, small and overexposed. Moving slowly uphill towards the desk I searched for a patch of shadow. At one point I thought I'd found one, but it moved: a passing cloud.

'Bonjour Monsieur,' I said, acknowledging his gesture by sitting down.

'You are English,' he exclaimed.

My confidence plummeted. One 'Bonjour Monsieur' and he knew I was English. However, he proceeded not in my language but in his, with a voice that was low and sonorous. His speech was not hurried, yet the words exited at an alarming rate, filling the space between us with sharp corners and severed vowels, but no sense, for he spoke too fast for me to follow.

There was a gap. I asked how much. He told me: 3000 francs. A month, presumably. I couldn't manage half of that.

Monsieur Lefarb had begun drawing a small diagram of the apartment, pointing out special details and a room which was not to be used, but I had lost interest. He was just a man behind a desk wearing a shiny brown suit with dandruff specks on the collar, and speaking too much and too fast to a man who didn't want to listen. I left and bought an English-language magazine and sat in a café to have a large *café crême* I couldn't afford. The magazine itself was pretentious, much of it devoted to fashion, though it was not supposed to be a fashion magazine. The theatre pages were critical of all but the most bizarre and experimental of the current Paris shows.

In the classifieds, however, I found someone looking for a young Anglophone to share an apartment in Belleville.

One hand in her hair she opened the door and I saw the kitchen directly ahead with a bedroom on either side. She introduced herself as Eliane. We went straight into the kitchen and without asking she poured me a mug of coffee. It looked like bitumen, but I wasn't going to taste it and see because of the grease smeared on the rim. Plastic shopping bags under the sink were stuffed with rubbish overflowing on to the floor: orange peel, coffee filters, slops from last night's dinner, or maybe last week's lunch.

Breezing out of the tiny kitchen and trying to stop a hand continually pressing on the side of her nose, she announced that untidy though she may be, dirty she was not.

I sat at the other end of the room while she drew her legs up into a lotus position on the unmade bed. 'I like to lead a Bohemian life,' she explained, pointing at the rug on the wall and paisley scarf draped over the lampshade. She pressed the side of her nose again, squashing it almost flat. Were there just the two rooms, I asked, plus the kitchen? Yes, that was correct. I could use all her utensils and pots and pans. We could cook and eat together as often as I liked.

I didn't like.

I crossed the city to see another place advertised in a different magazine. I joined a queue on a staircase and finally got a look inside. I couldn't work out why there was no furniture, not having considered an unfurnished flat before. The walls were leprous and the building squalid. Several of the applicants seemed quite keen and had begun to argue amongst themselves.

The queue had grown. A line of hungry-looking immigrant men stretched out to the street. Their wives and children begged outside the métro at Barbès Rochechouart just five minutes away. I spent the evening in a cinema behind the Place de l'Etoile watching another film I had little desire to see.

It was the morning after another excruciating night on the wicker chair that Birgit told me she was going to Rio the following day. I asked if it would be a long holiday, imagining a cushy flat-sit. She said she was emigrating to start a new life. She came from Germany originally, so what was there to keep her in Paris? What indeed? She had a friend living in Rio who said it was hot. She told me not to worry and to accompany her to a party that evening in Montmartre.

This was the day I spent traipsing round the British Council and the American Church and getting my feet wet, since the soles of my shoes had eventually worn through, creating holes the size of pennies, apparently overnight..

At the party, Sylvain, a friend of Birgit's, said I could move into his place until I found somewhere.

I had shelter but relations with Sylvain became strained. I told him persistently how sorry I was to impose; he said it was nothing. But I felt he wanted me out of the way. I felt awkward whenever our paths collided in the narrow rooms. I would look down and edge past, wishing I were somewhere else.

I began to get miserable. I could find neither work nor a place to live, and I had no friends. Sylvain was now the only person I knew in Paris, but I avoided him, staying out late in the evening so as not to burden him with my presence.

Everyone tells you not to worry, things will get better, just give them time. You never believe them. I wouldn't have done. There wasn't even a flicker at the end of the tunnel as long as I continued degenerating: feeling sorry for myself, drinking to ease the loneliness, vomiting up the panacea, feeling sorry again . . . Recycling my own pathetic anguish.

I got up one grimy morning and stepped on last night's sticky wine bottle – I'd started bringing the stuff back to Sylvain's apartment – and went spinning into the table, hitting its sharp corner with the side of my head.

I came to with a resolution: to pull myself together.

I cleaned up the mess I'd made while Sylvain still slept. Collecting my strewn belongings I confined them to a single bag from which I extracted my towel and some money, and went out in search of a public bath house. Sylvain's shower cubicle, lodged illegally at the end of his minuscule kitchen, was too cramped for the purging I had in mind.

A Scatter of Transparencies

He stopped.

A premonition or a black spot. Like a black frame in a film, it was almost subliminal.

The water beneath him was choppy in the wake of a riverboat. Muddy clouds blocked the sun and the temperature dropped. A fresh wind picked up off the water. The pole weighed heavily while he was not moving and the wire seemed as if it was about to slice into his feet. His walking shoes felt as thin as rubber sheaths.

He flinched as another black frame blanked his mind, and the sweat on his arms and temples bit like acid as the wind cooled it.

Then he remembered: in the Charing Cross toilets, standing at the urinal, he had felt pain and seen something his mind had refused to accept. Banishing it from his consciousness, he left the station calm and prepared for his walk.

He set up the wire without a hitch, securing it at Hungerford Bridge, then, using a length of nylon string, walked round the South Bank to Waterloo Bridge. Once in position at the centre of the bridge he drew the string towards him and began to haul the wire across, using a portable alloy winch which he attached firmly to the iron railing. By the time he'd acquired the correct tension on the wire a crowd had gathered, keeping a cautious distance from him and each other. Those not alone muttered in tones of concern and curiosity to their companions, but no one came forward to lay a solicitous hand on his forearm and suggest that he desist from this madness. Without even a glance at his audience Gargan climbed up on to the railing, steadied his pole and stepped off on to the wire.

He proceeded more or less regularly at quite an ambitious speed, thinking of nothing other than the mechanics of his progress. His balance was perfect, all nervousness suppressed.

Spectators had gathered at his destination. Without moving his head he swivelled his eyes towards the South Bank and saw figures pointing at him. He tried to visualize from above the geometry of his walk: the river curving to the left, the two bridges perpendicular to the banks at their points of departure, equidistant from the point of maximum curvature, his line forming the third side of an uncompleted trapezium or perhaps an equilateral triangle. He considered as he walked a graphical extension of the two bridges and estimated their point of intersection to lie just to the east of Waterloo.

A riverboat half-filled with tourists, oblivious to the tightrope walker above their heads, startled him. The throb of its motor indistinguishable from the rumble of traffic behind him, the boat just slid into view beneath his legs.

Then came the black spot and he stopped.

The shock of remembering what he'd seen earlier and had dismissed from his mind. Now it emerged. As he teetered on a half-inch thickness of wire above the filthy swell, his security invested in a twenty-five–foot pole held between his sweat-slick fingers, the image returned, penetrating his calm. He saw it now with photographic clarity, the way it intimated his eventual bisection. What had he got? Or done? Nothing as far as he knew. Yet the image had been familiar, as if he had dreamt it and now the vision had become real. It was horrible, grotesque, inexplicable. Was he supposed to have done it to himself? It looked less like disease than mutilation. Someone, himself maybe, had taken a blade, and used it.

His foot slipped.

Its sensitivity had gone. He lifted it clear and bent his useful leg at the knee, trembling, shaking his numb foot, while manipulating the pole to retain balance. Feeling returned to the foot and the foot to the wire. He had to avoid thought and complete the walk. The reception committee had doubled in size, and was growing agitated. Was he doing it for them or himself? It was a performance, but the motivation was a mystery to him.

His walk was not to be concluded without further mishap. Images flooded his brain; dim pictures of himself wielding a blade – scalpel or razor? – seen from different angles like a reconstruction. Where did they come from? His memory or imagination? Clouded memories like fragments of returning dreams, or graphic suppositions of how his flesh may have been sliced? Both explanations were plausible and both held horrors and attractions. He didn't know if he preferred to be his own mutilator or someone's unwitting victim.

A fit of giddiness seized him and he felt his muscles turn to slush. The pole was pulling his arms out of their sockets; his kneecaps emulsified and his feet felt as if they'd been skinned. What the hell, he thought, it's only water, I won't break any bones. But the state he was in would do little to enhance his poor swimming ability.

He tried to grip the pole; it was like a steel piston slippy with grease, eluding his grasp and threatening to slide to one side and into the river, leaving him stranded like a swallow on a telegraph line with a broken wing. The pole slid to the left and lifted sharply on the right. He stooped low on the wire, caught the pole between chin and chest. For thirty seconds he stayed in the same position, feeling some strength returning to his ankles. Finally he rose, slowly, and found himself suddenly walking. He gathered speed without effort and Hungerford Bridge arched closer, as if through a convex lens.

He didn't look at the wire or the pole. He focused on the bridge ahead but could only actually see a thin slice of steel sinking again and again into his flesh. As he reached the bridge his foot stubbed the railing, almost causing him to fall. A spectator's hand was extended by instinct then withdrawn as if the owner had thought better of it. But Gargan had righted himself and grasped the handrail. He held the pole over the rail and the crowd moved back to allow him to drop it on to the path. With unexpected grace the tightrope walker vaulted over the railing and landed firmly on the bridge. A murmur went through the crowd but he didn't acknowledge it, for the jolt of his landing had shaken up the pictures in his mind. They assaulted him all at once like a scatter of transparencies in a harsh light. His legs gave way and he fell to his knees, clutching his temples. He was dimly aware of figures closing in when he lost consciousness.

A Convincing Texan Accent

I saw the 'actors wanted' notice just after I moved into the studio, which I found the day after I started my job.

A concerted effort to look for teaching work got me a part-time job in a high school in the 19th. The staff secretary there knew of a man who owned a studio in the same street which he was saving for his mother to move into should her husband die before her.

The class of twenty-three boys and four girls eyed me with mingled amusement and suspicion: I probably looked nervous, but they could not necessarily rely on me being timid. I introduced myself as the new English teacher. The syllabus was technologically based; arts and letters were not popular, English least of all since it was obligatory.

The first lesson I spent trying to match names to faces and battling through a photocopied text from the *Herald Tribune* which one of the other teachers had passed to me with a sympathetic wink. They did not want to know. Two particular boys sitting at the back concentrated on trying to make me look a fool. I found their challenge more invigorating than the general apathy.

One of the girls gave me a constant frank stare which spoke clearly of sexual knowledge she either had or wished to acquire.

It was a third-year class. Thirteen-to fourteen-year-olds.

My ground-floor studio comprised a fairly large room with tall windows in one wall giving on to a courtyard, a kitchen better suited to a person far smaller than the average, and a bathroom which did little to deserve its name. Bilious flowers bloomed violently on chocolate-coloured wallpaper throughout.

And I was pleased.

Investigating more thoroughly after my first night in the

studio, I guessed there was going to be a small problem with damp: behind the wardrobe a sheet of water coursed down the wall. When I pressed my fingers against it, the water thrust out over the tips as if the wall was a vertical slate in a cataract. Unsure what to do I shunted the wardrobe back into the corner, almost causing it to fall apart.

Close examination of the wallpaper revealed patches of fungi growing in amongst the flowers. When I closed the door between the main room and the kitchen I saw that even the back of the door was papered over.

Keen though I was to discover what other delights hid in the shadows and perhaps beneath the carpet, I craved the open air. Being on the ground floor with only a small courtyard, not much light got in; at least, not during the latter part of the day.

The Parc des Buttes Chaumont was close by. I later grew to love the park like few other places, but that day I just passed through, skirting the lake and heading down towards Belleville. I lost myself among the thin streets made narrower by the greengrocery displays of identical shops. The air smelled strongly of squashed fruit, fresh bread and Gauloises.

With no plan of where I was going I cut across to the Place de la République. Then, because it appealed to me, I followed the Canal St Martin to the river. I found a bridge and crossed. My wanderings were no longer completely abstract. I had crossed the river and was therefore on the Other Side. The river was a dividing line and I was either on my side or the Other Side. I was not necessarily unhappy on the Other Side, but I was aware that I was there. Whichever side I was on, I was always aware of the line which separated me and half the city from the other half.

I mooched up one bank and stepped on to another bridge with alcoves and a stone bench. I sat down to watch the water and thought about the Thames, about how it divides London more significantly than the Seine splits Paris. I remember always feeling uneasy in south London, impatient to get back north of the river. The *quartiers* in Paris tend more to homogeneity. Each one has its baker's, a *charcuterie*, small general store and a *café-tabac*. There might be a bank and a bookshop. A fish shop maybe. Either the apparently random design of curved and ruler-straight streets, or a wide tree-lined boulevard. Always a fair amount of dogshit and piss stains.

In London you can rely on very little once you've got the video shop, bookmaker's and pub. There may be a little shop selling food, but the chances are, unless it also sells drink, it won't stay open as late as the video shop.

Walking on the Left Bank again I read the notices pinned to a board outside the English bookshop. So many rooms offered cheaply now I didn't need one any more. English lessons. English lessons in exchange for rooms. Right at the bottom was a small, frayed photocopied notice which said: actors wanted. I copied down the telephone number and went straight to the nearest call box.

The voice that answered said yes, they were still looking for actors and if I could muster a convincing Texan accent – my heart sank – I was welcome to come along to the auditions, which were being held that weekend in a theatre near Montmartre. I took down the address, went over the letters twice with my pen and jumped when someone rapped impatient knuckles on the glass behind me.

The rest of the week dragged by. Teaching hours stretched to between ninety and one hundred minutes. My one double period took several days. I went to bed earlier at night to destroy more time in sleep. One evening I went to see *Paris, Texas* for accent tips, but made the mistake of attending a dubbed screening. The Beaubourg Cinémathèque was showing a couple of old westerns, but Jack Palance and Audie Murphy could have been speaking in Bostonian or Californian accents for all I knew.

Having had all the time in the world, I actually turned up late to the audition on Saturday. But it didn't matter because I was able to slip almost unnoticed into the foyer-bar of the theatre, where a desultory handful of obvious acting types and a couple of ordinary people sat waiting. I lowered myself on to a chair which shivered and creaked, threatening to collapse.

'Break a leg,' quipped a friendly Irishman beaming in the manner of one who had been saving up a joke. Instantly my face broke into a broad grin, overcompensating and signalling my embarrassment. I sidestepped awkwardly to a battered old sofa which was slung so low I had to look up to see the other auditioners. The Irishman looked alternately at me and at the weave in his thick brown trousers. He was one of the ordinary-looking people whose presence reassured me. He was speaking again, I realised.

'. . . done any acting before?' he asked, picking at a loose thread on his trousers. I told him I'd done something in London. He looked impressed.

'Just fringe stuff,' I emphasized.

He asked me if my agent had fixed up this audition. I told him I didn't have one. The Irishman, Thomas, had seen an ad in the same magazine I had bought when looking for a flat, and had thought to himself, why not have a go, you never know, etc etc.

Meanwhile, a door across the room had opened and disgorged a smallish nervous man who left quickly. A head came round the door and called for the next person. Behind the bar an Australian girl served a glass of something green to a boy whose hands were constantly occupied sweeping thick swathes of greasy brown hair from out of his eyes.

Thomas was called. The brown-haired boy sat in a chair against the next wall and we did not acknowledge each other. Thomas came out shrugging and said it went all right. He bent over me as if to impart some tip, but the door opened and it was my turn.

'Good luck,' said Thomas as he ambled out, forgetting it was bad luck to say so.

There were three men in the room; guys, I suppose you would have to call them. One, with very thick dark eyebrows and bushy hair, lay on the floor, propping himself up on one elbow. He looked about twenty-five. A man of similar age and bright-green werewolf eyes swung his long blue-jeaned legs under the table he sat on. The third man was older, in his forties, with a kindly, distracted look about him. He stood in the centre of the room with one hand poised palm-down in midair and the other rubbing at his lip to aid concentration.

The boy on the floor – Dick, I learned later – drew his leg up slowly at the knee and glanced keenly across the room at Ed, who jumped down from the table.

'Let's take it from the top,' someone said.

Charlie, the man in the middle, began taking little steps towards me. Dick looked down again and played with a torn flap in the linoleum.

'Let's do it,' said a voice, probably Ed's, and Charlie approached me smiling with a hand outstretched to clasp my arm.

'You must be Jonathan,' he said, looking at a scrawled list.

'No,' I said. 'There's somebody outside . . .' My voice trailed off.

'Then, er . . .' Charlie searched for my name on his list. His hair fell in his eyes and he brushed it away. Dick lit a cigarette. Ed took a swig from a plastic Evian bottle. Charlie looked at me, clearly having failed to find my name.

'Midwinter,' I said. 'Adam Midwinter.' It wasn't my real name. I didn't much like the real one and my feeling was it couldn't be good for auditions: too unusual or something. Thus I explained my earliest rejections, anyway, before I switched to Midwinter. In fact, I could hardly recall my real name any more. I had stopped using it altogether.

They gave me a script and pointed out the speech I was to read, sketching in a bit of background. Then they stepped back and gave me the floor. I read through the passage once before speaking. As always, my eyes stopped on random words and skipped whole lines, so I reached no overall comprehension of the speech.

I was awful. Dreadful, in fact. I flushed in embarrassment at my accent: a peculiar mix of cockney and Australian. I was so bad I almost fell over in my hurry to leave, which is why I was so surprised when they asked me to come back for a second audition the next day.

And even more surprised when after the second audition I rang them up and they said I'd got the part and could I go in that afternoon for a rehearsal?

New Members Welcome

She had picked him up off the ground and half led, half carried him to the Embankment, where she bundled him into a taxi. Out cold for most of the journey, he occasionally muttered confused snatches of sentences and periodically clutched his groin. After Edgware Road he displayed no further signs of life. The driver helped her carry him out of the car and up to her third-floor flat, where she laid him on the bed. Debating whether or not to remove his clothes, she decided against it. Instead, she wiped his face and neck with a damp flannel then left him, as he appeared to have slipped into a comfortable slumber.

When he woke he didn't know where he was. The room and the bed were unfamiliar. On the bedside cabinet was a photograph, like a publicity shot, of a man he had never seen. But he felt that if he were to go to the dressing table and look in the mirror he would see that very man staring back at him. He had to be dreaming. He wouldn't want to look like the stranger in the photograph; it had taken almost thirty years to get used to looking like he did look, like the man whose beard he trimmed and whose teeth he brushed every morning.

But he wasn't dreaming. Where was he? Whose room was this? Definitely not a hotel's, it was too personal, and what time was it? Early evening judging by the luminescent blue of the sky that he could see along with a dozen TV aerials out of the window.

As he opened the bedroom door, the woman was just coming down the corridor from a large orange room at the other end.

Her name was Su and she was Gargan's fan. She had followed him for years from walk to walk, having been alerted by half an inch in the national press reporting on his first walk when he'd dropped the pole and caused a modest pile-up outside the Bank of England. His second walk got live commentary on an independent radio station, since one end of his wire was attached to their building. Su had been listening to the station at the time on her car radio and had re-routed quickly enough to see the completion of the walk.

There were more walks through the early 80s, some of which she saw, then nothing for a year. She had assumed he had lost his head for heights and had chosen to exorcise his demons in a less public manner. But he had merely taken his wire to the Continent. It gave the Oslo correspondents something to write about that didn't involve whales, when a mad Irish Australian was arrested for attempting to cross the harbour on a rope.

Since Su had wanted to get away from London anyway – the end of an affair souring the too-familiar landmarks and even the furniture in her flat – she packed a small bag, leaving much of herself behind, and took a ferry to Bergen. She located Gargan in Oslo and followed him when he left Norway. Through Sweden, Finland, Denmark, Holland she went in pursuit, and finally to Paris, where she lost track of him. Believing him to be still in the city, she found work and accommodation. Although it was likely that he had left Paris, she stayed on for some time before coming back just a few weeks ago to Kensal Green. It was pure chance that she was passing through Green Park Gargan was doing his practice. 'Pure chance or destiny,' she added. 'After all, we have already met,' she said in a voice that seemed heavy with significance. Gargan looked up to see an intense burning look in her eyes.

'I'm sorry,' he said, 'but you must be wrong.' Racking his own memory to be sure, he added, 'We've never met. Possibly I've seen you beneath the wire, but I never speak to anyone while I'm walking.'

Su appeared to let this go, even if she remained unsure. They were both tired, having been talking for hours.

The room had an orange cast because of a long muslin shawl draped over the standard lamp in the corner. There were no chairs, only large cushions on the floor. Gargan was relaxing. 'Why?' he asked. 'Why did you follow me?'

She thought a moment. 'For the same reason, I suppose, that you do it in the first place.'

'Well, if you find out why I do it,' he said, 'let me know.'

Over the years he had tried to explain the need to walk tightropes in several different ways. Back in London now, he was leaving behind a 'performance period', during which he had considered the audience central to the activity, and himself an extrovert. Now it had become 'geometrical'. He liked to see the world in terms of lines, angles, intersections, shapes, patterns, structures. It excited him to insert a straight line into an existent geometry and alter it. But whether this served as motivation he had no idea. Geometry made sense, but he suspected his reasons for walking went deeper.

'Would you like some of this?' she asked, indicating the gin. 'Or something else? I've got a lovely coffee liqueur.'

Gargan declined. 'You've been too kind already.'

'Rubbish,' she said, rising to her feet and crossing to a cabinet from which she took two small glasses and a squat brown bottle. Instead of returning to her cushion, she came over to where Gargan sat. Filling the glasses, she handed one to him and sat on a cushion which she pulled up next to his.

'I don't know what I'd have done today,' he said, 'if you hadn't been there. It's so unlike me to fall.'

They sipped their drinks and Su reached behind her to press play on a cassette deck. Nina Simone grumbled over the sound of her own piano-playing. Dimly Gargan felt threatened. This woman had been following him for years; she'd told him about herself and he'd said a little, and now they were in her flat; it was late and they had coffee liqueurs and the blues.

'I've just thought,' he announced as he reached in his back pocket for his wallet. 'How much was that taxi?'

'Oh forget it,' she said. 'Put your money away.'

'No, come on. How much? It must have been expensive.'

'It wasn't and I don't want you to give it to me.' Her tone was firm.

'Well, let me buy you dinner or something.'

'You don't need to pay me back at all,' she exclaimed. 'It's me who still owes you, for all the times I've watched you walk the wire. But if you want to take me out to dinner, I accept.'

She smiled at him. He smiled too as the wallet disappeared.

'When do you want to have dinner?'

'Oh, we can talk about it later.' She stretched like a cat. 'You're not rushing off, are you?'

'I have to. Before the tubes finish.'

'They finished hours ago up here. They don't go beyond Queen's Park after rush hour and the last one from Queen's Park left about ten minutes ago.' She seemed pleased.

'There must be a bus.'

Her mouth was set. 'Don't go.'

Gargan said nothing.

'Wasn't the bed comfortable?'

'The bed was fine . . .'

'Sit down again,' she invited him.

They sat close. She turned the cassette over and increased the volume. She poured more liqueur and sat back. Their shoulders and arms touched. 'Here.' She handed him his glass.

'Thanks. It's nice.'

'Very nice.'

He saw that she was grinning and asked what was funny.

'Nothing,' she said. 'I'm just happy.'

The drink helped. Reaching once more for the bottle, her hand brushed the top of his leg.

Accident or design, the touch was arousing.

'Just one more . . .' she murmured.

To conceal his excitement he shifted his weight on the cushion but the discomfort persisted. Su's hand appeared on his leg. His penis responded and a jolt shot through him.

He remembered.

He clambered to his feet. 'I've got to go. It's not you. I'm sorry, I can't explain.' He knew whatever he said would sound ridiculous. She followed him as he lurched to the door, tried to restrain him, to turn him round and tell him it was all right, there was nothing to be nervous about. But he was opening the door himself, between blurted apologies and pathetic reassurances that it wasn't her. She scribbled something on the back of a tube ticket and stuffed it in his hand, and then he was gone, bounding down the stairs, his head bursting.

Just before he pulled the front door to behind him, he heard her voice clear from the third floor above. 'Call me, Gargan.'

The bus had come only a few minutes after he reached the stop. He slung himself into one of the seats above the back wheels and tried to go to sleep. But it was futile. What was he going to do? How could he have forgotten? Remembering wasn't like waking up to the truth; more like slipping back into the nightmare.

Action had to be taken, which meant a rational approach. Questions: who was wielding the blade? Himself, almost certainly. Why? Good question. Very good question. Once he knew why, he would have diagnosed the need and might be able to get rid of it.

That poor woman. How good she'd been; helped him out, then offered him warmth and company. How banal his response must have appeared: he couldn't take the pressure and was too nervous, too gauche just tactfully to defuse the charge between them. The appearance could not have been further from the reality. He was excited like a boy on the verge of his first experience. But his arousal could not fail to remind him of the mutilation. He would have to phone her, like she said; her number was in his pocket, on the back of the tube ticket. But what could he say? Lie and say it was nerves? She would know he was lying and he hated that because people always knew when he was lying. They knew because his hating it made him no good at it. Yet how could he possibly tell her the truth?

Across the aisle he was distracted by a discarded copy of the *Financial Times*. It promised light relief – people took those pink headshots so seriously. He picked it up to discover it wasn't the *FT*, but *Loot*, a paper of the same colour composed entirely of classified ads. You didn't have to pay to place an ad; a service to people for whom the cost was normally prohibitive. A few jokers and lunatics always lurked among the columns.

Gargan scanned friends/romance. Leather, rubber, domination, subservience, submission, subnormal, subhuman, submarine – watersports: all tastes catered for, somewhere, by someone. All you had to do was write enclosing a photo to a box number.

Not much to ask, a photograph, only a small part of your soul; and presumably they'd send it back if you were substandard.

He flicked back a few pages. Hi-fi, telephone accessories, cars, lawnmowers, sprinklers, personal messages, meetings, accommodation wanted, offered. Something in meetings had caught his eye and he looked back. 'Needles and pins, nuts and bolts. Alterations undertaken. Invisible mending not guaranteed . . . but who wants it? If you are committed to piercing or just curious, come and meet us, informal atmosphere, Wednesdays 7 p.m. New members welcome.' It gave an address in Bethnal Green.

When the significance of the words 'alterations' and 'piercing' soaked in, Gargan threw the paper down in disgust. New members welcome. He felt nauseous and the buffeting of the bus didn't help. It couldn't be far now, surely. He just wanted to get off, but not until Trafalgar Square.

The Square at night became London's axis. All bus routes led there and started from there to go elsewhere. Young people dredged themselves out of nightclubs to piss against the National Gallery. The thought of them vomiting on the top deck brought a recurrence of his nausea. He sat down on a wall.

'Oi!' a voice bellowed in his ear. 'Who you lookin' at?'

Gargan raised his gaze from the pavement to a youth with CLASS WAR tattooed across his forehead, his hair dragged into several thick stubby spikes, giving his head the impression of an unexploded mine. Suddenly Gargan began to feel increasingly unwell.

Lartna

He was lying on his back staring up at the blue sky. The sun was behind his head, so he felt its glare on his forehead. The back of his skull rested uncomfortably on the sandy ground. He had been asleep, had slept well, but now he was awake. There was no hurry to get up. Today would be like any other day: aimlessly wandering around in the unrelenting heat, always returning to the same spot at nightfall. There would be little to do, no responsibilities; he had the freedom of a boy. When would he become a man? Would there be an initiation ceremony and a prescribed ritual to follow?

For now there were no demands upon him and he could just lie there as his dark brown skin became even darker. He wondered if he would see the girl today. Trailing through the bush waiting for him to make a move. Then what? Rebuff him or let him walk by her side? Maybe they would find themselves drawn to an abandoned shack and in the sweltering shade of the afternoon explore each other's secrets.

He felt excitement in his crotch but took his hand away when he felt the earth under his head vibrate with the approach of footsteps. They were several, whoever they were, coming in his direction. The pounding feet had an urgency about them which did not presage well. The men, eight in all, arrived and stood in a semi-circle at his feet. They told him to stand up. 'Let us go,' the oldest man said and they set off across the bush at quite a pace. They walked for an hour or so as the sun slowly angled overhead. Although he knew all the men by sight he did not attempt to engage them in conversation. Their destination proved to be a piece of raised rock like a humped hill. It was to a stone slab which lay on top of the rock that the men directed him. He was to lie across its width, and to close his eyes and relax. The latter he could not do, however, and he watched as one man obeyed the silent bidding of the man who was obviously the leader and walked towards the slab carrying a stone knife. A second man came close and the two of them stood over him, one on each side.

The second man grasped the foreskin, stretching it out as far as it would go, and the first man severed it with the small stone knife.

In the Familiar House

For once I was glad to fall into a routine.

I taught in the morning, went to rehearsals after lunch and spent evenings either at the cinema or walking around until I felt like going back to the studio, where I read or listened to music. I ate mashed potato, frozen peas and fish fingers, which reminded me of England and childhood. I also ate a lot of bread. I was no longer drinking and didn't smoke, but money from teaching didn't go very far. I had been told we wouldn't be paid for rehearsal time but it didn't bother me too much because the script was interesting and the people seemed pleasant.

Ed and Dick, young as they were, turned out to be joint producers. Charlie knew the boys from an earlier production and agreed to direct on the same terms that myself and the two girls donated our acting services: that we had to wait until we were performing to get paid. With goodwill this arrangement was acceptable. The boys assured us that once the money started coming in, their first priority would be to pay us. I don't think I was naive believing them. The girls saw no reason to mistrust them, and they'd worked, like the boys, in Hollywood.

Coming back from the first rehearsal, during which my accent became at least American, I came out of the métro and crossed the street so I'd pass by the *boulangerie*. I had a crush on a woman who worked there, a fat girl called Lucinda with a cherubic face and bright pink lipstick. I bought bread there twice a day whether I needed it or not. She was the best way to start the day, despite the seven-minute walk from the studio, passing two *boulangeries* on the way, even in sub-zero temperatures and before the blood in my legs had thawed out. (Each night my room relocated itself inside the Arctic Circle. The wall-mounted heater could not even melt the ice on the inside of the thin-paned window directly above.)

As I approached the shop she stepped outside. Instinctively I stopped and half turned away, noting a thumping in my chest and tightening of the facial skin. I followed her up the street. She walked slowly. I dropped back so she wouldn't see me if she turned round. I took my eyes off her when an engine revved up behind me. It was one of the city cleansing department's motor-bikes fitted with brushes which smeared dirt over a wider area. When the bike had passed she was too far ahead for me to tell which doorway she had disappeared into.

The following morning I got up early enough to go to the *boulangerie* before my class. Elasticized by the attempt to make it friendly, my smile slithered into a grimace. I was behaving like a love-sick fourth-former. Fourteen years too late.

The class was cancelled. I normally took half a class while the other half stayed with a regular teacher and if the teacher didn't show, both halves got a free period.

At rehearsal I began very slowly to feel my way into the character, despite the distraction of rehearsing in different surroundings. (The theatre where the auditions took place had been hired for just two days.) Our initial job was to rehearse to such a standard that we could audition to get a run in one of the English-speaking theatres. We had a date in two weeks' time at a small place close to St Germain. We had to convince the proprietor that we could sustain a three-month run.

We worked mainly in the tiny apartment Ed and Dick shared on the Ile St Louis, but also in the open air on milder days when we could find an empty corner in a park.

Walking up past the *boulangerie* I saw Lucinda out of the corner of my eye preparing to leave. I quickened my step, to precede instead of follow her, to find out where she lived. What I'm not sure about is what I hoped to gain from knowing her address. I suppose it was like when I was a kid and I fancied a girl called Jackie Smith so badly I looked up her address in the phone book and walked past her house four times a day, glancing nonchalantly at the upstairs windows.

When I stopped after two hundred yards to untie and reknot

my laces, looking back the way I had come, there was no sign of Lucinda.

The next rehearsal was held in Ed and Dick's apartment. I was beginning to get familiar with the lines and my character's identity crisis was making more sense. Fudakowski, a Polish-born American, does or does not go to Vietnam. Lansdale and Campbell, the other two male characters played respectively by Ed and Dick, do go to Nam. When they get back to their small Deep South town they find Fudakowski in a state of mind which would indicate he had been to Vietnam, yet half the time he maintains he didn't go. The townsfolk are also divided: some remember him going, others recall seeing him around at the store and the diner. Lansdale and Campbell mistrust him implicitly. 'The little fuck can't be in two places at once,' Campbell roared in his gruffest voice.

On my way home I was accosted by a prostitute as she climbed out of a cab. When I was unable to provide a light for her cigarette she offered me *une pipe* for fifty francs. Fellatio was not at the front of my mind as I stamped my feet on that dark frosting pavement. I told her I had no money. She said a credit card would do. I scowled as I turned away. She pressed close behind, suggesting other forms of payment. I walked more quickly but couldn't shake off the feeling that I was being followed. Several times I looked behind to see no one there.

About eleven o'clock the next morning after my class I went down to the PTT office to order a telephone for my studio. On my way past the *boulangerie* I saw Lucinda coming towards me. Summoning up immense courage I said *bonjour*. I was so excited I don't know if she spoke or just smiled in return. After that we always exchanged a few words when I went for bread.

At rehearsal Lansdale and Campbell began to show their contempt for Fudakowski, calling him fuckface, though it wasn't in the script. I was grateful for the insulation provided by the character; otherwise I should have felt the insults myself.

Somehow my telephone was delivered and installed while I was out. It had not been connected, however. I arrived for the afternoon rehearsal a little bit late: Charlie wasn't there; Ed sat at the window staring outside; Dick was perched on the steep flight of steps that led up to a galley kitchen. He was drinking bottles of beer. Neither turned on my arrival. I said hello. No one replied for a moment, then Ed mumbled something, reaching for a bottle. I crouched down on the floor and pretended to study my script.

Presently, Charlie knocked and came in. He apologized for being late and suggested we begin. The boys didn't move. 'Hey, guys,' he said, clapping his hands together. 'Let's go to work, OK?' Ed swung his leg sulkily from the windowledge to the floor and Dick took another swig of beer.

When we finally got some work done it was a strange, threatening experience. Dick was drunk and consequently Campbell was loud and aggressive. He became physically violent with me, so much so that Charlie had to stop the rehearsal.

'This is great though,' Dick grinned broadly. 'It adds a new dimension. This is what it needed.' The rehearsal began again but Dick continued as before, having gone beyond simply trying out a new interpretation, and it was not clear whether it was Dick or Campbell who held Fudakowski, or myself, in such low regard.

In the *boulangerie*, whereas at first it had been me who gabbled, now Lucinda had more to say. I found myself becoming less interested and, because it had gotten so cold in the mornings, sometimes went to the shop nearer the studio.

My telephone remained silent.

A sense of urgency in rehearsals grew as the day of the audition approached. The section of the text we would perform featured only the male characters, but we did some work with the two girls to help us flesh out what we had. They played Lansdale and Campbell's wives. It was rumoured that Campbell's wife conducted a spasmodic affair with Fudakowski, but although such rumours greatly enhanced his self-image, he denied them vehemently for obvious reasons.

Dick returned to his earlier, easier style of delivery, but retained an edge of entirely convincing malice. I found his taunts hard to shrug off after rehearsals. There were times walking down the street when I caught myself feeling depressed, as if Fudakowski's problems were my own.

For the audition we did the best run-through yet of the section we had chosen. Dick behaved reasonably and we appeared to be working together. The proprietor, generally regarded as a dour man, was enthusiastic and the audition a success. 'We did it!' shouted Charlie. That night we celebrated at a drinking club on the Ile St Louis where Dick held a small card up to a window to gain entry. Jessica and Linda were there too. I drank three bottles of wine then danced for hours under a silver-mirrored globe with Jessica's poodle.

I walked the six and a half miles back home, arriving around 7 a.m. On the way up the Avenue Secrétan I asked a greengrocer setting up his stall if he would sell me an orange even though he had not begun trading. He wouldn't. I had nothing at home except water in the tap, so went straight to bed, throwing clothes on the floor as normally I wouldn't, and slept most of the day but with horrible dreams.

I went to an estate agent's in a deserted area of a redbrick city. All the shopfronts were dusty and empty. I pushed all my weight against the door to open it. Inside, the carpets, furnishings and room-dividers looked temporary. Behind the facade, where walls didn't quite meet and pictures had been omitted from frames, all was black. A man rose from behind a flimsy desk, a smiling mask imperfectly attached to his head. A large industrial stapling gun sat on the desk. He made his way across to me, arm outstretched. There was a black gap between wrist and cuff which I tried not to look at. I could feel his eyes piercing mine, although they only stared straight ahead. I shook his hand. It felt like paper so I let go prematurely.

He gestured mechanically towards the back of the room. I stepped past thick curtains hiding expanses of blackness and through a doorway. 'Where are your clipboards?' I asked as we stepped outside. 'Your information and brochures?' He continued to smile and marched jerkily up the leafy residential street, which gave every indication of being more than just a block away from the street where I'd entered the shop.

Within seconds we had walked hundreds of yards. He stopped in front of a large house set back from the road in sprawling overgrown gardens. We spent hours tearing our way through the undergrowth then arrived at the front door completely refreshed. His thin, brittle hands twisted the key and I was led into the hall. Like a prospective buyer I was shown round but the house seemed familiar. I touched the walls lightly with two fingers and felt the man's eyes drilling into me. I found myself pressing my body up close against the wall. I could feel several pipes and wires through my clothes and they were pulsating. The beat was regular. Standing back I examined a pipe and saw that there was movement inside. I touched it and my finger recoiled in pain: it was a hot water pipe.

The man's hands feathered over mine and led me to more rooms; hallways and corridors, galleries and stairways. Only a couple of rooms were carpeted. In one an old clock ticked on a marble mantelpiece and a wardrobe hovered mutely in the gloom.

The pulse began to thump in my temples the higher we went. There seemed no end to the stairs. As we approached a landing with three closed doors the throbbing in my arteries got worse. The man's origami fingers skated over a doorknob and ushered me into the room on the left. It was a bathroom, its fittings intact. The banging in my head was joined by a desperate clanging. Water pipes and drainage pipes beat a tattoo against the wall and the bath. The taps began to turn in the bath, the basin and the bidet. They all just turned and at first nothing came. Then they began to run red. I was too horrified to think of turning back, then it was too late and he'd closed the door behind me. The bowls were already brimming and when I looked down into the bath I saw the body surfacing.

Not surprisingly I spent what remained of that day nursing an exquisite hangover.

I just about managed to locate the nearest launderette and wash all my clothes and sheets. It was a bit expensive but about time I went.

When I got back the telephone still wasn't working.

Vertical Slashes of Red Paint

As he sat in a Central Line train rumbling eastwards he realized that he was still as depressed as he had been upon waking up that morning. This happened occasionally: he was distressed by a bad dream and when he woke up the feelings persisted although the details vanished. Few remained from this latest dream; just a vast sky and a bush-like landscape.

Perhaps the seeds for anxiety had been sown the night before in Trafalgar Square when the anarchist had turned nasty, prompting a sprint to the nearest cab. He couldn't afford it but felt sure his pursuers could even less afford one in which to follow his. Financial differences helped him out for once and he made a mental note not to be so disparaging of the *Financial Times* in future.

Bethnal Green was not as he expected it to be.

It was worse.

Gangs roamed the streets like rats. The only graffiti were the work of neo-fascists: 'FREE JOE PEARCE', 'JAILED FOR TELLING THE TRUTH. JOHN TYNDALL. JOHN MORSE'. Gargan was glad when he finally located the address. He went over in his mind again his reasons for coming. He had no intention of allying himself with groups who did this kind of thing on an organized basis whether seriously or for fun. It was an investigative mission, to see if he could uncover some reason why he was doing such a thing to himself.

Prepared for the worst, if anyone so much as flicked a blade of grass or sharp edge of paper in his direction, he would be out of there like a shot and never pass within two miles of Bethnal Green again.

A short path led beneath stunted trees to a paint-blistered

front door. Lights showed behind curtains on the first floor and it took a while for his knock to be answered, then a man appeared wearing leathers, a ring through his nose, and hair in a ponytail slung round over his shoulder. Fair enough, thought Gargan.

'Yes?' the man asked.

'I saw your ad,' said Gargan, in a voice which he tried to make sound confident without being aggressive.

'So?'

It wasn't going well.

'It said new members welcome. I er . . .'

The man said nothing as he opened the door wider and motioned to Gargan to step inside, leaving just enough room for him to squeeze through. Gargan could take this. Just. The door closed behind him and he felt the man's breath on his neck.

'Straight up, is it?' Gargan asked, pointing to the staircase.

'Yeah, that's right. Upstairs. My name's Radcliffe, by the way.'

Gargan swivelled round to return the greeting but Radcliffe was standing so close that Gargan thumped him in the stomach. There was no injury, only embarrassment, and Gargan stammered his name, confidence draining from him with each step he now took up the stairs. At the top they turned right along a gallery towards a door at the end. Gargan looked down to the hall and felt dizzy. At the door he stopped and Radcliffe's hand, surprisingly light and delicate, reached round to grasp the doorknob and fling the door open.

It was a cross between 60s hippy and late-80s industrial. Coloured light bulbs and rotating psychedelic shades driven by heat from the bulbs. But the walls were painted black. A stereo played Psychic TV. Gargan couldn't see anyone at first, until his eyes readjusted. Shapes slumped in armchairs and among floor cushions became people. And they were all looking in his direction.

'Let's go through,' Gargan's guide said, pointing across the room to a door.

There was only one light in the inner room: a single jaundiced bulb hung in a dirty, once pretty lace shade. A white sheet was nailed to a far wall, daubed with vertical slashes of red paint. In its centre was an inverted wooden crucifix. Beneath that and a yard closer to Gargan stood a line of people. It looked stage-managed, as if he were expected. They looked at his eyes, he looked at their genitals.

The first man had rings through his foreskin and nipples linked by a light chain. He was smiling. The next man wasn't. His body was an acupuncturist's dream, bristling with needles. Next to him stood a woman tattooed from head to foot and wearing long eyed needles laterally through her nipples. Number four was a hermaphrodite whose nipples were pierced with rings to support several more rings of different gauges. His/her cock had been mutilated by a stainless steel nut and bolt. Finally there was a woman whose labial hooks, rings and needles gave the impression of a toothed monster.

'What do you think?' asked Radcliffe, who had now dropped his trousers to reveal a broad brass cylinder which elongated his scrotum forcing his balls out tightly at the end. An evil-looking skull was tattooed on his circumcised penis.

'Impressive,' said Gargan with composure. 'Very.'

'How about you?' asked the man with the rings and the smile.

'Well, I don't have anything. I'm just . . . interested . . .'

'You either pierce,' interjected the hermaphrodite, 'or you don't. And if you don't, dear, then you're in the wrong place.'

He had to keep it light. Otherwise, what these people had done to their bodies could seriously screw up his mind.

'Look, er . . . I think . . .' The door opened behind him and churning, grinding music invaded the room. A man slightly the worse for drink lurched through the doorway.

'Are you gonna stay in here all night,' he demanded, 'or are we gonna make a start?'

The interruption was a welcome one for Gargan, defusing the antagonism that had built up. One or two of the piercers left the room while Radcliffe, adopting to Gargan's amazement a role like that of guardian, put his arm around Gargan's shoulder and spoke of the night's impending business.

'Bloodletting,' he began, and Gargan's heart sank, 'is practised for many different reasons, each one perfectly reasonable to those who do it for that particular reason.' The circular logic, like a snake swallowing its own tail, confirmed that this was after all just a nightmare. He wished. Radcliffe was talking again: '. . . therapeutic, psychological, erotic, sensual, intellectually stimulating . . . all or none of which may be relevant for the members of the group.' He looked at Gargan, who said nothing. 'Let's go through. I think you will see the attraction.' Gargan allowed himself to be led.

A white sheet had been laid out in the middle of the room. Gargan remembered the red paint on the sheet in the other room. He had been mistaken. The men and women – many naked, others clad in ripped leathers or denims – were grouped around it. A razor was tossed. It spun and the person in whose direction the blade pointed – a man with a shaved head, antichrist earring and sundry attachments evident in his groin, whom Gargan judged to be between sixty and sixty-five–picked up the razor and lightly nicked the tip of his cock. In the coloured lights the blood looked like tar as it leapt towards the sheet.

Gargan was not staying. His own blood thumped in his temples and his stomach had begun to react. While their attention was centred on the bloodletting, he realized, he should be able to slip away.

The last thing he saw before he managed to open the door and disappear was the hermaphrodite about to go under the knife for the tattooed woman, whose eyes glittered accusingly in his direction.

Arilta

He lay on his back staring at the sky. It was the same but he was different. Having undergone the initiation ceremony, the lartna, he was now a man. But he felt much the same. Perhaps the process was unfinished.

The moment he started to think about the girl he felt the vibrations of approaching footsteps. Eight men arrived and assembled at his feet while he still lay prone. They helped him to his feet and as a party they set off into the desert. The seriousness implied by the taciturn aspect of his guides precluded idle talk.

When they reached the hill two men knelt together to form a living table upon which he was instructed to lie down. A third man stepped up and sat astride his supine body, grasping his penis and putting it on the stretch. Another man, the operator, then quickly approached and with a stone knife laid open the penile portion of the urethra by slicing upwards through and along the full length of the underside of the penis.

Following the custom of this ceremony, known as the arilta, the blood was encouraged to flow into a shield which was emptied on to a fire close by. In severe pain, the initiate was then allowed to place glowing pieces of charcoal into the ashes of the fire and urinate upon them, meanwhile holding his penis above the burning embers; the steam is said to ease the pain.

Pain or Pleasure

Gargan took Su to his favourite restaurant, his favourite because Rada worked there, but he owed Su dinner.

'I saw you boarding a Paris train,' Su was saying, 'but I didn't have a ticket. There was enough time before the train left. Or there should have been. I complained. Said it had gone out early. But I was wasting my breath. I don't even know if they apologized. They certainly didn't offer me a refund. So there I was with a ticket to Paris and no train for four hours. What could I do but wait? There was no way of knowing if you were staying in Paris, or if you'd connected with a train back to England. It was likely you would stay in Paris since you hadn't to my knowledge done a walk there. I've always liked Paris, so that was another reason to stay.

'I stayed in a hotel that night. Very cheap place: wall-to-wall cockroaches and hot running water – running down the walls. Next day I found myself a *chambre de bonne* in the 14th. I checked the papers every day but figured you would probably wait a week or two. When my money began to run out I got work teaching English to adults somewhere near La Défense.

'Not long after that I met this man. One of my students.

'Although it was two months since I'd arrived in Paris and there'd been no sign of you, I decided to stay. Not for this man but for me, because it pleased me.

'It was only later that I learnt he was not the gentle, selfless man he had appeared to be. When his wife's menopausal depressions passed on, he went back to her. Strange the way a person can make you believe you mean the world to them, when the very next week you mean nothing. I tried to believe that I had meant something to him. It's like a puzzle to which you can never be sure of having the right answer.

'Later I met an actor. We had a fling. I liked him a lot.' She gave him a look clearly designed to be meaningful, but Gargan didn't have a clue as to the significance. She hesitated then pushed further. 'You remind me of him, you know. Have you ever done any acting?'

Gargan's recollection of his own time in Paris was fogged. He didn't know if his memory was at fault now or if he had failed to store information when he was there. It wasn't as if there were gaps in his memory; he could hardly remember anything. When he did recall an event he was not able to place it in context. It was almost as if he had never in fact been to Paris but someone had made him believe he had.

On this particular evening he was also distracted by Rada.

There had only been one woman in Gargan's past, apart from his mother, and she belonged to a forgotten time, which made his recollections of Paris seem crystal clear in comparison.

Now there were two women on his mind: one who clearly wanted him and one whom, in spite of himself, he longed to know. He'd never spoken more than a dozen words to her yet he knew he wanted to sleep with her, not necessarily to make love, just to lie together and wake up in the same bed.

Could Su see the way he was looking at Rada? he wondered. He hoped so. It might dampen her enthusiasm. He felt a complete bastard for having wanted to go to bed with Su, when the only woman he cared for was Rada. But for all his longing and desire, he knew it would never lead to anything because he would lack the courage to tell her how he felt.

In this way, theoretically, his problems with the two women were resolved. But his pulse quickened when Rada approached their table and asked, 'Something else for you?'

If he hadn't ordered and drunk most of that second bottle of wine, he would have felt awkward when they got back to Su's place in Kensal Green. He wouldn't have known what to do with his hands or how to hold his head. And he probably wouldn't have allowed Su to hold it for him, as she had for a while, cradling him gently among the floor cushions.

They drank some more and talked a little about going to bed.

Couldn't she see the way his gaze went straight through her looking for Rada's face? They couldn't go to bed, he said. Couldn't. His firm refusals slurred into blurred negatives. They relaxed so far they almost drifted asleep in the cushions, but Gargan's bladder prevented them from doing so. He must have disturbed her slumber when he got up to go to the bathroom.

He was sitting on the edge of the bath examining the extent of his mutilation when he realized she was standing in the doorway. There seemed little point in the instinctive rush by his hands to cover himself, so he let them drop. She didn't appear shocked or horrified, just . . . sort of . . . interested.

'I'll go now,' he said, getting to his feet. But she took his hand and said, 'Come and sit down.' In the orange room she had a closer look and said there was no reason for him to go.

She liked it, perhaps; an even more pressing imperative that he should go. What strange exotic pleasures must be waiting beneath her skirts? An extreme case of infibulation, maybe, sewn up at puberty. It happened. Time to go.

She said she still wanted to go to bed with him. What difference did it make? she argued. Was he still turned on by the thought of sleeping with her? Yes, in spite of everything, he was. They had worked each other up into a state.

Sensation at that point being what it is, Gargan never knew if he was experiencing pain or pleasure.

Nagarlala

He knew that he was now a man as he foraged in the vegetation around the waterhole. No more lying on the earth all day, but there was no sense of nostalgia for lost youth, no bowing under the burden of responsibility. Just this foraging.

A splash in the water. A clump of weeds knocked in. Resting for a moment, he heard another splash. There was something in the water. He watched the surface; it stirred, dimpling, bending, sloping. What was there beneath the movement, causing it?

Moments later he saw the water part as if something were emerging. Nagarlala, spirit child.

The nagarlala approached and told him he was the father. It came as no surprise. The tiny figure then told him how he was to be called and asked where the mother was. He told the nagarlala he would take him there, but first he had to wash him. For this only a freshwater spring would do. Two days and nights he carried the spirit child, through desert and across chains of small hills. In a suddenly verdant sweeping valley they came across a spring bursting forth. He washed the child in the incandescent stream and left him immersed for the required three days. Thereafter, they made the return journey in a matter of hours and reached the place where the woman had been left.

She didn't stir as he moved alongside her, still carrying the spirit child. He placed the child gently on the woman's stomach and immediately turned and walked away.

Bad Actors

There was a first-night party.

Plenty of drink and plates piled high with stuff to eat. All provided. A Christmas tree bedecked with baubles and lights towered in a corner. An eclectic choice of music was played through speakers so powerful that conversation was obliged to be shouted or intimate.

Ed and Dick were extremely vocal and most heads turned their way. Charlie was eating snacks and talking to Jessica while Linda nuzzled the poodle. The fifty-odd other people crammed into the St Michel apartment, home of a former US cultural attaché, comprised friends and supposed influential associates of Thunderbird Productions (Ed and Dick Ltd). Congratulations were passed round with the peanuts. The boys gulped them down so fast they'd get indigestion. Charlie demurred before praise and the girls just laughed and played the game.

I admit it: I was pissed off because no one had come up to me, shaken my hand and said I'd done well. In the dress rehearsals I'd been really pleased with my performances and I put too much pressure on myself for the first night. The greater the expectation the deeper the disappointment.

I floated towards the far end of the room. No one held me back. A man bent over the cassette deck. I sat down on a large, squashed sofa. There was a woman, ten or fifteen years older than me, already sitting there.

'Do you mind if I smoke?' I asked her after a while.

'No,' she said, glancing sideways as she emptied another glass. A couple of minutes passed and she turned towards me with great care as if undue movement might wake the sofa.

'Why,' she asked slowly, 'are you not smoking?'

'I don't smoke,' I answered.

She found this funny, which surprised me.

Some time later, after we'd been talking, she said, 'Those guys gave you a hard time.' I wasn't sure what she meant. 'Those two.' She nodded towards the main crowd of people where Ed and Dick still held court. 'On stage. They didn't exactly make it easy for you.'

'What d'you mean?' I asked. She didn't say anything. 'They don't like him,' I continued, relaxing. 'They really don't like him. He stayed behind, you see. He didn't go . . . When they went to Vietnam, he didn't go . . . at least it seems like he didn't go. Maybe he did. But that's not relevant. To this . . .' I looked at her. Was she listening? 'As far as they're concerned he didn't go. So he's a wimp . . . Nobody likes a wimp.'

'They are bad actors,' she declared, looking their way again and drinking. 'Horseshit. They're horseshit. They don't like you and I could see it. I shouldn't be able to see it.'

I watched her, to see what she'd say next. This was good. I liked it. She was like a gust of fresh air in the métro.

'What about me?' I asked. I mean, I'm not proud.

'You were OK,' she said straightaway. 'Different. Better than them. You acted, you see. You were acting. They weren't. They couldn't.'

She didn't like them.

'Your accent slipped,' she continued, 'a few times. But you got it pretty good, considering.'

'Considering what?' I asked, draining my glass. She refilled it for me a trifle unsteadily.

'Considering you got no help from them. And you're . . . what . . . what are you? English, I guess?'

'Close enough,' I replied.

'It's a difficult accent,' she said. 'Difficult for Americans if they're not from the South. I am from the South, so I know.' She poured the rest of the vodka into her glass and chinked it loudly against mine.

This was more like it, this was fun.

'They seem to think they're OK.' I indicated the crowd of adulators.

She told me about *them*. They were expats. There was one

Englishman – Julian, our photographer. A couple of weeks previously we'd had a photocall at his studio. Lots of umbrellas and flash guns. The poodle had run slaloms round the tripods and ran out of steering. Within seconds a tripod became a bipod and the weight of the camera brought it toppling down, sending the bill rocketing upwards by around 5000 francs.

Here he was tonight though, Julian, melting into the crowd around Ed and Dick. All camera damage forgiven. Provided they paid up and used him again. The photos, after all, were pretty good. They had been printed in the programme. The publicity materials – posters, fliers, programmes – had all been produced to the highest standard. The boys had spared no expense.

Apart from Julian the party guests were Americans. Some of them spoke basic French now and then. They all had money and they got into the arts. Expatriate American art wherever possible. Like Thunderbird Productions. And like Jimmy Koch, the American artist whose mutated photographs of once familiar skylines and cityscapes were as sought after in Manhattan as in St Germain. And Jo Kozinski, writing about the Parisian underbelly but for the East Coast market. The expats liked to know established figures, obviously, but most of all they liked to talent-spot and promote emergent names in the manner of patrons. They had to get rid of their money somehow.

None of which has got anything to do with the fact that after the party I asked my new friend, whose name was Jenni, to come back to my studio. Which invitation to my great delight she accepted.

Another Man's Child

It was a shock to learn that he'd had a conversation with Su in the night, since in the morning he had no recollection of it. Apparently Su had a dream which woke her in the early hours. As she jerked awake she made Gargan jump. Eyes wide and staring he demanded to know what was wrong.

'A dream,' she said.

'What time is it?' Gargan asked.

'I don't know. Why?'

'What're you doing tomorrow?'

'Going to work. What are you doing?'

'Don't know,' he said, then added, 'I've got to go to Nunhead.'

With that, according to Su, Gargan's contribution to the conversation ended. She asked him why he had to go to Nunhead but his eyes had closed.

When he woke in the morning Su was in the kitchen. He could hear her moving dishes around and turning taps on and off. He glanced at the bedside cabinet and saw the photograph he'd seen when she'd brought him here the first time. He picked it up and studied it. Who was he? he wondered. An interesting-looking man, intelligent, not handsome but the planes of his chin and jaw were striking. He didn't really look like an ex-husband, though he didn't know if there were any. Nor did he look like the Frenchman who went back to his wife. The actor maybe?

'Coffee?' Su had come in. He put the photograph down and said good morning. Yes, he would love some coffee. She went to get it, leaving a swish of perfume in the room behind her.

'What time do you have to be at Nunhead?' she shouted from the kitchen.

Nunhead!? How did she know about Nunhead? *What* did she know about Nunhead? All *he* knew was he'd found himself thinking about the place on several occasions, or rather just of the name. He couldn't recall ever going there and when he *had* thought of it, he'd forgotten it moments later.

He wished he knew what the hell was going on.

'What d'you mean?' he shouted above the noise of the kettle.

'I just wondered what time you had to be there, that's all. Don't want you to be late. Though it's only eight now.' He heard her pouring water into mugs. She carried them into the bedroom and, handing him one, sat on the edge of the bed. He sat up, dragging a pillow behind his back for support. She looked so different all made up. It was hard to believe this was the same woman he'd gone to bed with.

'Why did you ask me about Nunhead?' he said, blowing on his coffee. He was amazed when she told him about the conversation they'd had in the night. She said it was a common phenomenon: as a little girl she had sleepwalked into the kitchen where she had sat down and talked coherently to her parents for ten minutes before they told her to go back to bed and she did so without a murmur. She believed none of it when they told her about it the following morning.

Su crossed to the dressing table where she checked her hair in the mirror. 'Come round for dinner tonight,' she said.

'I don't know yet what I'm doing tonight,' Gargan answered, not wanting her to make assumptions.

'Well, you've got to eat, so eat here.' She plucked a hair from her shoulder.

'I may want to eat somewhere else.' He tried to keep the irritation out of his voice. 'I don't know yet. I don't really like to make plans.'

'This evening is hardly planning.' She glanced in the mirror.

'It is to me,' he said, pulling the duvet up to his chin. 'I like to live from day to day. Hour to hour almost.'

'Well, all right,' she conceded. 'But be practical. You can't afford to eat out all the time.' He clucked in annoyance. 'You're not working, are you?'

'No, I'm not,' he shouted, 'but it's not your problem.'

'You can't afford to eat out if you're on the dole.'

'Hey, what is this, an interview?' She looked round, fastening the zip on her handbag.

'Maybe I have independent means. An inheritance, a title, a modest stipend. Maybe I run guns or push drugs. Could be I'm a ponce, or a whore ... You don't know. But it's not your problem. OK?'

She looked unruffled. The make-up and smart dress were armour. 'I'm going to be late for work,' she declared.

'I can be up, dressed and at the front door in three minutes,' Gargan announced.

'No. Don't hurry. Let yourself out,' she said and with that she left.

It was almost four o'clock when the phone woke him. He let it ring. It wasn't his, after all, so he wouldn't feel right answering it. He pressed the pillow over his head and recalled a Christmas many years ago when he had crouched in a corner at home terrified to answer the phone when it rang. He couldn't remember why he hadn't been able to answer the phone, but the feeling of abject loneliness was very clear in his mind.

The phone stopped ringing and Gargan uncovered his head. A short while later, showered and dressed, he stood by the bed and picked up the framed photograph. What was it about the man's face that made Gargan want to look at it again? The man's nose was slightly bent, like Gargan's, his eyes deep-set and inscrutable. Gargan turned to his left and faced the mirror. He held the photograph next to the glass and stared now at the photograph, now at his reflection, but the faces were different, even apart from the obvious things like glasses and facial hair. The noses were bent in opposite directions.

Rada was on, so Gargan went in.

'Dobro vece,' she greeted him when he had sat down.

He asked her how she was: 'Ka ko ste?'

'Dobro.'

Gargan's conversational Serbo-Croat exhausted, he ordered in English and she smiled as she tore off the order and placed it in the dumb waiter. Gargan noticed a man come in from the street and sit down at a table a few yards away. He looked hungry, for more than just a meal. His hair could have done with a wash and his eyes stared nervously, avoiding contact.

Gargan wasn't surprised later when the man left without paying. He rose quickly without appearing to have even stood up – the great skill of the 'runner' – and slid to the door like something viscous. Rada was at the far end of the restaurant collecting somebody's *coq au vin*, oblivious to the incident, until that seventh sense, common to all experienced in her trade, told her something was up. She looked round, dropped the *coq au vin* on the counter and made straight for the door. Gargan made as if to get up and help, but what could he do that Rada couldn't? All anyone could do was stand in the middle of the pavement, hands on hips and curses on lips, head shaking from side to side. She returned glaring. Before she noticed Gargan he was already shaking his head slowly and tutting.

'Not fair, is it?' he said, as much to the air as to her.

'I was at the other end. I can't watch everyone all the time.' She was angry.

'He was too quick,' Gargan threw in. 'Too quick. You couldn't have stopped him. It's not fair when it's so cheap to start with.' She looked at him. 'I know what it's like. I worked as a waiter once. It happened to me.'

'Did you?'

He couldn't believe it! She had asked him a question. This was what he wanted, the proof that she meant something by the way she looked at him. He mustn't ruin it. He must say the right thing. Should he tell her where he'd worked? How long ago it was? Tell her about the three squaddies who'd had their garlic pizzas with extra garlic then done a runner, even saying good-night to the cashier on the way out? Tell her about the heiress slumming it as a receptionist who'd fallen for him, in whose car they'd driven up to Barnet one night after work? How he'd placed a hand lightly on her leg and then they had driven back and she had dropped him off in King's Cross.

But it was too late to tell her anything because she'd gone.

He thought of Su to see if he felt anything. Nothing.

Rada was coming back. He decided on impulse to say something which had been at the back of his mind for a week. One afternoon he had called in at the Yugoslav tourist office to find out how to ask someone out for a drink in Serbo-Croat. Before Rada had a chance to ask about his dessert he spoke: 'Dali bi ste zelele da idete na bice?' She looked quite blank. It occurred to Gargan that he shouldn't have been so trusting. The translator could have been playing a Slav joke.

'Bice?' She looked puzzled.

'What?'

'Bice?'

'Yes. I think so. Doesn't it mean drink?'

'Drink? No. Drink is pice.'

'Pice. That's what I meant to say. Pice. How about it? I mean, if you'd like to.'

There was that smile again. 'Where,' she asked him, 'did you learn to speak Serbo-Croat so well?'

'A friend of mine,' he half lied. 'A Yugoslavian friend. He lived in London.

'What was his name?'

'Zoran. He was a waiter. Long darkish hair. He pretended to be Greek and called himself Nikis Socrates so he could work here.'

'Yes,' she nodded. 'I think I know him.'

'Yugoslavia's a big place.'

'Yes, but the world is so small.'

'Where did you learn to speak English so well?'

'With the person I live with.'

Gargan's heart sank. Did she mean live with or live with? He couldn't ask her. 'What about the drink then?'

'I don't really go out much,' she said, shaking her head. But then she smiled at him again.

'I'm pregnant,' Su said.

'What?'

Smile or no smile, Rada had rejected his offer. It was selfish and calculating, he knew, to go back to Kensal Green, but his ego was very demanding and the temptation too great.

'How?'

'Well, in the normal manner, I expect.'

'But how do you know? How *can* you know?'

She did seem to know though. And as it sank in he realized he wasn't as surprised as perhaps he might have been. *(Wandering through the bush carrying a child . . .)* He had received a warning of some kind. *(. . . whom he delivered to the woman . . .)* Yes, he'd dreamt it, he must have done. Her announcement made sense after . . . after what? He might be inventing a dream to explain this, the inexplicable. And suppose there had been a dream *(. . . the spirit child surfacing from the ether-water of the pool . . .)*, had it merely foretold the future or actually created the pregnancy?

'It's not you, honey.' He couldn't be a father. The baby would be born deformed. 'How could it be? How could I know so fast?'

He snapped to: 'What?'

'Don't worry,' she told him. 'It's not yours. Remember the actor in Paris I told you about?'

The actor. In Paris.

Gargan lay awake next to Su for a while thinking about his situation and the difference made to it by this new revelation. On balance it probably took the pressure off him. She could hardly make too many demands if she was carrying another man's child, so he could come and go as he wished, as long as she wanted him. For the time being it was a safe place: if she had razor blades he didn't know where they were.

The Stranger

He walked for miles thinking that he ought to feel thirsty, yet he felt no thirst. Mountain ranges were drawn past him on either side and broad spans of birds wheeled overhead waiting for him to drop to his knees, but he walked on, his head disassociated from his feet and his feet from feeling.

The nervous system reawoke, slowly as the budding of a flower, and pain intruded as a dark figure emerged from the heat-haze on the horizon. The newcomer floated steadily nearer and the bush-walker narrowed the mutual approach. His feet weighed heavily like lumps of wet sand and the bones in his lower legs cracked and shattered afresh with each step. Sweat throbbed from his pores, congealing the dust on his skin. Sand pricked the back of his eyeballs and scraped its way into his lungs, and just when his eyes were gluing shut and his kneecaps spinning round into dislocation, a strong arm encircled his shoulders.

He was led off at ninety degrees and soon they were marching between two high walls. The earth was the same, suggesting these incongruous walls had just arisen or been planted there. His guide turned to the left and the walls turned too, without appearing to have shifted at all. Turning again and again into a circle, the walls wrapped themselves around a doorframe.

The stranger gently guided him to the threshold where he began to resist, a token struggle, tugging at the other's beard, unwilling to enter the shell of a house.

The stranger turned his faceless head and left him standing in the centre of a darkened room. He watched through the open doorway as the black figure of his gaoler disappeared in the distance of the walled dusty corridor.

He looked up at the higher reaches of the interior walls, where half a dozen tiny empty oblongs were the only windows and all that could be seen through them was the white sky. Deep in the far wall hidden by shadow was a closed door.

He heard a distant rumbling from the doorway. It wasn't possible to see anything unusual through the heat-induced vibration of the air distorting the twin walls and twisting them into restless spirals. The rumble had increased in volume. Something was coming. He could feel its approach beneath his feet, with the force of an earthquake or a tidal wave. Now he could see it thundering towards him but couldn't tell what it was. Maybe a storm of black dust, but as it got closer he could see it was a viscous liquid. And that it was red. Splashing like surf on rocks it hit the walls and instantly found the doorway. It caught him in the neck and picked him up and threw him against the far wall. As the level in the room rose swiftly only natural buoyancy kept his head above the froth. In the turbulence his legs were beaten this way and that like strips of liver. Soon its peaks touched the ceiling and the tiny windows were breached but the unceasing force of more pouring in through the doorway was greater and as he gasped for air the boiling blood thrust into his mouth and he gagged.

Unconnected Phone

It was a long way for her to go back to her place and she was tired. She lived in Pontoise about fifteen miles north of Paris. She was tired and not feeling very well.

It was morning by the time we got back to my studio and I had classes. The first night had been a Thursday and the next morning was a busy one for me at the school.

I made coffee and let Jenni sleep in my bed while I went over the road. The kids were quieter than usual, which was a relief because my head and stomach felt as if they'd switched contents. I did crosswords on the board with the first class and hangman with the next lot. Nothing too demanding, for them or me. There was just one sticky moment when I used the word 'bit' in the phrase 'have a bit to eat'. They pronounced it 'beat' which resulted in general hysterics. General except for me, that is. I felt foolish when a patient teacher explained to me later that 'la bite' was the slang equivalent of 'le pénis'.

I went back to the studio at lunchtime and Jenni was sitting up in bed reading a Zola paperback. She looked much better. Shyly I retreated into the kitchen and prepared an omelette which we shared, with me sitting on the bed. I'd given her a baggy shirt to sleep in. It gaped a little bit and I kept looking away. Nothing had happened and nothing had been said. I said I had more classes and didn't want to be late and she asked if she could stay and read since she was so comfortable.

I went and sat in the park all afternoon. The classes had been an excuse. I sat on the stone bench on the little observation platform at the top of the park. The pond, the streets and cafés of the *quartier* and the rest of Paris were beneath me. I tried not to think. When I finally returned she was asleep. I sat and watched her breathing but soon felt obscurely guilty and went into the kitchen. While I was preparing a meal she got up and came into the doorway.

'How are you?' I asked her.

She yawned and stretched. 'Sleepy,' she said.

I experienced a weird mixture of feelings: guilt for looking at her, excitement at how she looked and disappointment that she seemed not to realize how the sight of her aroused me. I attacked the steak vigorously in the frying pan, prodding with a spatula. She passed through into the bathroom. I made as much noise as I could with my pans and cupboard doors. I told myself I was being stupid. She didn't have to make allowances for me; I had invited her back; she didn't owe me anything. I just couldn't work out if something was *happening* or not.

It was only after we'd eaten the steak and potatoes and were for some reason sitting on the bed that something did actually happen. We sat there talking for about half an hour and all I know is that at some point I kissed her briefly on the lips. It seemed I hadn't misjudged the situation, because she immediately gave me a big hug.

For the next hour we remained on the bed just kissing and holding each other. It didn't feel real. I wondered why it wasn't an enormous release for me and I think it was because it felt so unreal, as if I wasn't there and someone else was doing it, or I was there but I was playing a role. I observed myself and couldn't stop doing so. I felt as if I ought to be on stage. Which reminded me. I sneaked a look over Jenni's shoulder at my watch. Seven-thirty. I should have been there an hour ago. My entrance was at 8.45. If the telephone had worked it would have been ringing. I explained the situation to Jenni and she said she wanted to come with me. We left the studio eleven minutes later and had to fight through the Christmas shoppers.

The second night went quite well. I was reprimanded for lateness but I performed well. There was still a lot of work to do, but plenty of time to do it: the run was three months.

Jenni came back with me and we made the mistake of going to bed and rushing everything. It was cold and methodical and we ended up sleeping back to back in my narrow bed.

The following day was a Saturday. We went out walking,

crossing the park and heading south, through Père Lachaise and down as far as the river. We were both a little worried that it wouldn't work but we told each other it would.

In the evening we took the suburban train from the Gare du Nord to Pontoise. Her studio was smaller than mine and cosier. It consisted of a room and a kitchen. There was a midget bath in the kitchen and the toilet was outside. Jenni cooked dinner then we relaxed. She said how late it was. When I prepared to go she walked me to the door and across the street. Coloured light bulbs and decorations had been strung between the houses for Christmas. Watching her feet she said she hadn't meant to sound like she was kicking me out. I didn't reply for a moment, which she said was ominous, but I said I was trying to think of how to phrase what I wanted to say. 'I thought you had wanted me to go after last night.' Still looking down she said, 'No, not at all.' So we turned round and walked back, holding hands.

We were together the next two weeks virtually all the time. Nights we spent either at her place or mine. Whenever I got back to my studio I went straight to the telephone and was consistently disappointed. She came to the performances and I gave up the teaching job at the end of the first week when we got paid at the theatre. Ed and Dick handed out cash: 300 francs to everyone, themselves included. Apologetically they assured us it would get better, that when the bills were paid off we would get at least 700 francs a week.

We spent long mornings in bed, the bluish light edging sideways through the lace curtain and falling across the silent telephone. One day we looked at photographs Jenni had taken weeks ago and I massaged her shoulders while she concentrated on the pictures. I slid my hands under her arms and covered her breasts very lightly with my palms. She shivered and dropped the photographs in the bed. Stretching back into my chest she dropped her hands on to my legs and pulled them out straight, then turned round kneeling to face me. Several photos were being creased under her knee but she lifted my chin and made me look at her. I stooped to kiss her neck. She ran her hand across the base of my stomach and let it fall into my lap.

The photographs went everywhere, sliding underneath us.

Some ended up so creased the images were unrecognizable. Jenni picked up a good one and studied it. I sat up. 'Look,' she said. It was upside down. But when I looked carefully I could see it was far more interesting than the right way up. It was a view of the city taken at night with a long exposure so that the sky was white and the lights burned brilliantly. Upside down the sky became snow on a wide boulevard and inversion made little difference to the buildings, which now rose out of the snow. Scattered bursts of light were horse-drawn carriages and the whole thing looked like an Impressionist painting.

Other inverted photographs of Paris skylines revealed a small corner of a Canadian town with a husky-dog sled team about to set off on an expedition, an Alpine ski resort with huge hotels, a snowbound busy gaslit square in Imperial Russia, and an Icelandic city hemmed in between the freezing sea and steep icy mountains.

It might not mean much now, but it meant a lot then. It was a small, shared discovery.

Jenni had already arranged to go away for Christmas, to see friends in Belgium. The night before she was due to go we were making love, lying alongside and kissing, holding, caressing each other. Slowly and with some awkwardness I began to lift and slide my body on top of hers. Suddenly I was watching us both. Then I was myself again but there was somebody else there, and it was me. I was watching me lying on Jenni's right side whilst fully aware of my body being where I was, on her left side. Which one was me? I sensed my own presence within myself. So who was this other person, who seemed also to be me, lying there? In fact, it didn't feel as if I was in the company of an imposter, but simply in the company of myself. At the time it was deeply disturbing and I felt threatened.

I spent Christmas Day in the studio waiting for the phone to ring, but it wasn't connected. I began to get miserable until I thought to myself that I was better off with an unconnected phone than a phone I couldn't answer. It seemed to me I had experienced that one Christmas, or dreamt it one night.

Jenni came back on New Year's Eve and we went to a party

held by some friends of Sylvain's in Pigalle. At midnight everyone toasted the New Year in. For Jenni and myself it felt wonderful to be together again. I got extremely drunk and Jenni had to take me home. I had no memory of anything at all between just after midnight and 12.15 the following afternoon when I was woken by the noise of Jenni having a shower.

Later in the day when we were sitting on the bed drinking coffee with only a couple of candles burning, Jenni asked me if I would like to see a poem and I said yes.

This is what she showed me:

'Parties'
voice-filled rooms
with faces, mindless
words filling spaces
senseless sounds falling
on ears deafened by silent years
spent learning movements
signifying implied understanding
assumed agreement
meaning nothing.

Victoria Line

He couldn't breathe, couldn't move his tongue or stop his stomach twisting. He gagged.

He opened his eyes and saw dirt, his mouth was full of it. He heaved again and succeeded in clearing his throat. Hauling great gulps of air into his lungs he spat out as much soil as he could, but particles continued to grit between his teeth, causing considerable discomfort.

Although it was throbbing he lifted his head and looked about. A cemetery! Graves and tombstones crowded around and there was a memorial slab standing at the head of the grave on which he lay: 'Alexia Pryce. A very dear child taken too soon from this life, aged thirty-two' Someone had been digging. Clods of turf had been ripped up and much soil turned over. He looked at his hands: they were filthy, the fingernails black. The excavation was no deeper than ten or twelve inches which meant he had been a good four or five feet short of hitting wood, and for this at least he could be thankful. But despite that, lying in the dirt only a few feet above the deceased Alexia Pryce – whose name rang bells, though he couldn't think why – he had something else to worry about, for he was completely naked.

After walking some way, as carefully as possible to protect his lacerated feet, he came across a gravel path. More painful maybe, but only by using it could he be sure of finding his way out. As it was the path led him to another, which in turn led to another. Each looked the same. The same motley procession of headstones in varying states of repair slipping by on either side, and the same untrimmed, overgrown borders sprouting dandelions and brambles; the same heavy trees standing darkly in between. His horrible suspicion that the paths curved in a spiral soon proved correct. Gargan stood in a small circular conjunction of paths and set off immediately down one of them.

He was aware that he was in a mess. There was, to start with, his incision. Deeper now, it caused him pain from time to time, and anguish. He wanted to stop the process but was wary of taking a preventive measure such as clearing the house of razor blades and old newspapers, in case this had an adverse effect like waking a sleepwalker. If when asleep in the early hours – he had come to terms with the fact that he performed the operation in his sleep – he should fail to lay his hands on the blade, he might grope about and find the scissors, for instance. It seemed wiser to retain the razor blade since it was practical and efficient.

Establishing the motive was imperative. Was it a subconscious urge? Was he a paranoid schizophrenic? He couldn't go to a doctor and become an exhibit paraded before students. The piercers of Bethnal Green had not shed any light with their blood, so he had to find out for himself. Once he had done so he might be able to find a way to stop it. To this idea he clung.

He turned on to another path. If the pattern was how he imagined it, he should by now be approaching the perimeter.

His next problem was Su. To continue seeing her would do nothing to advance his cause: she was not repulsed by his modification. As for her effect on his tightrope walking, her enthusiasm was now a distraction. Her face singled out from the crowd was the one which would make him fall. Then there was Rada, the only person Gargan cared about. He'd thought, cynically, that sleeping at Su's would stop him incising, but that was no good if the alternative was sleepwalking in the nude and eating soil in a cemetery at dawn.

The trees were thinning out somewhat now and Gargan could hear the occasional car changing down through its gears. He'd never been inside Kensal Green Cemetery but assumed that was where he was, since the gates were only a few hundred yards from Su's flat. He became increasingly conscious of his nakedness the nearer he came to the edge. It was still very early but there were always two or three people out at this time on strange contrived pretexts. He began to glimpse houses between the trees. Eventually he reached a railing and vaulted carefully, for the spikes were sharp, and crept along in the shadow of overhanging trees.

He'd passed no one by the time he recognized the familiar architecture of a small local BR station partially hidden at the bottom of the hill. This would be Kensal Green. He couldn't see the name yet and there were no streetnames visible to confirm his whereabouts. A Mini swung out of a side street and the spiky-haired driver pipped his horn, grinning at Gargan, who growled and hurried on. He reached the end of the street and found the railway station ahead of him. The name was obscured by trees and he could only see n e . He ran on, willing Ke sal Gr en to appear, fearing all of a sudden that it might not.

It did not.

The missing letters were Nu h ad.

Nunhead.

He prayed Su would not have left for work before the cab got to Kensal Green. She should have seen his clothes on the floor by the bed and worked out what had happened.

Nunhead though! How had he walked so far in his sleep? He hadn't even been drunk. Once, very drunk, he had walked across Paris to reach his bed. Waking up at lunchtime he couldn't believe his good fortune at being there, because the last time he could remember being conscious was around midnight near Pigalle. He deduced that he'd walked rather than taken a cab by the thickness of dogshit on the soles of his shoes.

'Good party was it then?' the cabbie asked as they passed through Camberwell Green.

'What?' said Gargan, startled.

'Last night. This morning. Good party?'

'Yes.' It was easier to lie. 'Not that I remember much.'

The driver laughed and Gargan joined in with false bonhomie.

'What's your 'ead feel like?'

'Not too good.'

'Some of this'll clear it.' The cabbie pulled out a thermos flask and stuck it out behind his back for Gargan to take.

'No thanks,' Gargan said, feeling queasy. The colourful

anorak hanging on a hook in the cab would have been more useful. He slumped and sat out the rest of the journey in silence.

Su helped him clean and apply antiseptic cream to his feet which were badly cut and bruised. The more she did for him the worse Gargan felt inside, because he did need her help but didn't want to be in that position. Only when he was resting with his feet up did she ask him where he'd been. He simply told her he'd been sleepwalking and left it at that.

'It's not working,' he said.

'What?' she asked warily.

'Me being in London again. I'm obviously not meant to be.'

'Why not?'

'These things weren't happening in Europe,' he declared. 'Incising. Sleepwalking. And I was walking the wire regularly.'

She cut in: 'Until France.'

'If I didn't walk for some time that's my business. It's all my business.'

'There's no need to get like that,' she said calmly.

'I need to get a hold,' he said. 'I'm wondering if I should go back to Europe. Just for a while.' She said nothing. He felt rotten. 'I might not . . . I probably won't . . .' Still she was silent. 'I feel I need to regain control of my life.'

'Sounds to me,' she said, 'like you're in a mess.'

'Yes,' he leapt to answer. 'Yes, I think I am. Just a few problems but I need to sort them out . . . I want to find out what's making me do these things.'

'How,' she asked, 'will going back to Europe help?'

'I don't know,' he replied.

To do it alone would be difficult. First he would need to gain entry into the derelict hospital and secure one end of the wire. At the top of the Wellington Arch he would have to find another secure place.

Then there was the walk itself. And finally the escape.

He went back to the house to practise. The street was quiet as if everyone had moved away. Outside number sixteen there was an orange Reliant Regal Supervan III that never seemed to move. Gargan's building was virtually unfurnished. He didn't use the ground floor; the rooms were empty. On the first floor there was a kitchen, a toilet, and his bedroom, which contained very few books, some clothes, a bureau, a small table and a mattress. There was one more room with a single feature.

He tested the wire with one foot. It was taut, running from the front of the house to the back only eighteen inches off the ground. Not a great test but it was useful for practice. He stepped on to it, jumped to see how safe his attachment system was. It held secure and there was just the right amount of give in the wire. He walked, springing his ankles and heels, to the far end then returned at a gentle trot. He lifted one leg and hopped the full length of the wire. Coming back he dropped to a crouch and almost crawled. This took its toll on his ankles and exhausted his calf muscles. He wondered how Henri Rochetain had been able to sleep on his wire. For 185 days he had remained 25 metres aloft, above a supermarket in St Etienne, even sleeping on the wire to the great puzzlement of doctors.

Gargan slept on the wire that night. Part of him wanted to prove it was possible and part of him just couldn't be bothered to get off the wire and go to bed.

He squatted, achieving a perfect balance. The balls of his feet hugged the wire, his arms dangled in front, his head sagged on to his chest. He moved from time to time in his sleep but never enough to upset the balance.

He dreamt the wire was as sharp as a blade, cutting, slicing into him as he crouched upon it. Like a scalpel guided by a surgeon it squeezed into his flesh, bisecting his body neatly in seconds. He fell, half on each side, to the dusty earth. The wire ran on to the horizon where it disappeared in a heat-haze. As he walked, his counterpart tracked him. Soon the wire on his right had become a wall stretching ahead. He looked behind: there was no wire in the distance, only the wall and both he and his counterpart had become whole, each a replica of the other.

A man was behind him holding him, forcing him to look up at a window in the wall. Large drops of blood suddenly spattered like red rain on the inside of the glass. It began to pour down the window in streaks from above. The man lifted him up and pressed his head against the glass. The blood bubbled on the floor of the room and swirled around a man's foot.

He saw his other self standing in the room like a reflection, the window having become a mirror. But then the man behind him increased the pressure on the back of his neck and forced his head into the window, smashing the glass. He was pushed through the frame. Broken shards of glass creased like paper under his touch. He plunged head first into the blood-pool, curved up from the bottom and broke the surface to find himself all alone; the window through which he had entered was a picture in a frame and the level of blood was rising.

It took all morning to shake off the depression which clung to him like a hood after his dream and the fact that even sleeping on the wire, he had still managed to sleepwalk and cut himself.

He spent the afternoon making some special purchases and going to see Rada at the restaurant and talking with her at some length, then after dark he turned into Grosvenor Place and made for the rear of the derelict hospital. Using a route discovered years ago when he'd been working at the restaurant next door, he gained entry through an open window. He landed on an old bent metal sign and waited for the crash to stop resounding in his ears. He listened to the silence which seemed to hum and buzz like a fluorescent bulb. Carefully he stepped over to the door which hung wrenched off its hinges.

Suddenly there was a terrible clattering din and something propelled itself out of the shadows towards him. It flew over his head and out of the window. A pigeon.

He allowed his heart to slow down and his nerves to stop jangling, then proceeded into the corridor. Rooms opened to left and right, some like dark cupboards, others lit dimly by skylights and glass roofs. One small room told a story all its own: the door was flung open, an empty dusty chair sat on castors in the middle of the floor, and a white coat was sprawled over a bench as if hastily removed. Gargan could almost see the chair still swivelling.

In a room on the left of the corridor a large cabinet had all its drawers pulled out displaying thousands of test tubes, syringes and swabs. Broken glass lay scattered all around.

There was an indefinable menace hanging in the air, much more frightening than the threat of a security guard stumbling across him.

The corridor led him into a large room with workbenches and washbasins. At the far side of the room on the left was a concertinaed door to a lift shaft. On the bench nearest to this were dispersed hundreds of transparencies. These too had been here years ago. A jar of liquid stood exactly where it had before, next to a window, where during the day it caught the light and was red. After nightfall it was black.

Of these props his memories were crystal clear. He remembered also the restaurant next door and how he had waited on tables night after night, joking with Alex the heiress receptionist during slack periods. But there was nothing beyond the restaurant, with the single exception of a midnight drive up to Barnet in Alex's car. She'd taken him to King's Cross afterwards but he couldn't picture it in any detail.

His heavy bag swinging at his side, he found his way easily through derelict wards, corridors and laboratories to the higher floors overlooking Hyde Park Corner. In one room there he found exactly what he wanted. The open window had a direct view to Wellington Arch and the ceiling was propped up by reinforced metal poles. Gargan tried to budge the poles with his shoulder but they were rock steady. To be safe he would split the strain between three poles by attaching the incoming wire to a four-ring steel junction and securing that.

He set his bag on the floor and took out the hardware. It reminded him of the piercers' paraphernalia in Bethnal Green.

It took two hours to fix the wires to his satisfaction. He felt strange: he didn't really want to do what he was doing, but since he was doing it he wanted to do it well. He lowered the wire out of the window, then inspected the clamps, picked up his bag and left.

It was another hour before he emerged from the derelict hospital and walked round to get his wire. He had to stop in the middle of the road to wait for an Escort van to go by. Leaving just enough slack behind him, he passed the war memorial and proceeded down the path to the big arch, which he scaled in forty minutes spurred on by the knowledge that the Arch housed London's smallest police station. There could barely be room for two officers and an angle-poise lamp. After two hours' work weaving in and out of the horses' legs on the top of the arch, and using some of these to anchor the wire, it was beginning to get light. The amount of traffic round Hyde Park Corner had doubled.

He sat down to relax. He extended his telescopic pole to check it, then closed it again. He would feel when the time was right. Su was coming at nine. By telling her that meeting him in the tube station with his bag was more important than watching him walk, he had managed to get rid of the disorientating threat of her presence under the wire.

Maybe another reason for delaying was to wait for a crowd to gather. He still didn't particularly enjoy performing but occasionally he gave in and indulged in some small display of showmanship, which he always regretted. Such moments seemed superfluous to the tightrope walking, but when he thought that, he always raised the question, what is the point of it anyway?

It gave apparent order and purpose to his otherwise chaotic life, but he didn't think those needs had always been there. The tightrope walking might almost have invented them.

The traffic was steady now. One or two pedestrians stood and stared. He wanted to get at least halfway across before the police wondered what all the fuss was about. On this occasion he couldn't afford to spend time in the cells. He swung his left foot on to the wire.

He began a little too quickly and had to slow down. The pole, though light, had taken the momentum of the quick start and seemed to pull him faster than he wanted to go. He reined in on the pole, causing it to bounce off his groin and creating a hiatus in his progress. He pressed on when all was steady.

He looked up at the war memorial and his heart missed a beat. The wire swayed inches above the muzzle of a rifle. How could he not have tightened it sufficiently? Was it slipping?

His feet kept taking him forward. The nearer he got the more the wire sagged. When he got there it would snag. He was high enough for the fall to be fatal, or paralyse him. He poured curses on whatever caused him to do this. Why couldn't he lead a normal life? Go to work, come home, go to bed, get up, etc. Maybe have a girlfriend. Rada. *Rada*. He wanted her, now more than ever. She was all he wanted. Why couldn't their paths coincide? Why not? Her face filled his mind, blocking out all vision. Shoulder-length dyed-blonde hair, dark arched eyebrows and deep-set kind eyes, fine strong nose and a smile like a warm evening. Her features conspired to create a magnificent paradox: penetrative and sympathetic, yet aloof and ambiguous. He watched her face dip and angle slightly, sliding into that smile and holding it, until she turned away with a single heel twist.

When he was finally conscious of sight again, he had passed over the war memorial and was just coming over the road. Whether he had been close to falling or not he never knew.

A number of people had gathered and he felt strange, as if he were doing something private in a public place. He gazed at the black hole of the window in the peeling white wall of the hospital, still a long way away.

No, Rada had said earlier that day. No. But how could he have expected her to say otherwise? He hardly knew her. She knew him even less well. But he knew her better than the extent of their relations should have allowed. He loved the beauty which came from within her and lit up her face.

'Watch out!'

The wire swung wildly in the wake of a huge lorry. The shout came from below. Gargan stooped low to stay on the wire, which slowly returned to normal, though still slacker than it was safe to be.

The police appeared as he approached the far side of the road. Their instruction to him, delivered through a loudhailer, brought laughter from the crowd: 'Come down!' Gargan was banking on the police remaining outside the hospital, waiting for him to come out. They would never have explored the building; he doubted if even the security guards had.

The swing in the rope was less pronounced now he pushed

himself into the incline. He clung with his toes like an inverted sloth and the crowd beneath applauded, causing him to prickle with a mixture of resentment and pleasure.

Losing his pole safely and quickly, Gargan dived through the window and landed heavily. He darted to the doorway and across the next room; round a series of work benches and stacked chemical racks; over a sheet of hardboard which rang hollowly; down a flight of stairs two at a time, making more than enough noise to attract the torches he saw playing on the far wall. The bearers couldn't see him from where they were. He moved quickly and quietly, changing his route, descending another flight and creeping under the room in which he could now hear the guards moving about. He reached a corridor he didn't recognize, but he felt he was going in the right direction. TOXIPATHOLOGY, said an arrow pointing the way he was going. He crunched broken glass; the circular window of a swing door on his left had been smashed, from the inside. On a table inside the room was something that looked like a heart or a lung long extracted and gone hard, host to various fungoid substances. He stepped closer and prodded the thing with a pencil that lay on the bench. Its matter didn't yield, nor did the thing itself budge. Maybe it was a tumour but he hoped not, considering it was the size of a large fist.

A sound distracted him: something knocked to the floor upstairs. He left the room and proceeded to the end of the corridor, where he pushed through swing doors and down more steps. The lower he got the damper it was. The walls were moist and he had to be careful not to slip on the moss growing on the stone steps. At the bottom was a locked door and an open corridor leading to a hallway. The door probably led down but forcing it would be foolish. He went along to the hallway and looked around. This was familiar. If he took that small staircase and went left . . . He ran up the steps and turned into the narrow passageway he had known would be there.

He nudged the door closed quietly, then locked it with its bar. Now he went straight down, a narrow spiral stairway. He was no longer in the hospital but beneath it. Now it was just a question of finding the right way, using his memory of previous explorations, fresh knowledge garnered from maps and his sense of direction. The important thing to remember was that it was possible. You could get to every conceivable corner of London without ever rising to street level.

There were several different sorts of tunnel. The tube was only the most obvious. Gargan used a variety: tube tunnels, tube service tunnels, GPO tunnels and sewers. His immediate access from beneath the hospital was to the dirty passages and tunnels of a disused section of the Underground. From here he worked his way into the subterranean infrastructure.

All the time, as he crept along the sooty walls, crawled through junctions narrow as slim cigars, pulling his weight by his fingernails, and waded disdainfully through marshes of crap, he thought of Rada; not of the woman he was on his way to meet, Su, who knew only what Gargan wanted her to know about her complicity in his escape. Not of her, but of Rada.

The riskiest sections of his underground hike were live tube tunnels. Here there was a real possibility he would be seen, but the station he was aiming for was not equipped with video cameras. He wormed his way through a service shaft and dropped into the tunnel leading to Green Park. Almost immediately though he felt a tremor growing to a steady vibration in the rails. This part of the exercise he had never practised. Last time he'd been down in the tube tunnels was in the middle of the night, when only cleaning and service vehicles were in use.

The advancing train threw a splash of light on to the wall by his head. There had to be enough room to hug the wall and let the train go by. There had to be. But still. It only had to nick him in one place, one loose hanging part of his clothes, one ankle bone, or the back of his head.

The train was coming. He ran. He knew it was stupid, but he ran. Seconds before the train's lights turned the corner, he fell headlong into a hole beneath the track. He landed on his feet and hands in a crouch, avoiding serious damage, and the train thundered overhead.

He was in a service dugout. As he climbed out of it his legs were shaking. He ran along the right-hand rail and covered the distance to the station in no time.

The platform was not busy. At this time of the morning this was a station where people got off rather than on. There was a middle-aged woman reading a copy of *Reader's Digest*. Two women stood together, dressed in brightly coloured tights, floral skirts and turned-up striped collars with pearls. Then there were three Oriental men in suits and briefcases, and a bearded man in his 30s contravening the no-smoking regulations.

But no Su.

He climbed up on to the platform, arousing the attention of the bearded man, who pulled on his cigarette and looked away.

She'd got the platform wrong. He found her on the other side, holding on to the locked hold-all he'd asked her to bring. He thanked her, said goodbye and dived back into the tunnel to begin the second leg of his escape: from her. She thought he was going back into the tunnel to change.

Twenty minutes later Gargan stepped out of a tunnel and on to the southbound Victoria Line platform at Victoria Station. He made his way up to the main-line station.

He checked his bag again before getting on the train: money, passport, wallet, spare clothing, essential toiletries. He wondered what he'd forgotten, because there was always something. He ran down the list of things without which he couldn't leave the country, and he seemed to have everything. Even his ticket.

Just the Two of Us

I assumed she'd written the poem that day as I slept off the effects of my drinking, but in fact she wrote it after the first-night party, the occasion on which we met.

My guess was that the poem was not hers and was in her handwriting only because she had copied it from a book or from memory. When she revealed its authorship I pressed for more. I wanted to read everything she'd written, in an afternoon. But she made excuses.

As soon as the New Year festivities were over it was back to work; back to the theatre. And back to school. When I went in to chivvy them over my final paycheque I was asked if I would do them a favour: one lesson a week. They were short-staffed and would be very grateful. I agreed.

The general return to work obviously excluded the PTT. My telephone still was not connected. The PTT office requested that I 'patienter un petit peu'.

In Pontoise one night, that which so far had been absent from the Christmas period arrived. I drew the short straw that morning: going out for the croissants. When I opened the door to the street there was snow everywhere.

By the time I got to Paris it was all slush.

Over the short break Ed and Dick had done some thinking. We now had understudies, but only one per group. The boys and I had Tom who, being Texan, doubled up as dialect coach, and tripled up as stage manager. The girls had Liz, a New Yorker.

A strange thing happened after the performance. A woman whom I had noticed in the front row – I tried to ignore her because she stared so insistently – came backstage and burst into our dressing room. She marched up, scrutinized me and seemed about to speak when suddenly she faltered. She tried to speak but was too flustered to make sense. It transpired she thought she knew me, until she got up close and something drained her of conviction.

We talked for a while; she was living in Paris. Since Jenni was staying in Pontoise that night, meaning simply that I didn't have to be anywhere at a certain time, I took the woman up the road to La Palette for a drink. We ended up going back to the studio and she stayed the night, which I regretted later. She was very keen to see me again but I said I couldn't. She even asked for a photograph and I said if she really wanted one she could call the theatre. She collected one the next day.

We all got paid at the end of the first week in January. Three hundred francs each. Ed and Dick apologized and mentioned the extra expense of two new people. They told us not to worry: houses, which had been full for the first week, were slackening off now, but would pick up again.

In Jenni's studio we shared a bath. It was tiny but deep, with two levels. There was a ledge which I sat on, as deep as a normal bath, and a deeper level where Jenni sat with her back to me and her head between my knees. On the landlady's radio we found a station which played jazz piano through the night. We sat in the bath for over an hour sometimes, listening to the music. We found shapes in the pattern on the thin blue curtain that hung in the doorway. I thought I could see a threatening face, but Jenni saw polar bears, which when they were pointed out to me I could also see. I always tried to concentrate on them and blur the human face, which I didn't mention to Jenni.

We walked a couple of miles to Osny one afternoon before it was time for me to go to the theatre. By chance we discovered an overgrown cemetery with dozens of statues arranged in tableaux hidden in the trees representing the Twelve Stations of the Cross. At the end of the trail was an area of open ground where an altar and open-air chapel had been constructed. There was a collection box nailed to the stone brimming with coins although the place seemed uncared for.

Something that afternoon brought us extremely close. I don't know whether it was the small three-legged dog which befriended us or the fresh beauty of the scene: the full silver moon in the early blue sky, the trees, the crosses and statues, and across the railway line a small fire burning on a construction site. Whatever it was, I felt tears welling up in my eyes. They fell silently and struck the ground. In front of me kneeling down to touch the dog, Jenni was shaking. She too was crying.

I felt supremely happy.

At the theatre Ed and Dick were getting worse. We had discovered that they were both models and we spent many hours, the girls, Tom and myself, fortifying ourselves by bitching about them. They spent an awful lot of time sitting in front of their mirrors. The dressing room was built for two, but the three of us shared it. The girls had the only other one. I often felt like a visitor in their private bedroom, perched on a stool at the back, craning now and then for a glimpse of my make-up in the mirror. Beneath the two mirrors surrounded by lightbulbs were two tiny tables attached to the wall where Ed and Dick somehow found room for their things: bouquets of flowers, telegrams and cards, make-up, emergency medicines, lemons, bottles of Evian water, religious tokens, acting manuals, tissues, whisky flasks, cigarettes, ashtrays, breath freshener, deodorant, chewing gum, and back copies of fashion magazines in which their modelling photographs appeared.

They took hours to warm up. Ed stayed in the dressing room. His vocal exercises swelled to fill it with sound, so that I felt my presence diminish further, while Dick strode around the downstairs bar tossing his stetson into the air and strutting.

If they were intent upon the erosion of my personality it didn't bother me.

Because I had Fudakowski.

It took two hours.

We were in bed at my studio. We had been there all afternoon and evening, in bed together for much of that time. The day was Sunday, my evening off. It took two hours of making love to convince me there were just the two of us, which is to say, just the one of me. I kept telling myself that the feeling of observing myself from a distant vantage point was an illusion; the face in the window was just my reflection and the human features disguised as flowers on the wallpaper just my imagination. I was myself again. The sensations were mine. The obsessive self-observation had disappeared.

At some point I fell asleep and began dreaming.

The telephone rang.

Not having heard it ring before and having almost given up hope of it ever doing so, I didn't recognize the noise. It was just a bell, an alarm of some kind.

Crossing the room on weakened legs I hovered over the grey telephone while it rang again shrilly. I picked up the handset.

A thick voice spoke in French with a heavy accent. 'Allo,' I said. He continued speaking but the sound of his voice was mutilated by interference. There were gaps in his speech but they didn't correspond to the gaps when I was asking questions. He was repeating a word, I could tell that much. Presumably a name, either his own or that of the person he had expected to answer. But due to the confusion and crackles, I couldn't make out the name. It was just a two-syllabled grumble. Scarman or Barber, Harden or Margan, I didn't know. I motioned to Jenni to pick up the second earpiece from its cradle.

When the caller had finally gone, apparently hanging up in mid-sentence, by which stage he was no longer speaking French but possibly English, I asked Jenni what she thought he was saying.

'It seemed perfectly clear to me,' she said, pausing.

'Well?' I asked.

'Gargan.'

The name had that vague significance things sometimes have in dreams.

The Rail

The Rai

The journey produced a surprise.

She was sitting in the hovercraft departure lounge when he first noticed her. They were evidently awaiting the same flight. He could only see her profile, and it was entirely familiar to him, yet he couldn't place it. He could get up and stroll around the seating area to see her from the front, but didn't want to because that would destroy the spell. Viewed head-on the face would be a stranger's. Gargan had experienced the coincidence before: that a person in profile or from behind bore a startling resemblance to someone he knew. It was usually an hour or two before he was able to put a name to the memory.

The woman, obviously American judging by her glasses, trousers and build, got up and joined the queue. The walk was familiar too, casual yet confident. He had no idea where he'd seen it before but felt sure he had. He stood alongside and took in her profile. The way she picked up her bag and put it down again as the queue slow-marched to the gate, even that was familiar. Gargan was half scared now that she would feel his gaze and turn on him accusingly. *Don't we know each other?* It was feeble. It didn't even deserve a rebuff.

He stayed behind on the tarmac and was almost thankful when she turned left into the smoking compartment. He wasn't going to add a smoky atmosphere to the risks of nausea he had heard so much about. It was his first trip on a hovercraft and he was expecting it to be less than enjoyable, especially since the item he had forgotten to pack was seasickness pills. He knew where they were: he could picture them hiding in his salvaged bureau in the pigeonhole second from the left.

He took a single window seat on the right then gave it up when four girls wanted to sit three across the aisle and one in his seat. He sat at the window end of the row behind and was instantly imprisoned when an Australian couple moved in to occupy the two seats between him and the aisle. Their knees wedged behind the seats in front and they took out a number of books and notepads. The brown paper bag in the seat netting facing him was more of a taunt than a comfort. If he was going to be sick he wanted to do it properly, have plenty of room to do it in and preferably a bowl to aim at. But how would he get past these people and their books in time? He ought to do so now and sit elsewhere, in smoking if necessary, but the great machine had begun to lift itself off the ground and was already turning round to face the sea. The bodywork rattled ferociously, as if it were trying to shake loose every rivet.

The hovercraft flew down the steep ramp and shot out on to the water. It proceeded steadily without the slightest roll or sway, but Gargan would not be falsely soothed: he knew they were still in the harbour and once they left its shelter the craft would yield to the sea.

But he was proved wrong and for once was glad to be. It was steadier than many bus rides he had taken. They passed ships to starboard and in no time were in sight of the French coast.

He delayed his exit to coincide with hers, but saw that she was talking to the man in the next seat. She looked up, laughing at something he said, and Gargan saw her face. The illusion remained intact. The face was familiar. Everything about her connected with a memory which Gargan could not trace.

He hurried out of the hovercraft and down to the French tarmac, slightly unnerved for a moment. He slowed down, hoping she might draw level, but she didn't appear. He continued towards the queue for passport control, craning his neck to look for her but without success. Then, when his part of the queue snaked round the next hurdle, he saw her at the back. She was no longer talking to the man, but he was right behind her.

Somehow he lost her between passport control and the train, so he concentrated on assuring himself of a good seat, then went to look for her. She was sitting by the window in the next carriage with the same man at her side. Gargan went back to his seat and spent the journey waiting for her to pass him on her way to the buffet car. It was only on arrival in Paris that he realized the frequent passage of the minibar meant the train had no buffet car. He got off and waited on the platform until she appeared, the man in close attendance.

'Excuse me,' he said. She looked at him. 'I'm sure I know you. Do you recognize me?'

She pondered a moment before saying, 'No.'

He was even more sure now he heard her speak. 'I'm sorry to be insistent, but I'm sure we've met.'

'No, I don't think so. Did you ever go to California?'

'California? No. Never. But maybe you've been to Europe?'

'I was in England and just arrived in Paris, as you see.'

'Do you have a sister? A cousin? It's just that you remind me of someone. Very strongly. You must have a twin sister.'

'No. Really I don't. I have no family except my parents.'

'Oh.' He was disappointed. 'Sorry . . .' He began to move away, but she didn't seem to want him to go.

'Do you know Paris?' she asked.

'Yes, very well. I've stayed here before.'

'I need to find a room. Do you know where I should go?'

The man, alongside now, frowned.

'Well,' Gargan said. 'There are plenty of small cheap hotels not far from here. I could help you look if you like.'

'You don't have to do that. Just tell me where to go.'

Gargan thought a moment. The man sighed with impatience.

'It really would be easier if I showed you,' he said. 'I don't remember the name of the street, but when I walk out of the station I'll know which way to go.'

'It's very kind . . .' she began.

'No, really. I've nothing else to do.'

'Well, if you're sure.'

'I'm sure.'

She turned to the other man who moved away a short distance, clutching a bag. She followed and there was a brief discussion which Gargan could not hear. The man was clearly angry and held the large blue bag even tighter. Voices were raised and the man surrendered the bag unwillingly, though he didn't move away. The woman took the bag, muttering, and turned back to Gargan.

'Let's go,' she said.

They walked to the exit. Gargan slowed down for the woman, whose bags were evidently heavy. He pointed to the biggest one and asked, 'Shall I carry that for you?' She hesitated. 'I'll let you have it back,' he added, 'as soon as you want.'

She smiled and nodded wryly. 'That guy,' she said. 'He didn't want to give it back. He wanted me to go stay at his big fancy hotel. Uh-uh. No thank you, I said. That's not what I came to Europe for. You know what I mean?'

'Yes,' said Gargan, changing the bag strap over to his other shoulder. 'You came here to sell lead weights.'

'Yeah, really,' she laughed. 'Books. That's what's so heavy. They're my travel guides. See France in a Week, you know, that crap. My girlfriend told me, just take one, JB, a good one, it's all you'll need. What did she know, I thought. She never even went to Washington. Turns out she knew though. She usually does. She's like a sister to me and sisters always know. I know. My girlfriend told me. Do you have sisters? Why am I talking so much?'

'No I don't,' he said. 'Are you just on holiday or are you staying for several months?'

'Yeah, feels like it, right? No, I'm having a quick look around, then I'm going to Provence to see the lavender farms.'

'Lavender farms?'

They turned left out of the Gare du Nord and walked towards the Rue de la Chapelle.

'Yeah. I'm getting a train from Lyon station. Is that right? Lyon?' She pronounced it 'lion'.

'Lyon, but I knew what you meant.'

'Americans speaking French. Too funny, right?'

'The accent is difficult,' he said.

'I get a train down to Marseille,' she said. 'Then I'll hire a car and drive up to Aix-en-Provence and all around there.'

'I didn't know lavender farms existed,' he said.

'Sure. I want to study them so I can go back and grow lavender in Oregon. So that's what I'm doing. What do you do?'

'I'm a tightrope walker,' he said before he could stop himself. He bit his lip, cursing inwardly.

'A tightrope walker! In a circus?'

'No. Yes. Sort of. I don't like to talk about it,' he invented. 'Superstition. My great-grandfather said if I talked about it I would fall off.'

'I see,' she said, not seeing at all.

He changed the subject. 'Your accent, it doesn't sound Californian,' he said, though he didn't know how he knew.

'My folks were from Alabama but I was brought up in California. I only just moved to Oregon. That's where I have my farm. But I think I have a Californian accent, all the same.'

They crossed the road, Gargan changing the bag over again, and headed off to the right.

'Yes,' he said.

She sighed with relief. It was the third hotel they'd tried. At the first one JB had waited outside while Gargan went in to ask if they had a room. He knocked on the dirty window and nothing happened. As he was about to knock again he saw movement. A wrinkled forehead was all he could see, making its way towards him. An old man stood below the window and Gargan shouted, 'Est-ce que vous avez une chambre libre pour une nuit?' Slowly the man raised a hand and slid open the window. Gargan repeated his question. The man shook his head and closed the window. Turning, he shuffled away. Gargan rapped on the glass again. The man turned and came back. Gargan asked if he could suggest any other hotels in the neighbourhood. He grunted and closed the window before trudging back into the shadows.

In the second hotel, three doors up, the proprietress didn't like the fact that JB was American. In the third one they were lucky. JB followed Gargan up to reception on the first floor. The man knew no English and JB no French, so Gargan translated.

'We have two empty rooms,' the hotelier said.

'What's the difference?' asked Gargan.

'One is 85 francs, the other is 90 francs,' said the man, whose accent, like Gargan's, revealed him to be a foreigner.

'What's he saying? Huh?' JB wanted to know.

'He says there's one at 85 and one at 90.'

'So what's the difference?'

Gargan asked him.

'One is on this floor,' he said. 'The other on the third.'

'Which is which?'

'This floor is 90. The other is 85.'

'But is there any difference in the rooms?'

'Yes. The one at 85 is higher than the other.'

Gargan brought JB up to date and added, 'I haven't quite worked out yet why the one on the third floor is five francs less. Maybe it's not as good, you see.'

'It's cheaper because you have to climb more stairs, dummy.'

The proprietor confirmed this.

'Have you decided yet,' JB asked, 'what you're going to do?'

Earlier Gargan had admitted his plans were uncertain. 'No,' he said. 'But I hadn't really planned to stay long in Paris.'

'You'll be staying tonight, won't you?'

'I don't know,' he wavered. 'I hadn't counted on doing so.'

'Stay tonight. Be my guest here,' she offered.

'You don't need to do that. It was a pleasure to help you.'

'So what did you . . . I mean . . . You just helped me, right . . . because you're nice?' It seemed faintly incredible to her.

'I'm not so nice really,' Gargan said self-consciously. She continued to stare at him as if he'd just stepped out of a flying saucer. The hotelier broke the silence with a question.

'What'd he say?' JB asked.

'He wants to know how many rooms we want.'

'Well, are you staying? We can have fun. Hang around this afternoon. Get something to eat tonight. Do you like hanging around?' She made hanging around sound like an activity.

'Yes,' he said.

'Tell the man we'll have both rooms then.'

'Both rooms?' he said, momentarily taken aback.

'Yes. If you're staying. I'm going to wash and change. You wanna come down in an hour or so and we'll go hang around?'

'Sure,' he smiled, picking up his own bag and turning to the staircase. 'See you later.'

The room was small and dark, three times as long as wide. The bed was low, much lower still when he sat on it. There was a wardrobe containing a few unhappy coathangers but no surprises. At the end of the bed stood a small table and chair and beyond that the window, next to which a thin partition hid a washbasin. Gargan ran the taps, getting cold out of both. There was a strip light above the mirror but no switch. He imagined it would be at the other end of the room if anywhere.

He pulled back the thick nets and opened the window, diluting the room's thick brown air by the merest of shades. Leaning on the rail he looked down into the street. A handful of people waited at the bus-stop. A train scraped the rails of the overhead section of métro line which bridged the busy junction at the bottom of the Avenue Secrétan. A woman watched television in an apartment across the street and a dog squatted noiselessly in the middle of the pavement. Gargan could clearly imagine this street thronged with shoppers in the evening, hunting for bargains at dozens of fruit and vegetable stalls.

He watched the street for an hour, relaxing.

After splashing his face with cold water and running his wet hands through his hair he felt refreshed. At the door he paused and flicked a switch: a sickly glimmer lit the ceiling above the washbasin. He flicked it back and left the room.

They got a few croissants and walked up to the Parc des Buttes Chaumont. JB said she loved the park. Gargan said he thought he remembered it from before. They were standing on the suspension bridge talking about the French as seen through visitors' eyes, the climatic differences between Oregon and Provence and their common views on US foreign policy, when the rain started. It was just a few drops at first, but heavy ones, exploding on impact with the skin like little plastic bags full of water. Gargan enjoyed the sensation but the slate wall of approaching cloud did not augur well. JB produced an umbrella from her bag and as the heavens opened they ran off the bridge.

JB held the small umbrella a little too much over to her side, though she wasn't to know and Gargan wasn't about to tell her if it meant her back would get as wet as his was getting. He had never seen such rain. In a matter of seconds the earth had turned into a quagmire and was fast deteriorating into a soft-bottomed lake. The splash effect reached above the knee.

'Do I really look like somebody's sister?' she asked him, raising her voice above the ceaseless drumming on the umbrella.

'Yes. Well, I don't know. You do look incredibly familiar, but I can't think where from. It's strange,' he continued as the rain made its way down the back of his neck. 'Each time I look at you I feel a sort of jolt because you remind me so much of someone and yet at the same time I feel easy with you as if I've known you for ages.'

'Maybe you knew me in a past life,' she joked. He laughed, despite the rain crawling down his spine. 'No, I mean it.' She wasn't joking.

'You believe in that?' he asked.

'I better believe it. I'm a psychologist. I do special research into areas of parapsychology. I'm writing a paper.'

'I thought,' Gargan said, as the rain reached his pants, 'you were a lavender farmer.'

'I'm that as well, but first I'm a doctor of psychology. I have regular patients and I do research. The lavender farming relaxes me. Believe me, I need it.'

'I don't believe in past lives,' he declared. 'I've never seen any evidence.' The water ran down the backs of his legs until it could go no further: beneath the knees his trousers were already plastered to his calves. 'How do you do it?' he asked her. 'How do you get to someone's past life? Hypnotism?'

'Yes.' She nodded. 'But it's not me who reaches the past life. It's the subject under hypnosis. I just help. Have you ever been hypnotized?'

'No. Never. I've always rather wanted to be but I think I'm a bit sceptical. I don't see how it can work.'

'Well, it does. We can do it if you like, when we get back. If we get back,' she added, looking about.

While JB changed, Gargan went out to buy a pair of trousers and a shirt, such items to which the description 'essential' had not extended when he had packed his bag. Travelling light had been necessary to avoid arousing Su's suspicion. He wondered if she'd missed him yet, but put the thought out of his mind and hurried back to the hotel to change.

'I want you to stare at a point on the wall. Choose a point and stare at it. Just keep staring at the same point.'

He did so. 'I can't stop thinking,' he said.

'Don't worry about that now. Just keep staring at the wall.'

He was thinking about why he had agreed to this session. True, he was interested in the possibility of discovering past lives, and if something were to be revealed it might cast some light on his present life. He had nothing to lose, after all. It was not dangerous. He trusted this woman to bring him out of a trance if it began to look like he needed it. Once again it was that familiarity between them that engendered this trust.

'Just keep staring at the wall.'

He stared at the wallpaper, at the particular flower he had chosen, and listened to the car horns and shouting voices rising from the street. He tried to ignore them but couldn't.

'It doesn't matter about the noise,' she said.

He wanted to believe her, but couldn't help thinking the distraction would prevent him going under.

'Now, I want you to close your eyes and start relaxing your body. Beginning with your feet. Are they comfortable? You must be comfortable. Change position if you're not.'

'I'm fine,' he said, shifting slightly.

'Relax your legs. Just let the tension flow away. Relax the muscles. And now your waist.' He began to feel the relaxation happening. His legs felt free. 'Your stomach. Relax your stomach. All the muscles in your stomach. Just relax them.' Her voice was soft and caressing. 'Your chest now. Loosen up. Flex the muscles then let go. And your hands. Clench them. Let go. Relax . . . Arms. Let the muscles become nothing . . . Shoulders now . . . You notice your breathing has changed by itself. Take even deeper breaths now and relax your face, your scalp.'

He was conscious of being physically relaxed. He knew he was leaning out of the chair. A little further and he would fall, but it felt right, it felt good. His breathing was deep but unforced.

Air entered and left his body of its own accord. He felt as if he were floating. *It won't work, it won't work*, part of his mind kept telling him. But he wanted it to work.

'Your breathing is getting deeper and deeper.' She was right. And slower and slower. If he gained nothing else he would at least emerge from this experiment completely relaxed. 'I'm going to count to five. When I get to five you will go deeper. You don't have to make any effort. It will just happen . . . One.' He wanted to laugh. At least, part of him did, the saboteur in him. He suppressed the urge. He had the impression that she was swinging a watch before his eyes.

'. . . four . . .' What happened to two and three? Surely it wasn't actually working? 'Five.'

Was there a difference or did he imagine it?

'If there's anything worrying you, say so now. Any fear or complication, let's get rid of it now. Is there anything?'

'I can't stop thinking,' he said, without ruffling the surface of the river in which he was floating. 'I keep seeing images and thinking words. I can't shut my mind off.'

'It doesn't matter. You are going into a trance despite that. I'm going to count to ten. When I get to ten I'm going to ask you something. I'm going to ask you to start going back in time. To start remembering. More than remembering. You're going to be there . . . One . . . two . . . He slid deeper and deeper, like an angler fish floating in limitless depth. '. . . six . . . seven . . .' Movement before his closed eyes again. *Deeper and deeper dives the line of his division.*

'Ten.'

Like a métro train stopped in a tunnel. Completely dark. Submerged. It starts to move again and the line goes down steeply. I am the train. The rails have gone now and I'm just flowing like a stream of lava through rock which draws apart before me like curtains.

'I want you to go back. Go back to when you were five. Go to your fifth birthday. What were you wearing? Was there a party? Who was there? What did you eat? Was it night or day? Were the lights on or off? The curtains open or closed?'

The curtains.

'I can't,' he murmured, 'remember anything . . . except . . .' the face in the curtains. In the patterns his mother told him were leaves . . . '. . . the curtains . . . the face . . .'

'What face? Whose face?'

'Curtain face. Lives in the curtains. Lives in the central heating vent.'

'Who?'

'When I got up it was cold and I sat by the central heating vent but the curtains were still drawn and the light from outside outlined his face in the curtains.' The words spilled out of his mouth like beans.

'All right, all right. I'm going to count to five and you're going to go further back. When I get to five you will be at your third birthday.'

Sinking.

'. . . four . . . five.'

Sinking into something vast and suffocating. Getting smaller and smaller. Not falling but sinking into a mass which inflates around me. Feeling powerless at the mercy of whatever substance surrounds me. Its colour is the same as the inside of the eyelid. The same as the face in the leaves in the curtains, in the knots of wood in the shutters.

'. . . back again.'

. . . detaching itself from the . . .

'. . . the beginning . . .'

. . . mass expanding like heated glass . . .

'. . . five.'

aaaaaaaaaaaaaggggghhhhhhthump. Nothing. Thump. Silence. Crash. Thump. Twisting, pushing, yielding, falling.

'. . . bring you out of the trance.'

A presence behind me pushing, pressing. I'm turning to see. The face.

'. . . three . . .'

The screaming red face . . .

'. . . five.'

'RAI!!!'

Lavender Farming

'So what does rai mean?'

'I don't know, Gargan. You said it, not me.'

The train squealed round the bend and into the station. Gargan sprung open the door and they squeezed in. The signal blew and a youth who was leaning out levered himself back in.

'I don't remember saying it.'

'That doesn't surprise me,' JB said. 'You were reliving something very traumatic.'

The doors leapt open at La Chapelle and Gargan thought he remembered the mauve seats on the platform.

'You mean birth?' he asked her.

'Yes,' she said, pulling down a vacant seat. 'It's a pity you couldn't go beyond that. It was obviously too much. I had to bring you out.'

Gargan wasn't so sure she had brought him out. It seemed to him the shock of seeing the face had flung him back into the real world. The face had been bloated and streaked with blood, swarming in front of his own face, growing bigger and bigger, subsuming him. The nightmare sensation, so immediate and tactile, yet impossible to define, had accompanied it.

An ingress of passengers jostled them. Gargan rubbed his eyes and focused on the name of the station. Charles de Gaulle Etoile. 'Hey, come on,' he shouted, grabbing JB by the wrist.

He tried to shake off the experience but it clung to him. He sat down on one of the blue seats and massaged his temples. He shifted on the seat. JB put a hand on his shoulder.

'Stay sat down,' she said. 'You need to relax.'

'We're not starting that again,' he said.

'No, we're not. But you have to relax.' When Gargan felt better they made their way out of the station. He chose the escalator so that the very first thing JB saw as they surfaced was the Arc de Triomphe. She was impressed. Gargan admired the curve of the arch. Strolling down the Champs Elysées they talked about the division of time between lavender farming and parapsychology. She had enough time for both, she said, because she had no one else to think about: her second husband had died some years ago.

'Hey!' she shouted, pointing at the Eiffel Tower. 'Is that what I think it is?' Gargan nodded. 'This is better than any bus tour. I was going to take a bus tour tomorrow but I don't need to now. I hate those things but I wanted to see Paris.'

A minute later they were crossing the river. Dusk was beginning to settle and the lights to sparkle. They walked in the direction of St Michel. Opposite the Orangerie a bright yellow bird flew in front of them. It landed and hopped towards the water then flew off. A *bateau-mouche* glided by, washing them in its warm creamy lights, and the yellow bird reappeared, fluttering in the glare of the bulbs, becoming luminescent before flitting away. They watched it become a speck.

They had couscous in a small, dirty Tunisian restaurant. Gargan was unnerved when the proprietor welcomed him like a regular customer. Gargan avoided eye contact with the man and was glad when JB had eaten enough and they could go.

They went down into the métro and a rubber-wheeled train swished out of the tunnel. They got on.

Gargan wasn't sure what to expect of the night to come. They were walking from the métro to the hotel, concentrating more on keeping the umbrella up than on making conversation. Did she think they were going to sleep together, and if so why had she booked two rooms? So they would have enough space for their stuff? Or had they been destined to sleep apart from the beginning? He decided it was up to her.

They paused in the doorway while the umbrella was shaken dry. On the first floor landing they paused again. Gargan said, 'Well, here we are then,' suddenly wanting JB but not knowing what to say or do about it. 'Yes,' she said, inserting her key. 'Goodnight.' She smiled at him, paradoxically, as she pulled her door to. Normally there would have been no mistaking that look, but this did not feel like a normal encounter. Gargan fed the steep banister rail through both hands to get to his room.

He locked the door and pressed the light switch. He decided he preferred it dark to almost dark and switched it off. Leaning out of the window and watching the last métro drag its illuminated oblongs round the curve, he thought of JB in her room. He went to the door, unlocked it and lay down on his bed.

He dreamt that JB came up to his room and entered as if it were all taken for granted. She went to the window and looked out as Gargan pressed up close behind her, then she led him back to the bed. It was over quickly, though much of it lingered. Soon she simply wasn't there any more.

When he was woken in the morning by heavy lorries the memory was indistinct but not fragmented. The images and smells he still retained were not attempting to slip out of reach, like a dream would. He lay back again and closed his eyes, but the traffic below his window churned and gnawed at his brain.

He slid out of bed and got dressed.

The dining room was the colour of old carpet and it smelt as bad. Only the cracked cups and the gleam in JB's eye caught any light from the netted window.

'More coffee?' she asked, already pouring the sepia liquid. It tumbled rather than flowed. He was surprised his cup didn't cave in. 'Did you sleep well?' Was she smiling or grimacing at the taste of the coffee?

'I think so. Did you?'

'Very well. Thank you.'

Someone snorted beside them. It was the proprietress, a deeply unpleasant woman, when in a good mood. She wore a fixed look of contempt and thrust croissants out in front of her as if threatening to use them.

'Non merci,' said Gargan.

'Is it far,' JB asked when the woman had gone, 'to the Gare de Lyon?'

'Yes,' he mumbled between mouthfuls of bread. 'Are you going to Marseille today?'

'Yes. Should I get a cab?'

‘Up to you.’ He siphoned off a layer of coffee and regretted it instantly. ‘Cheaper and easier to take the métro. Line 8 south and change at Bastille. It’s quicker than a cab.’

‘But I have so much luggage.’

‘I’ll help you.’

She smiled. ‘Thank you.’

They left the hotel an hour later.

The métro took longer than expected and the TGV left earlier than she’d thought. They rushed from ticket hall to platform.

‘What do you do,’ he panted as they marched up the platform, ‘when you get to Marseille?’

‘Hire a car and drive straight out. I’ll tour Provence for two weeks. I know where several of the farms are.’

‘Well, good luck.’ He pushed the last case into the train and she stood on the steps. The station announcer droned.

‘She said it’s about to go,’ he explained.

‘It was lovely meeting you, Gargan.’ She smiled.

‘Yes, JB . . .’ he began, then was interrupted by the announcer – ‘Attention à la fermeture automatique des portes!’ – and the blue Attention Départ light with its jangling bells. They hadn’t spoken about the hypnosis since the night before and he wanted to know more about the rai. ‘What do you think the rai was?’ he shouted.

He didn’t know if she heard or if his question was lost in the din. Her mouth was forming words as the door snapped shut, trapping her mutely behind the glass. The train was moving.

She was mouthing something. He had to run to keep up now. ‘I don’t know,’ her shrug seemed to say.

Endless Tunnel

I told the kid from my class who started to light up a joint in the street outside the school while I was with him that it wasn't such a good idea, and that's how he and a friend ended up smoking in my studio one afternoon. Not being a smoker myself I had to be persuaded to share the joint. The taste was unpleasant but evocative of the past. They rolled another, grinning. I said they couldn't stay long as I had to go out, which was true, I had to go to the theatre.

Before long we were all laughing at silly things that normally would not be funny. I began to form the impression that they were sharing jokes at my expense. The dope seemed very strong. Were they lacing the joints with something I didn't want to take? I tried to get serious. 'Look. This is just normal stuff. Isn't it?' Did they laugh uncontrollably because they were high or because they were conniving?

The only way to get them to go was to leave at the same time. Checking my watch I saw it was time to go anyway.

The afternoon light was an assault on the eyes. Shoppers jostled me like schoolkids in bus queues. The métro opened wide and swallowed me. On the train everyone stared. They all knew what I'd been doing and would eventually get me for it. The tunnel between Stalingrad and the Gare du Nord had been extended. It was endless. The darkness outside and the accusing pinprick eyes inside, condemning me. The recurring taste of the dope made me nauseous. The train stopped in the tunnel. I was convinced it was never going to move again and I was in hell.

I sat in a corner and dared not speak. Ed and Dick were making enough noise getting into character almost to conceal my presence. As usual, my preparation began in the wings two minutes before I went on. I took lots of deep breaths so that when I walked on, Fudakowski was breathy and nervous, as he would be in the company of Lansdale and Campbell.

I took deep breaths and my head began to swim. The sensation would go away on stage. My forehead throbbed. How long had I got? I listened. '. . . in back of the store' – 'Lansdale, *where* is my *car*?' A few more lines then I was to enter as usual to tumultuous derision. As my cue came up I cursed the afternoon's recklessness, still high as a kite.

It was miraculous. The effects of the drug vanished as I parted the curtain and walked on.

As if I had stepped out of my own body and into another. Into Fudakowski.

Campbell was glowering at me. Slowly, threateningly, he crossed the stage and grabbed my red tassled shirt by the collar. My mouth fell open. 'Fuckface.' He spat the word straight down my throat. 'Talk to me,' he said. After gulping for air I fed him his next line. 'What about?' I asked. 'Talk to me,' he began again, 'about . . . my car.' It was the way his voice always dropped half an octave for the last two syllables – *my car*. That's when he became terrifying.

I had wrecked his car. He didn't know for sure yet it was me who'd done it, but all his life he'd been itching for a chance to kill me, so he didn't exactly need a signed statement. He loved his car more than anything and hated me as much. I admired everything about him even though he scared me – *because* he scared me – and his car most of all. I had always dreamed of driving it and it seemed like I finally had, though a man who had no particular reason to defend me swore I was serving him in the store at the time the crash took place across town. But as far as Campbell was concerned I'd wrecked his car and should die. I never even had a right to live in the first place.

'It's a real nice car, Mr Campbell,' I stalled. He tightened his grip then let go and turned away. 'I don't know what I'm going to do with you, Fudakowski.' Which meant he just hadn't decided on time, place and method. Suddenly he whirled round and raced towards me, picking me up and pinning me against the wall. Thankfully it held, but this bit of business was not in the script. He was throttling me. I coughed and spluttered. He took one hand away but only to thump me in the stomach. I doubled up and collapsed at his feet. He placed the sole of his boot on my ear and with increasing pressure swivelled his foot.

At this stage I might have given up and walked off, but Fudakowski wanted more and I was in his control. 'I was in the store, Mr Campbell. You can ask Bill Hancock.'

He faltered, amazed that I should invent a bare-faced lie. But come to think of it, I did sort of recall chatting to Bill Hancock. And I did remember driving the car and it going out of control. Yet both these things happened at the same time.

After the show I raised my voice to Ed and Dick. 'You completely changed the characters,' I shouted. Ed had been far more cynical than usual, sitting around and letting Dick hit me. 'No. No, no,' said Dick slowly, as if speaking to a child. 'We didn't change anything. But if the interrelationships are fluid the characters will respond. To force the character back along a familiar route would destroy the balance.'

'An actor,' Ed chipped in laconically, 'must love the art in himself, not himself in the art.'

'Right, Ed,' Dick confirmed, looking at me. 'You were being an annoying little prick tonight. On top of the fact that you smashed up my car.'

'Fudakowski . . .' I mumbled, aware that the distinction meant as little to me as it did to Dick.

Ed and Dick both smiled, looking me right in the eye.

The following night they did exactly the same thing. After the show Charlie came through and told them what he thought, that if they wanted to play tragedy they'd hired the wrong director and if they tried it again he'd leave the group.

I slipped out of the dressing room while Ed and Dick were laughing about Charlie and playing football with Campbell's hat. I caught up with Charlie in the corridor and told him that if he left I would leave too. He nodded, rubbing his stubble, staring above my shoulder. I think he didn't quite welcome me aligning myself with his indignation. 'Anyway,' I said. 'I'll see you later, Charlie.' He walked away.

That night I was in the kitchen cooking something for me and Jenni. I was standing there vacantly stirring eights in the white sauce when I became aware of a presence in the doorway behind me. It was Jenni. She stood in my dressing gown in the doorway between the main room and the kitchen silently crying.

I still found it amazing that this should happen.

At the theatre and with Jenni it seemed like a stasis had been reached. Ed and Dick, scared of losing Charlie, who was easily the production's best asset, performed along Method lines.

There was just one minor hiccup. One of my scenes involved me sitting on an upturned crate fantasizing about Campbell's car. Lansdale and Campbell were behind me but I'd kind of forgotten them. I did little bits of business with my hair blowing in the wind, telegraph poles whooshing past, and culminating in me lighting a cigarette, but it made me cough and splutter because I wasn't man enough. I had to light it in a particular way with a Zippo lighter. First I had to hold it above my leg and bring it down, catching the cap on my jeans to spring it open; then push it back up the same way, spinning the wheel on my leg, so it rose in my hand to my mouth ignited.

Most nights it worked like a dream. Occasionally it failed to light and I had to repeat the action. That actually got more laughs, especially when I hammed it up. But on this particular night it caught on my jeans and the sudden release jerked it from my grip, so it flew out of my hand and sailed down the central aisle. I watched it go and thought, 'Fuck, what do I do now?' My ad-lib skills had gone with it and I froze. Ed and Dick would help me out. They'd worked in Hollywood, if only on cheap TV and video features; they'd think of something.

But they let me down completely. They did nothing. In desperation I think I said, 'I don't have a light.' They just sat there. Campbell would never give me a light, unless it was up my ass, but Lansdale was the kind of guy who would casually toss me a box of matches (which I knew he had in his pocket in case his lighter failed). But nothing. Assholes.

So I thought, why don't I just jump off the stage and go get it? The theatre was so small I was practically in the audience already. I knew I shouldn't leave the stage. It would break character. But I hardly felt I was acting anyway. By this time, being on stage was little different from not being on stage.

Eventually a kind-hearted man in the third row picked up the lighter and handed it to me.

Jenni still came to performances once or twice a fortnight. We stayed at her place most nights during the week. I would get the last train up from the Gare du Nord, walk up the hill and join her in bed. Thursday nights and weekends we spent at my studio. Life was comfortable. Time went by. It was the kind of life I suppose I had always hoped I would one day lead.

A Towering Presence

The episode with the American woman, JB, had left two things on his mind, like driftwood stranded after the tide had gone out. The image of the rai troubled him, and then there was JB's intriguing familiarity. He had been worrying at both problems since leaving the Gare du Nord himself, and only the thought of Rada gave him any relief. The stuffy train didn't help. But she did. Over and over in his head he repeated the name of the town where her sister lived: 'Subotica. Subotica. Subotica.'

His ticket would take him all the way to Subotica, but it was a long, slow journey. After Paris his next stop would be Cologne. The ticket had not been cheap but money was no object, even though he hadn't worked for years. *She was* very *rich, wasn't she?* What? *Very rich. Very rich. Therefore no problem.* What was this? What are you what am I talking about? What the fuck thefuckisgoingonnotandnodestuneranearaaaaaaaaaaaiaaaiiiiiie-iiiieiiieeiieeeeeeeeeeeooout out of the tunnel and the train hurtled through the bush on an undeviating track. He couldn't seem to rise from his seat. Looking down at his hand he saw the weave of the seat material was stitched into his flesh. He tugged and tore the skin over a knuckle. Maybe with his teeth . . . He bent forward and attacked the threads with little bites but skin came away in his mouth.

A man stood before him wearing a controller's black cap, beneath which no face was visible, only more black the texture of cloth. The man pointed out of the window. In the distance was a station-like structure. There were no other buildings. The track curved and the train thundered towards the station.

Looking back out of the window once the train had stopped in the station, he saw he had been mistaken about the size of the structure. The opening through which the train had entered was wide enough only for one train and now it was blocked. He saw a door opening. The controller stepped off the train with a faceless glance to the front. He clicked the door shut then inserted a short metal rod into the lock and twisted it. He marched away across rusting rails and disappeared through a door.

One minute the concrete walls of the station stared back at him through the windows, the next the glass was painted red.

The initial wave subsided and the walls were visible once more. The end of the station was a dam. The level rose before his eyes. Soon the train was rocking. If there were no windows open would not the air in the train provide sufficient buoyancy to lift it up to the surface and smash through the roof?

He put his head round the compartment door and saw the glass door at the front end of the carriage pushed open by a frothing red stream. He rose. The blood came faster. He left the compartment and tried to run but it felt like he was swimming. Blood outside pressed against the window and seeped through airtight seals. Behind him the glass door beat against the wall as the pressure increased. Blood washed into the compartments. He closed the glass door at the end of the corridor.

Suddenly a fountain erupted from the connecting doorway to the next carriage. It cascaded towards him. Trapped, he glanced around and saw the toilet. He locked himself in with premature congratulations. The toilet seat rose and fell, coughing blood. Overflowing it painted the white bowl scarlet. Blood dribbled up through the plughole and drained in through the air vent in the door. The light bulb fizzed, shone more brightly and winked out, plunging him into complete darkness. Fumbling wildly he couldn't retract the door latch. He kicked and thumped the door, splashing and thrashing blood as the level rose swiftly in the enclosed space. It became increasingly difficult to move arms or legs. His own blood hammered round his head, beating metronomically against the back of his eyes, threatening to burst through the retinas and spurt out through the pupils. A fresh surge splashed his chin. He swallowed some and retched.

('Reveillez-vous, Monsieur!')
more blood hit the back of his throat and he snorted
(a hand on his shoulder)
blocking his pas
('Reveillez-vous!')
sages drowning
('– eillez –')
in blood . . .
'Monsieur! Monsieur!'

He jerked awake and tried to speak but spat blood. His shirt was covered. He coughed up a thick red wad like a dressing. More blood poured thinly from his nostrils. The passengers leant towards him gesturing. One woman tried to help him to his feet as he struggled into consciousness and out of the compartment.

Countryside slid past the window. French, Belgian, German, he didn't know which. He wondered if he might still be dreaming. The toilet was unoccupied. He kicked the floor stud and waited for water to sputter into his cupped hands. He doused his face twice then positioned his still-bleeding nose under the tap. The bowl ran red, gradually turning pink. In the mirror the toilet seat jerked up with the motion of the train and fell down again. He pinched his nose and blew out the remaining clots. The toilet seat hiccupped again. He turned round and lifted the seat. At the bottom of the uncovered chute the track sped into a blur. He replaced the seat and returned to the mirror, dabbing at his face with wet towels. In the glass the toilet seat danced to the rhythm of the rails and out of the corner of his eye he saw the exterior turn red as the bowl overflowed. His heart hit the roof of his mouth and he whirled round. The bowl was white. He flung up the seat.

Nothing.

His trembling hand twisted the doorknob and he left.

The passengers seemed to hush and bow their heads when he reappeared before them. Or could they have been asleep all the time? He stepped over their legs and slumped in his seat by the window, accidentally knocking the shoe of the woman opposite. Her eyes remained closed. Did he only imagine she screwed them more tightly shut? His own eyes soon closed.

When the train jolted him awake he was alone. Where was he? He turned to the window and felt immediate dismay as a dark red blur slid into his field of vision. At the same time a female voice carrying an awful ring of gravity and doom announced the imminent departure of a train from platform three. 'Am Gleis drei bitte einsteigen und die Türe schliessen. Vorsicht bei der Abfahrt.' Her voice dropped ominously half an octave for the last two syllables – Abfahrt – and the effect disturbed him. As if this was the last journey one would take. And it was too late because the doors had closed.

The red blur was a string of Belgian second-class carriages.

Gargan stepped down to the platform, his head a whirl. The loudspeakers sparked again. 'Am Gleis neun . . .' Her voice was authority, but sounded like a victim of a cruel regime of which she was also an agent. '. . . schliessen. Vorsicht bei der Abfahrt.' A literal translation of the innocuous 'Attention Départ', yet 'Vorsicht bei der Abfahrt' inspired dread. A forty-year-old legacy that wouldn't let go of the language. Her voice descended on Gargan like a cowl, tightening round his neck as he stumbled down the steps. He pitched forward like a man blinded, using his arms as buffers. The pain behind his eyes was so acute he wished the eyes would stop resisting and just burst out on to his cheeks. He forged through crowds of tourists and made for a wall of glass doors. He almost fell getting through and once outside was immediately aware of a towering presence.

Cologne Cathedral. Inconceivably huge.

He bent backwards almost double to see the whole thing. His neck squirmed with pain. Between the minutely perforated twin spires was there a man walking on a wire? Gargan lowered his head, wiped sweat across his forehead, looked up again. The man was still there. He squinted against the sun to make out his features but the wire was too high and the light too fierce. The sun was burning too close, right next to the earth. It fired in his eyes, shooting sharp spasms through his head.

The sky began to turn red. The man and the wire and the spires stood out like a line-drawing then were lost as the sky exploded between the massive towers. Gargan's eyes boiled. The cathedral fell towards him. Slowly at first. Then its shattered stone was raining about his head and he was crushed.

Wired Lengthways

When he came to he was lying on his back and a man with chalky hands and torn jeans was kneeling by his side. He looked up at the cathedral. The spires towered intact. No wire stretched between them. The sun still blazed and the sky was white.

'Wie geht's?' asked the man next to him.

Gargan levered his torso up until he was resting on his elbows. The ground around him was rainbowed with chalk. He had fallen on the work of a pavement artist. Twisting agonizingly, he coughed up a little blood and apologized to the artist.

'You are sick,' the artist said.

'Bad night,' Gargan croaked. How could he tell the man the cathedral was too big? That he'd seen himself tightrope walking between its spires? 'Here.' Gargan drew some coins from his pockets and dropped them into a battered trilby. The artist shrugged as Gargan lurched away across the square. He passed a group of people huddled round a lottery booth inside which a fat man smoked, idly pushing a wheel.

Gargan's stomach ached. He was desperately hungry. 'Where's the nearest café?' he demanded of a startled passer-by. 'Verstehe nicht,' the man said, peering down his red nose. 'Café!' Gargan said, pointing to his mouth. The man coughed and moved aside.

Gargan ran from street to street but could neither see nor smell food. The streets crowded him, bounced him like a pinball from one obstruction to the next until he fled down a side street. A veil of cotton fluff blew from the trees and provided some protection against the throbbing sun.

The River Rhein was in flood. An entire walkway lay under several feet of water. Here and there a white bench or litter bin protruded. Short flights of steps down to the riverside walk now plunged into brown water. A notice prohibited entry.

Gargan walked along the higher path. Cyclists whisked by. A woman in a green serge suit walked a tiny ratlike dog which snapped shrilly at his ankles.

He was hungry and didn't know which way to turn. He felt pathetic. Leaning on a railing he watched the river swirl and threaten to engulf the supports of a bridge. The water was a rich, clay-infused brown, almost red. He rubbed his head but it wouldn't clear. The giddiness tightened like a clamp. He turned and rested his back against a wall. A woman drew his attention. Proceeding slowly she looked like a local out for a relaxing walk. She might know where he could go. 'Bitte,' he began, concentrating as hard as possible. She looked at him and he asked her where he could find something to eat.

'You are American,' she said.

'No, I'm British,' he said. 'Sort of.' She was older than she had first appeared, forty maybe, with a pleasant, open face, the merest trace of caution in her grey-green eyes.

'You are not well,' she observed. He shook his head, which made it hurt more. 'I live not far from here. I can give you some food and you can rest.'

He looked at her to gauge how serious she was. Totally, it seemed. They walked north by the river. She talked a lot, almost without taking breath, most of it over his head. She supported him when his legs seemed about to give out. There were brief moments of lucidity like tiny islands in the sea of delirium. He retained only a handful of nouns from the flow of her chatter: cats, cable cars, attic, road, doctor, graffiti, zoo, hair. Sometimes he looked at her but she didn't notice. He seemed to have become strangely taken for granted. The river pressed at its new banks. Something dangled in the air high above the river, moving in a straight line from left to right, swaying in its path.

'What's that?' Gargan managed to enunciate.

The words 'cable car' slotted neatly into her speech, which faltered not one instant to allow the insertion. So, provided the thing *was* a cable car, she did still know he was there and had asked a question. But why would there be a cable car crossing the Rhein? There were bridges. It came to him like a lightning bolt. How could the cars travel but on a wire? The thing had been put there to torment him. They wanted him to walk it and fall and drown. Was she a part of it? He looked at her. She talked on and on without taking a breath. She was pretending, acting a part. He'd go along with her as far as need be. Far enough to get some food inside him. Then he'd escape before she could do whatever she was planning to do: kidnap him, force him to walk the wire, or just ridicule and humiliate him.

His eyes were closed most of the time now. He was inventing the world in his head. The sensation was reminiscent of the worst stages of total drunkenness. You know it will pass because you've experienced it before. But while it lasts it's utter torture. Here at least he could trust this woman to some degree, to take him safely to her home. That's where she wanted him. What was she saying? Crossing the river? He squeezed open an eyelid but could only see her, blurring mountainously and obliterating all else. Her pressure round his back increased then disappeared and presently he realized he was sitting down.

The motion was strangely comforting. What was it? Rocking back and forth.

'Where are we?'

She didn't reply. Or at least she didn't appear to. Just the same uninterrupted chatter, from out of which again only a few words escaped unmutilated: carrying, impatient, baby, river. Did she say Su? Or was it soon, or soup? No, it had to be Su. That would fit with carrying and baby. It *was* all a conspiracy. This had been no chance meeting. The woman had ambushed him. It wasn't fair. What had he done? It wasn't as if the baby was his, yet she made him feel as if he ought to feel guilty for it. As if he ought to wait for her. Be a father to her child. A lover to her.

A thought struck him. The woman was Su. He would open his eyes and see her face. He'd been tricked. He fought against the noise and pain in his head and dragged his eyes open. Through the plastic windows was sky at the top all around and underneath, far, far below was the river and its two distant burst banks. The cathedral was a dark spiny silhouette in the distance. The river itself was thick and purple like a watery bruise. The wire above the cable car was of a diameter greater than that to which he was accustomed. There was no trapdoor in the ceiling of the tiny car. The window appeared impossible to open from the inside. So how was she going to make him walk it?

'How do you intend to make me walk it?'

'Sssshh. Quiet,' she murmured. 'You're delirious. Talking nonsense. Rest. We'll be there soon.'

'You won't, you know. You won't make me. And I won't see *her* either.'

She put a hand on his shoulder then fell back as he attempted to get up. He overbalanced on his weak legs and sprawled on the floor.

The outer skin of the car was thin fibreglass. There was no inner lining. A misplaced fist could possibly puncture the only protection they had. He tried to get up again and fell, jarring his knee and causing the car to dance excitedly on its running wheel, falter and continue, swaying wildly.

Then it stopped.

It still swung from front to back but was no longer moving forward.

Gargan and the woman froze. She looked petrified, having already crouched in a corner, pretending to be shocked and horrified. Gargan was thinking. This was an opportunity for him to escape. He tried the door. It was locked. He pressed his hands against the window and tried to force it down. Sweat lubricated his grip. He wiped his hands on his trousers. The woman continued to feign terror. The window slid down abruptly and Gargan began to climb out, right leg first, then he levered his thorax through the gap. Some people watched from the east bank. He saw the flash of sunlight on some tourist's camera lens. Standing outside on the running board and inspecting the top of the car he saw the woman's swift movement only out of the corner of his eye. They grappled dangerously. To the people watching it no doubt looked like she was striving to prevent a suicide, but Gargan knew she was trying to push him out. In his efforts to keep her at bay he lost his footing on the running board and fell.

Eight fingers clenched on the window frame took his entire weight. They felt as if they were being sliced to the bone by a long thin blade. The woman's arm snaked out of the open window and a hand grasped his forearm. The car lurched even more. The wheel would jump the wire and they'd both go down. She poked her head out. The wheel appeared to buckle, then it was rolling. The car was moving again.

Gargan high-kicked and acquired a foothold with which he worked his way back up to the window and climbed inside. His landing set the car off swaying again but its journey this time was not interrupted. Only in straightening up did the effort required for his recovery take its toll. He slumped on to the bench and was dimly aware of the woman's face bending over his.

The cable car rolled into its descent. The woman had come out of her corner and asked Gargan if he was all right. He wasn't. At the bottom he had to be helped out and shielded from the wrath of the operator who demanded to know what had been going on, insisting that such behaviour would not be tolerated in his cars. Whatever she said to the man, it shut him up. Gargan had little choice, drained of strength and willpower to fight the head pains, but to allow the woman to lead him away.

Consciousness retreated further and further. Even the chaos inside his head dismantled its clanging scaffold and gave way to a steady dull ache. All thought was cancelled. He knew nothing until he tasted food in his mouth and a hot drink, coffee or tea, he didn't know which. The food was excellent: a large bowl of some hot, spicy meat dish. Chilli or goulash, there was no telling. He gulped it down greedily, filling his gut with as much air as food.

The woman sat in a low chair at the other side of the kitchen. It was a large, homely room. A huge pan simmered on the stove. Gargan's food had been served on a great round table of thick dark wood. There was a cat eating out of a bowl on the floor. It seemed to be eating the same food as Gargan.

'What's your name?' he asked, concentrating hard, with his mouth full.

'Heike.'

'Thank you for the food, Heike. It's good.'

'What is your name?'

'Anthony,' he lied.

He sat back in the chair, full, and his eyes closed in spite of himself. The chair was low-slung and reclined. The weave of the cushion material reminded him of something. It seemed to pluck gently at the hairs on his arm, teasing them into its own fabric. The cat purred like a diesel engine. Somewhere in a distant vestibule a clock chimed.

The woman came and took him from the chair. She had no face. She led him down a corridor floortiled with black and white lozenges. On a mantelpiece near the door by which they left, a piebald cat ticked.

She left him at the top of the incline and shinned down the massive steel pylon to the river, disappearing into the water without seeming to have entered it at all. The wind glanced over his face. He looked to the front and began walking. The wire was quite thick and taut. It presented no immediate problems. At least not until he noticed the dark shadow of the cable car dangling like overripe fruit from the wire. He wondered why it was growing steadily larger and stopped wondering when the wire beneath his feet began singing like rails before a train. Although the car was still some way off he pictured the wheel rotating on the wire and it seemed to him it would not be possible to step or jump over the wheel and be sure of his footing. The wheel trundled closer like a mechanical toy. Without having had the time to cover the distance it was upon him, squealing angrily.

He thrust his arms before his face and connected with something. The animal uttered a piercing shriek as it leapt and scurried away. A form larger than the cat moved closer and overshadowed him. He felt her hand on his shoulder exerting a little pressure.

He jumped. It was the only thing. The other wire was seven feet away but his feet brushed the top of the wheel and he fell short. He threw his arms forward while his toes caught the wire he had meant to leave. He did reach the far wire. With his fingernails.

And he lost part of one. The pain was barely noticed as his body plunged into the abyss between the two wires, which were far more flexible than he would have wished. They almost met above his head, pulling his spine into a deep inverted arch. He bounced back up and looked left to see the next car coming, only yards from his clinging feet. Making sure his grasp on the wire in front of him was secure, but without thinking to glance right, he unhooked his toes, falling down and across until he was hanging only by his hands, which were burned by the striations of the wire.

Then he saw the car on his right which had been lumbering up the incline during his acrobatics and whose wheel was now two or three yards from crunching his fingers.

He jumped and landed on the roof of the car, just managing to sling an arm round the bottom of the wheel bracket. Having twisted his body while landing, he was now looking south. The cathedral was floodlit by greenish lamps. It was far too big for its context, like an object of inappropriate gauge dropped in the middle of a toy village. It shimmered against the night sky, appearing to hover, like twin rockets incandescent with ignition fire.

The car jolted as it rolled over the pylon and into its descent. He jumped off before it reached home, just a small drop to a patch of grass. He landed with a thud which jarred up to his head and rattled the brain inside his skull.

The Hauptbahnhof was the liveliest place in the city at that time of night. 'Am Gleis sieben bitte einsteigen . . .' She was still there. His heart sank lower. He stood in the entrance hall. People sat about with great suitcases. A group of interrailers unrolled their sleeping bags and settled down for the night. A man sitting in a tiny booth surrounded by cans of Coca-Cola and wearing a silly hat looked sorry for himself. Left-luggage lockers banged open and shut.

He was on his train, in one of the last few empty compartments. A gang of men was suspended in a cradle high up in the vaulted ceiling working on the superstructure. They were agitated, obviously concerned that something was wrong, as they shouted to other men on the ground, who strained to hear. One of the men in the cradle pointed upwards at something, maybe at the ropes holding it. Gargan felt anxious for the men. 'Am Gleis zehn bitte einsteigen und die Türe schliessen. Vorsicht bei der Abfahrt.' The carriage was tugged forward. The cradle swayed dangerously. Looking back, as the train picked up speed, Gargan saw one end of the cradle collapse and a man toppled like a sackful of old meat to the track below. The train accelerated. Gargan felt like a fugitive, as if the sense of foreboding he'd felt when he first heard the announcer's message should have enabled him to foresee the accident and prevent it.

Hours later, before light, he got up and left his seat. Those compartments which had been occupied were now empty. Some had blinds drawn but cracks revealed the interiors. In one seat in the next carriage he saw himself and his stomach turned over. But it was just his reflection in the glass. The train screamed on into the night, dancing and skittering over the rails. In his dreams he finds himself off the train a mile ahead of it, squatting down and straddling one of the rails. His penis is wired lengthways on to the rail, which begins to hum as the train narrows the gap.

Peeled Ripe Tomatoes

By mutual agreement (or so I kidded myself because I felt like a bastard for suggesting it) Jenni and I spent a week apart. I had hoped that during the week I would miss her and look forward to the weekend, when we would enjoy a happy reunion. It's amazing, the crazy ideas you can convince yourself are brainwaves.

I spent the mornings in bed enjoying the spaciousness of the single bed once more and listening to favourite pieces of music at a volume louder than Jenni cared for. At lunchtime I only had myself to worry about, so I could go without if I wished or if I couldn't be bothered. Afternoons I walked in the park or sat with other individuals in dowdy cinemas watching horror movies, which Jenni never wanted to see. At the theatre I relished complete anonymity, hiding alternately behind Fudakowski and myself.

I knew she would ask me if I had missed her and I would not be able to lie. There would be no point in saying I had when I hadn't.

We met again on Saturday at the zoo. I was nervous because I wanted to be excited by seeing her again. Either that or for her maybe to have cooled off a little. But that would have been too neat.

I waited for her outside the monkey house. I could tell nothing had changed as she hurried towards me, eyes wide and shining. We held each other tightly and I tried to work out what my feelings were. Was I excited or was I bored? I couldn't tell, being too distracted by my own questions.

We wandered round the primates. Did I still love her? I wondered, admiring the fall of her hair from the back. I didn't feel the same as I had in the first couple of months when I'd been on a high. When we were *in love*. Weren't we in love any more? Jenni seemed to be. What was wrong with me?

A mandrill jumped from a rock and pressed his raw, scarlet arse to the glass like a pair of peeled ripe tomatoes.

In the beginning I had wanted her strength of feeling to match mine. I had not been disappointed. She loved me fiercely and tenderly in the same breath. I got what I wanted. So what was the problem?

Together, in so far as I was standing just behind her, we watched a lemur's acrobatics. It leapt to a higher branch to join another and pick its fleas. Her hand appeared from the folds of her coat and took mine. My hand was passive. I didn't squeeze her fingers like I would have done once. Maybe I actually wanted to but was too obsessed by my own doubts. She withdrew her hand.

A male orang-utan climbed on top of his mate and they began having sex. If it were two months earlier we would have exchanged a look and laughed together. As it was, I moved towards the exit past a group of chattering, jeering baboons.

Jenni caught up with me at the bears' enclosure. I watched her as she concentrated on the animals. She *was* beautiful and I *did* love her. I think I knew I did and hadn't stopped doing so.

The problem was simply that I'd got what I wanted, so had nothing left to yearn for. I'd gone from being alone to being with someone, which was what I had wanted, but now I wanted to be alone again. I was here and I wanted to be there. Realizing that once *there* I would probably want to be *here* again didn't stop me wanting to be *there*. Like in summer when I often wanted a chance to wear my thickest sweaters and coat, yet when it got to winter I was impatient for summer to come round again. Like when I chose one restaurant in preference to another and regretted the choice. I was in the thick of an emotional relationship with a beautiful woman and I felt I'd rather be on my own.

How convenient it would be, I thought to myself as we left the zoo complex, to be two people rather than one. You'd be able to do *both* things at the same time: wear a T-shirt *and* thick jumpers, eat in two restaurants, be one half of a relationship *and* an individual in your own right.

Instead I had my self and my dream-self, whose adventures were becoming an increasing source of distress.

That very night I was taken again by the man with the papery hands to a residential area in a redbrick town. He led me through streets of drab terraces and eventually through a narrow back door into the same large house as usual. It was so familiar now. (Was that because I'd seen it in so many dreams or because I'd actually been there and the dreams reminded me?)

He showed me round the rooms on the ground floor and the upper storeys. I looked in each room and just as I was turning to go, saw the shape of a woman walking towards me. I pulled the door sharply closed in each case. It seemed to be the same woman in every room, yet I was still shocked by her sudden appearance each time. Her face, though I only glimpsed her features, had a terrible aspect.

I felt pressure beneath my skin, as if some unearthly sweat were forcing its way out. The sensation increased in intensity as we neared the top of the house. I saw the woman again, emboldened, leaning naked in doorways. At the end of a dingy corridor three replicas of the woman jostled for position in a photograph which curled forgotten in a drawer somewhere. Each vision pricked me with fear and foreboding. Everything led, as I was being led, to the bathroom at the top.

I twisted the doorhandle myself and as I did so I imagined I heard bells echoing dully in a distant tower. My guide was retreating down the hallway, striding backwards at an impossible speed. The door opened and the scene inside was so immediate and shocking it seemed to be printed on a flat screen filling the doorway. But the screen collapsed inside and became the bathroom. The same woman was there, backing away from the door, struggling with an unseen assailant. Blade-slashes appeared in her flanks and torso. Blood leapt out and spattered us both. She was losing strength. More wounds were torn open. As my eyes moved I glimpsed the flash of silver but no distinct weapon or actual attacker.

She struck her heel against the bath, full of steaming water, and toppled over backwards into it, cracking her head against the wall. She slumped loosely into the water, spilling some and turning the bath red as she disappeared.

A ringing telephone distracted me, allowing me to tear my eyes away and dart out of the room. In the hallway there was no sign of the papery-handed, masked man. The ringing was coming from a room on a lower storey. I made my way down the steep stairs, clinging to the banisters. After each ring I was convinced it would stop, but it didn't. I descended two flights and found myself suddenly inside the room with the telephone. The ringing was so loud it filled the room and made it hard to breathe. Each new ring that was emitted jangled against the previous set of notes as it lodged itself between the floor and the ceiling. I wanted to take a handful and crush them together to make more space. But I was too weak. They thumped my head as they rose like black bubbles on sticks. When I could no longer bear it I took the easy way out and answered the telephone.

The abrupt, empty silence was pregnant. I could hear a clock ticking on a mantelpiece in another part of the house. I said hello. A man's voice asked for Mr Gargan. I said I was unable to help, and felt inadequate, for here I was in a house which felt so familiar it might have been mine and I didn't know the person asked for on the telephone. The voice pressed on, very serious, using words weighed down with significance like murder, wife, police, money. I told the voice I didn't understand and hung up. Turning to leave the room and feeling suddenly drowsy, I saw a bed against the far wall. The sheets were pulled back on one side. It looked slept-in and comfortable. I went straight to it and was about to get undressed when I discovered I already was. The mattress was soft and lumpy. I burrowed down and came across a sticky patch. The mattress was damp. I extended my leg to the other side of the bed and collided with another leg, not one of mine. It too was wet and sticky. I sat up and pulled the sheet back.

The woman from the bathroom lay there, cut to ribbons.

She smiled at me.

'Who was on the phone?' she asked.

Neutral Ground

He stepped down from the train and walked along the platform, trying to assess what it felt like to be in Switzerland for the first time.

Su was waiting at the end of the platform.

Alert, Gargan jumped back on to the train, certain that she hadn't seen him, and he left by a door on the other side, climbing into another train and then down on to the next platform.

He reached the front of the locomotive and glanced left. Su was craning her neck, looking for him among the stream of passengers arrived from Cologne and Munich. Twisting his head round the other way, he walked quickly towards the main body of the station, obscured from Su by other passengers going in the same direction. He didn't risk looking round to see if she'd seen him; he just kept going. But where to? he suddenly thought. He didn't know anyone in the city, apart from Stan, and he hadn't seen him for several years. The writer probably wouldn't even recognize him, never mind have anything to say to him. In any case, *he* wasn't the reason why Gargan had come here.

He'd left Cologne in a hurry, eager to be gone, catching the first train south, which took him only to Munich. When he alighted there at a quarter to nine in the morning, he already knew he didn't want to stay. The booming station announcers and red, sweaty people sent him straight to the departures board, searching for whatever would get him out of the country the quickest. There was a southbound train at nine. It brought him here, another step closer to Yugoslavia and Rada. She *might* be waiting for him, was all the hope she was able to give him.

He manoeuvred for a position at the newspaper kiosk from

which he could observe Su but she could not see him. She waited until all the passengers had disembarked and left the platform, before she walked along towards the end of the train, peering in through the windows. At the last carriage she seemed to shrug, then collect herself and return, looking herself like a passenger from the north, though minus luggage.

She came back on to the concourse. Gargan sought out the English-language newspapers and selected the one which had the broadest sheets. He paid for it and hid behind page seven as Su passed by the kiosk. A photograph caught his eye. It showed a man – clearly recognizable as Gargan – hanging half out of the window of a cable car, apparently attempting to jump, and a woman inside the car, whose pose suggested to the reader that she was trying to save the man. But Gargan knew different: Heike was in league with Su. She had tried to make him walk the wire by forcing him out of the cable car.

Gargan blanched. The camera-toting tourist on the river's east bank had indeed been enterprising. Gargan folded the paper and looked around for Su. She was examining the arrivals board. There was nothing due from Munich for several hours. She swung her arms by her side and looked about.

How had she known he would be in Zürich? Cologne was obvious. She'd seen an early edition of the newspaper, had flown there immediately and somehow known to follow him here. She had to be working with Heike.

Su was walking away from the arrivals board towards the exit. He followed, keeping his distance, and his eye on her red coat. Outside the station the crowds thinned out. He didn't have to stay too far behind, because the last thing she expected was that he would be following her.

She went into the tourist information office and came out two minutes later carrying a map of the city. She paused in the middle of the pavement. Twenty yards away, from behind his paper – the front page folded away so the familiar legend wouldn't attract her attention – he watched her. He was shocked to see how pronounced already was the bulge in her stomach. Then he remembered it was not he who had impregnated her. Nor did he know how long before she met him the conception had occurred.

She sauntered off down Bahnhofstrasse.

Shoppers here thronged past him, swathed in gold, fur and cosmetics, pausing to covet the contents of shop windows. The entrance to a bank yawned on his right like a grotto.

She stood on a corner, consulting her map. A tram came between them and stopped. Before it moved away another one came from the opposite direction and stayed after the first one had gone. It was hardly possible and not at all safe to cross and he couldn't see anything through the windows of the trams, so tightly were the passengers packed. When the road was clear, Su had disappeared. He ran across the tramlines and up a perpendicular street. There was no sign of her. He ran back down to the corner and looked up and down the boulevard, in case she'd moved on or retraced her steps. Nothing. Once more he jogged up the side street and a little way down the first road off it, but she'd vanished. He checked back, glancing into shop windows. There was a department store on the corner where she'd been standing, but he didn't feel up to coping with the thick waves of perfume and heat that welled around the air-conditioned entrance.

It began to rain as he approached the Zürich-See. At first he found this refreshing and the smell of summer rain richly evocative. Soon, however, it was coming down in sheets, slicing into the surface of the lake, sending mallards scurrying under the wooden pier. Great grey clouds engulfed the mountains across the water. A pleasure boat berthed at the end of the pier and disgorged its tourists. They ran under newspapers, magazines and city maps towards the overhanging shelter of the ticket booth where Gargan was keeping dry. A tram soon pulled up and they all got soaked as they pushed and shoved to get on. Gargan picked up a map that had been dropped in the scrum.

The mallards ventured out then retreated. The boat waited passengerless. Lake and sky merged like lacklustre mercury.

The downpour eased off slightly. Gargan finally found a good use for his newspaper: he covered his head with it and stepped out into the rain.

He noticed a girl standing in the doorway of a café and did a double take. She looked like a cross between a coffee-bar jazz singer in a rainy northern port and a peasant girl from the south with her hair dyed blonde. Like Rada, in other words, leaning in the doorway of the restaurant on Panton Street, where she'd once caught him pressing his nose against the glass, peering through from outside, seeing if she was working before going in. She'd been in the doorway all along, watching him.

What are you doing there? he'd asked her. *Going out*, she'd said, *to buy cigarettes. I'll go with you then*, he declared and did so. *You see*, he said, *I told you we'd go out together one day. It was fate*. She smiled under her dark arched eyebrows.

This had been the first time he'd seen her in the daylight, without any artificial light at all. She *was* beautiful. Older perhaps than sixty watts suggested, and no less appealing for that. She wore some powder on her cheeks. Maybe the man Gargan assumed she went home to at night liked that. It was more than likely that someone waited for her. She always said *I can't*, when he asked to see her, rather than *I don't think so* or *it's not that I don't want to*.

As they stood at the roadside waiting to cross back to the restaurant, Rada turned and looked at him. *Appraisingly*. Maybe. Her eyes were large grey discs shot with a strange flash of yellow around the pupil. He'd felt a great sadness.

But this girl wasn't Rada. She was a Swiss imposter, now disappearing back into the shadows of the café. Gargan moved on. The rain began coming down more heavily again. He didn't care. The newspaper was turning into papier-mâché, matting into his hair. He threw it away. Instead of emptying, the streets were athrong with umbrellas of every circumference and colour.

The attraction of the rain was beginning to wear off, unlike the intensity of its fall. He sheltered near a tram stop and took out his map to pinpoint his location. If he carried on going north he would come into the area where Stan lived, provided he did still live there. Shelter and food. *If* he was still there and *if* he remembered Gargan.

He trudged out from under the tram stop and splashed up the hill. The rain struck at an angle, coming from behind. It seemed doubly unfair, like shooting someone in the back. He climbed up through the university district, avoiding trams and trolley-buses at the last moment, through the grounds of the university hospital, until he found himself high enough to look down over the city at the head of the lake. Clouds continued to muscle over the mountains, threatening several feet of rain. Eventually he found himself on Hochstrasse, trying to recall the number of Stan's house. He wished he had his address book.

The rain made it difficult to see where he was going. It was like a wall of steel always just in front of him whichever way he walked. He began to feel he had to get out of this downpour, which was now causing him as much pain as discomfort.

He examined the names on the letter boxes. R S Kennington. That was him. That was Stan. Gargan pushed the bell. A minute or two elapsed and Stan opened the door seconds before Gargan was going to ring the bell once more.

'Come in, Gargan,' Stan said, curiously unsurprised by his visitor, who stepped gingerly over the threshold, wincing as his clothes stuck to legs and arms. He only really appreciated quite how wet he was now he was out of the rain. Stan peeled off the jacket, then Gargan dragged his feet out of his shoes.

'Sorry to arrive unannounced,' Gargan began. 'I didn't plan to come here. I didn't know till this morning that I was coming here at all. I didn't have your number and I seem to remember something about you being ex-directory.'

'It's all right.' Stan hung the jacket on a hook, next to a thin red coat also wet. 'I was expecting you.'

'The old morphic resonance again?'

'You could say that,' he nodded obliquely. 'It's good to see you, anyway, Gargan,' putting an arm round his shoulder, 'whatever the circumstances,' and he pointed the way to the stairs. *Whatever the circumstances*. A startling thought crossed his mind and was gone. He meant the rain: Gargan had only come to see him to shelter from the rain. True, but that wasn't the point.

As he mounted the stairs he heard women's voices. So, Stan and his wife Liza had company. The same thought darted through his mind once more. It was nonsense. He dismissed it.

At the top of the stairs though, viewing on to Stan's sparsely elegant knocked-through lounge and diner, with full-length windows and generous thick rugs, Gargan had to admit that the foreboding had indeed been a prophecy. Sitting on the deep, comfortable sofa next to Liza and now looking in Gargan's direction was the last person he wanted to see. The shock of seeing her displaced questions like what had she told them? and how had she got here? Following him to Zürich was one thing, but coming here and *preceding* him was deeply mystifying. No doubt, however, she would explain in full and take the opportunity to gloat a little about the apparent success of her mission.

'Hello, Gargan,' she called across the polished width of parquet floor.

'Su,' he replied thickly, ascending the last step. 'Liza. It's good to see you again.'

'Hi, Gargan. Come on over. Sit down.'

His eyes didn't leave Su as he crossed the floor and sat down on a second sofa opposite Su and Liza. Stan drew up a wooden chair, turned it back to front and straddled it, folding his arms across the back rest and cradling his chin. Su watched the reflections caused by all this movement in the glass-topped coffee table between the two sofas.

'Your books must be selling very well, Stan,' Gargan observed, indicating with a sweep of his arm the handsome interior.

'Not bad. Not bad,' Stan said without enthusiasm but still with his swampy, southern-states accent. 'I just delivered my latest two, three weeks ago.'

'Still the same stuff?' asked Gargan.

'They call it dark fantasy now, Gargan, instead of science fiction, if that means anything to you.'

'It doesn't really, but I hope it does well,' he said lamely.

'It should do OK. Look, Gargan,' Stan's tone hardened. 'We have some sorting out to do. I'd like to ...'

'I'll deal with this please, Stan,' Gargan interrupted the writer. 'What are you doing here, Su? More to the point, how the hell did you find your way here?'

'I looked in your address book,' she replied, still concentrating on the table top.

'*What?*'

'When you sent me to your place to get your bag and bring it to you, supposedly so you could change after walking that wire into the old hospital, but really so you could run away to the continent.' She met his eyes for the first time. 'I took your address book from the bureau.'

'You had absolutely no right to do that. No right at all,' he shouted.

'I had about as much right as you had to do what you did,' she replied, beginning to lose her cool. Gargan spluttered, unable to articulate. 'You tricked me, Gargan,' she continued, bitterly now. 'There's no excuse for that.'

He had. It was true. But only in so far as he'd left without telling her.

'Look, Su,' he attempted to remain calm, 'I think this is all a bit unnecessary.' Stan and Liza watched Su with interest. 'I wanted to go away so I went away. I don't recall promising never to leave your side.'

'You sneaked off. Like a child.'

'Look. This is ridiculous. We only knew each other a couple of weeks.' Palms upward, he turned to Stan and Liza. 'I don't have to sit here and defend myself. It's my life. I do what I want.'

'Didn't you forget something?' Stan asked ironically.

'What? What d'you mean?' He began muttering to himself: 'This is crazy. Anyone would think I was on trial.'

Stan said: 'Gargan.'

Su looked down.

Gargan looked from her to Stan.

'The baby,' said Stan.

The sun had emerged through the rainclouds and a low shaft fell across the writer's face, glinting off his spectacles. Liza blinked in the sudden glare and turned to look at Su, who was staring at the hands clasped in her lap.

'What? What about the baby?'

'Going away without telling Su is one thing. But giving her a child and then disappearing is quite a different thing altogether.'

Gargan turned to Su, scarcely able to control himself. 'What the hell have you been telling them?' Su still looked down. '*Well?*'

She answered in barely a whisper.

'What?' Gargan shouted.

Stan tried to intervene and Gargan waved him down without turning from Su. This time he heard her: 'The truth.'

She was acting *extremely* well. Stan and Liza could be forgiven for believing her. Gargan felt as if knots were being tied in his brain.

He slapped his hands on his knees and rose to his feet; paced up and down the wooden floor, his wet socks leaving damp prints which faded after a moment. Su's head was down. Stan and Liza watched Gargan.

'Evidently,' he began, still walking, 'you believe what she's told you. I don't blame you either. Her act is good.' He paused, for breath and emphasis. 'But that's what it is. An act.' He looked at the writer and his wife. Liza looked away at Su while Stan's gaze didn't falter. 'The baby is not mine. It was conceived before I even met her. In Paris. She told me herself.' Stan began to look doubtful. 'She even has a photograph of the baby's father on the dressing table in her bedroom in London.' Gargan stopped at the large rectangular window through which the sun was still shining. He recalled holding the photograph next to a mirror and contrasting his face with that of the baby's father. Not only was the man clean-shaven and without spectacles – unlike Gargan, who wore cheap plastic frames and a short beard – but also their noses were bent in opposite directions.

'I saw your reaction when I told you I was pregnant so I pretended to play along with you,' Su was saying. 'Pretended to accept you were a different person. I couldn't be sure when we first met in Paris, but when we met in London I knew who you were. At first I didn't know if the beard and glasses were a disguise or an act of regression but when I got to know you a little bit better – if you know what I mean – I realized there was something wrong. Now it's time to stop running.' She breathed heavily. Otherwise the room was deathly quiet.

Gargan stared at the sun and tried to clear his mind. The sun grew bigger as he allowed his focus to slip, so that it filled his vision, mushrooming around his ears, ballooning over his head. Voices murmured behind him, growing indistinct from each other. What could they possibly import that was not completely trivialized by the sheer size of the sun? The chattering melted away to a hum of flies – mildly irritating but of no great consequence. The descending fireball bent its rays into a garden beneath the window. Neat and trimmed. Not a single blade of grass grew contrary to the general flow. Not even the pole rising out of the lawn disturbed the symmetry because it had a partner twenty yards away, joined to it by a length of twine. A clothes line. *A tightrope.* The hated urge tightened his stomach. If he smashed the window with his elbow and jumped carefully, he might be able to land on the rope and withstand the recoil. It might snap though. Or the poles bend. But the fall would be a minor one. The sun heaved between the inner rim of his iris, filling his pupil, no longer a void. He raised his elbow.

'Gargan.'

He whirled round to face the owner of the hand clamped on his shoulder.

'I said,' Stan started again, 'what do you have to say?'

'I don't know, Stan,' he sighed. He resented the urge to walk the wire, to walk *any* wire, *all* wires. 'The baby isn't mine.' He looked back at the window, losing interest. 'There's another man. He looks like me. She's mistaken . . . Never mind.' He turned back with restored vigour. 'She has no claim on me. No right to follow me around. I'm sorry she bothered you.' Leaning closer: 'Listen, Stan, I think she's crazy,' he whispered. In fact, he didn't know if she was lying or deceiving herself. He walked back towards the lounge area. Unconsciously, he followed a straight line in the wooden floor, placing his feet one in front of the other.

She refused to leave until he did. Her intention was clear. He allowed her to follow him to a tram stop on the hill. Waiting for the tram she stood at several yards' distance. He got on and sat down near the centre. She walked down to the rear entrance and sat in the second car, from where she could keep an eye on him. He was one step ahead of her in this respect, however. As the doors started to wheeze shut he leapt up and darted between them. She glared at him in defeat, turning as red as her coat, as the tram carried her away down the hill.

He turned off the main road immediately and took an oblique route down towards the city through leafy residential neighbourhoods. He guessed she wouldn't get off at the next stop to look for him, but would stay on until the railway station, knowing he would get there sooner or later. He wished he could drive, then he could hire a car. Hitching was out of the question; it was too late in the evening, and anyway, he didn't expect these people gave lifts to those whose situation obliged them to ask. His rail ticket would take him almost anywhere on the continent; it would take him south to Yugoslavia.

Descending an old cobbled alley he came into what was clearly a red-light district. Bars belted out gobbets of music. All the lights were red. A girl shivering bravely on a corner turned her lipstick and mascara towards Gargan. Her thighs seemed to meet just below her chin. She slurred a question in the local dialect. He struggled to tell her in his own peculiar version of German that he didn't understand, although he *did* understand, because there clearly wasn't that much *to* understand. She smiled what should have been a sickly grimace, given the convolutions of her cosmetics, but it turned out rather sweet.

'Komm her!' The strange words fell out of her mouth like a small cough. He did move a little closer. 'How are you feeling?' she asked. 'Better,' he said and meant it. 'I've got to catch a train.' She smiled again and he walked on. She called after him, 'Gute nacht. Schlaf wohl.'

He had about as much chance of sleeping well that night as she had. He had to get on a train going south, and he had to make sure Su didn't see him.

He crossed over the small river and came into the station. Su's presence was not immediately detectable. He looked for her red coat but couldn't spot it. The departures board, illegible from where he stood, was out in the open. Most likely it was being keenly observed at that very moment. He tried another tack: passing the left-luggage lockers he sneaked round to the platforms themselves. He attempted to mingle with customers at a bar selling overpriced drinks and snacks, but these were the late-night customers, an entirely different breed to those consuming by day. They comprised sly-looking thieves, pernicious, menacing no-hopers and a handful of paranoid youths. Gargan's welcome was minimal and he didn't outstay it. The distance from there to the platforms was, in any case, too great to be able to read the destinations and times. He crept closer. There was actually only one train waiting at this end of the station. He couldn't see if the details were written up anywhere. He moved a fraction closer and the widening of the angles revealed a row of covered telephone booths on the left. A red coat stood talking on the telephone in one of them. It was Su. She was looking at the wall, her back to Gargan and the train. Why? Suddenly she moved. He was wide open and had to run.

He made it on to the train as the station announced its departure and the last carriage, into which he had jumped, was jerked into life. He got his breath back and took a cautious look out of the window.

The red coat lay crumpled on the floor.

It had been a trick, a makeshift dummy, now collapsed.

She was on the train with him. He left his compartment and patrolled the corridors.

He found her in the next carriage, sitting in a compartment in which a man sat opposite her with a defeated look on his face. That man Gargan clearly recognized as himself. He felt his knee joints emulsify as Su rose and came towards the glass door. Without appearing to see him, she pulled the curtain sharply across the door and the windows either side.

Fuckheads

Who indeed had been on the phone? In the dream. I had to keep reminding myself it was only a dream. A caller with a strange, menacing voice asking for a man I didn't know; threatening in the manner of a blackmailer to reveal information unless payments were made. Information which, although scandalous, should have been of no interest to me. Especially since it was all part of a dream, I told myself again.

Dream or no dream, I found it difficult to shake off during the day. Jenni wanted to know what was wrong with me. So did I.

At the theatre there was something wrong with everyone. Liz and the girls were agitated. Tom, who knew more, was furious. Ed and Dick were just being themselves, or their characters, much more loudly than usual. Stomping around, slapping their hats against their thighs and punching the walls in actorly despair. I didn't realize there wasn't any sign of Charlie until Tom calmed down enough to tell me what had happened.

Charlie had resigned. Ed and Dick had arranged an extra rehearsal for the girls without telling Charlie. They wanted to exercise directorial control. Jessica told Charlie, who promptly resigned.

'I'm that far from going myself,' Tom told me, holding his forefinger and thumb an inch apart.

'Me too,' I stated bitterly, remembering my promise to Charlie and wondering if I meant it.

That evening I completely ignored Ed and Dick offstage. After the show as I was hopping around in the corner trying to get my trousers on and they were gazing at their reflections prior to makeup removal, Dick suddenly spoke.

'What's all this big silence treatment, asshole?'

Asshole was what they called Fudakowski when they were being nice.

I finished struggling against gravity and my trousers before answering. 'Charlie,' I said.

'Charlie,' Ed replied, 'no longer felt able to commit himself fully to the show.'

I snorted and left it at that. There was no point in going on. Discussion was out of the question: they argued like children.

I was really beginning to feel the pressure now. The next day they called a production meeting.

'Bad news,' they said.

As they told us right at the beginning, their first priority was to pay members of the group a decent regular wage. It had been necessary to postpone payments though, owing to costs and low receipts. We had been patient and understanding, for which they were grateful. Tonight they had hoped to be able to promise good things. And indeed they were able to do so. First though, the bad news: they would not be able to give us any of the backpay which was due. Nor could they pay us for the next week or so. They had just been given a further bill by the printers. But they would be able to pay us properly for the final month of the run.

Charlie's commitment to the show had unfortunately dwindled, as we had all no doubt noticed. Ed and Dick would be co-directors, if we needed any direction. The show was going well. We had a lot to be proud of. The reviews had been complimentary. And let's face it, guys, we are all working.

That much was true. We were working. Work was not easy to come by, paid or unpaid. The credit alone was worth a lot. It would help us get our next jobs, even though they could be months away.

After the show, as I was leaving the theatre, I saw Tom at the bar. He was bristling with anger and knocking back a string of whiskies. 'This sucks,' he told me. I had to agree. We had a drink together, then Tom said he was ready to leave and headed off to the boys' dressing room. I went the other way, out to the street and home.

Jenni could see I was tense. 'You need to relax,' she said,

sitting behind me on the bed and pressing her thumbs into my back just beneath the shoulder blades. Jenni made the thumbs describe a circle and travel down either side of my spine. She worked her way back up using the ball of the hand and the gentle, kneading pressure of her fingertips.

I didn't find the massage very relaxing. I wondered if I would have found it more so with a change of masseuse.

I pretended to be asleep the following morning when Jenni got up, had a shower and dressed. The light slanted in. Jenni put on the Vangelis tape. She sat at the round table in the middle of the room with a coffee, looking over to my corner every so often. At one point she hovered over the telephone, either undecided as to whether to make a call or expecting it to ring.

She spent ten minutes copying something (a poem, I discovered days later) from her notebook to a sheet of paper. She placed the paper in one of my drawers, got her bag and coat, and left the studio.

I sat up as she closed the door behind her and passed in front of the lace-curtained window. I remained in that position for an hour, watching the dust in the column of light sloping to the floor. I hoped the telephone wouldn't ring but that if it did the caller would ask for me and not some stranger. I hadn't killed anyone and naturally objected to being threatened with blackmail by a man who claimed to be from 'the hospital'.

What hospital? I had no recollection of being in any hospital. If the man kept calling in the middle of the night, dragging me from my bed if not my sleep, as he had again that last night, I was never going to get the facts any clearer.

Again I had to remind myself it had been a dream.

Later in the day, after a light lunch, I walked down to the PTT office. After a half-hour wait, clutching a numbered ticket, I was admitted to the first stage – reception. A young man straddling a chair, smoking a cigarette and scratching his chest through a thin poplin shirt asked me what the problem was. I told him I was receiving calls for someone who wasn't me. Could they check to see that my number wasn't incorrectly listed somewhere? Impossible, he said. Maybe my number already existed on someone else's line and should never have been given to me? Couldn't happen, the man told me. When I persisted he wrote my name down on a long list and told me to go and sit down.

I left after almost an hour with a lengthy queue still in front of me. It had been a long shot anyway.

I had a glass of wine in a neighbourhood café and wondered what developments there might have been at the theatre. When I thought about Tom, I realized there was a good chance he would not be there tonight. What had he said at the bar last night? 'I'm about ready to leave now.' Leave what? The bar? Leave the theatre for the night? Leave the show? From the expression on his face, which belied the amount of alcohol I knew he had consumed, I decided he had probably been going in to see Ed and Dick to tell them exactly what he thought of them. Then, I imagined, he would have resigned.

As it turned out, this had in fact been his plan. Things hadn't gone exactly according to it, however. As soon as he had got inside the dressing room Ed had taken the lead. 'I'm glad you're here, Tom,' Ed had begun, before Tom had a chance to draw breath. 'Because I have something to tell you. We don't need you around any more.' Dick had got up. 'You're fired, Tom,' he had grinned. 'You bastards,' Tom had said slowly. 'That's right, Tom,' Dick had smiled. 'We're bastards. But we like a peaceful show. And you are becoming a disruptive element. We don't really need that. Therefore, you gotta go.'

Tom had blustered but they had said they didn't have time to listen and had bundled him out of the dressing room.

I learnt all this some time later, after the show had finished. Tom called round at my studio one morning and we went out for lunch. He looked well. His hair had been washed that morning. It was longer now too. It shone. His walk was more confident. We sat outside a café in St Michel and ordered drinks and sandwiches. Tom told me about his last night on the show, and about the work he had coming up: a major supporting role in an American miniseries set during World War II. He told me all about the big names involved and smiled a lot as he watched the tourists go by.

It really struck me listening to Tom how directionless I had been. I knew then, however, that I would leave Paris within a few days. And I think I already knew where I would go.

They fired Liz the day after they got rid of Tom. 'You were only ever with us on a temporary basis,' they told a disbelieving Liz. 'Fuckheads,' was her only comment. I was quite surprised. It was the first unkind word I'd ever heard her use. But so appropriate.

The two girls and I battled on for some strange reason. Probably the undiminishing excitement of playing to audiences, however small. One night was actually quite busy due to a party booking. The front five or six rows were full of people who looked like Ed. The same bland mask stapled to so many heads. It was Ed's modelling agency. They'd sent along a coachload.

They enjoyed the show. Always lots of laughs in watching a little guy get humiliated. I would say it was only a very small percentage of that particular audience who saw the irony and appreciated my moral victory at the end of the play. Still, you can't have everything.

Having been lucky with the métro and arriving at Odéon twenty minutes early, I wandered into the Village Voice bookstore rather than hang around the theatre. I had only been in there a few minutes leafing through a pompous literary magazine when a brash American woman's voice assailed me from the café-bar end of the shop. 'Oh my Gawd!' she cried. 'It's Fudakowski.' She came up to me and told me I was 'so goddam funny'. When she turned away to beckon her friends to come over I slipped out of the shop like a reluctant star, or a criminal.

That same day after the show I was having a quiet drink in La Palette before going home. I think what I was doing was putting off going back to Jenni, who if awake would welcome me with too much affection.

Raising a glass of red wine to my lips I accidentally crossed sightlines with a fat man looking in the mirrored wall on the other side of the room. He turned to face me, rising immediately to his feet. I emptied my glass and fumbled round the back of my chair for my jacket. He was on me before I was able to get away. 'You're that Fudakowski, ain't ya?' he boomed down at me. A few people around us looked up. 'No,' I replied. 'I don't know who you're talking about.' 'You even talk like him,' he sneered. I realized I had spoken in a Texan accent. 'Whatchew drinkin', boy?' he wanted to know. 'Wine! You *are* queer, ain't ya?' I tried to measure the distance between my table and the door. 'You gotta drink *beer*, asshole. Not wine.' The trouble was, he was standing between the two. 'I'm gonna gitchew a beer and then we're gonna drink together.' My chance. He turned just an inch towards the bar and I sprang from the chair, vaulted over the next table, felling a bottle of mineral water, and ran to the door.

I sprinted to the river, along it, then across the first bridge. I dodged into the Châtelet métro behind the Hôtel de Ville. Instead of taking a train *direction porte de Clignancourt*, I tunnelled deeper to the RER and walked underground as far as Les Halles, eventually surfacing on the Rue de Turbigo. Half a mile underground, on foot. I stayed in the shadow of the shops and shied away from a bright display in the window of the Americana shop where Ed and Dick bought my ridiculous cowboy shirt.

Groups of people approaching sent me scurrying across the road and down side streets. A bus turning a corner urged its passengers to watch me squirm in the light shed by its windows. Cars slowed down to pass me.

Footsteps echoed in my wake. When I stopped they stopped also. Turning on my heel, all I saw were disappearing rats. I was being followed but not, I felt, by the fat man from the café. Several times I glanced back but saw no one. When was my pursuer going to show himself? I had the feeling I was on stage in a play I'd never read, being chased by an assailant known only to the audience of dark, blank windows lining my route.

My footsteps in the Rue des Vinaigriers were so loud and metallic I worried I might wake the residents. If I did, would they protect me from my pursuer? Doubtful. Wrongly perceiving the dark street to be a dead end I panicked. Sweat gathered round my neck like a noose. More footsteps behind me. I wheeled round. A young man in a baggy Italian suit glanced at me in surprise as he stepped out of a doorway and made off in the other direction.

There was a canal at the end of the street and a swing bridge. I crossed over and began the long climb up the Rue de la Grange aux Belles. I didn't lose the feeling of being followed. Even when I got back to the empty studio and folded myself into bed, I still felt convinced there was someone right behind me.

When I woke up, apparently alone, thin morning light falling like drizzle through the window, there was blood on the sheet halfway down the bed. I conducted a brief examination but found no likely point of its exit from my body.

The stain was red rather than a dirty brown: still fresh. I touched it: warm, damp, sticky.

Later in the day I decided I must have been dreaming that I'd woken up.

The Vienna Woods

'Vienna was easy. You followed me here from Zürich. But how did you know I was in Zürich?'

'Easy,' she said.

This conversation was taking place in a Viennese fish bar in the north-central area of the city. The train he had leapt on to had been destined for Vienna: not particularly good news for Gargan. He found a seat in the busy second-class rear section. A young Hungarian called Zolst had a large bag of cherries which he passed round the compartment. Gargan was convinced he offered not out of generosity but to see what people would do with the stones. The two men by the window, both Austrian, had access to the little bin whose lid wouldn't stay open and clanged every time it was touched. The crispy middle-aged woman next to Gargan reached across the man on her left to drop her stones in the bin. The man lifted the lid. The woman burned with embarrassment, clearly wishing she had refused the cherries in the first place. Gargan wrapped his stones in a tissue he found in his pocket. With a smile he conveyed his connivance to Zolst, who looked askance, making Gargan feel foolish.

Before long they crossed into Austria. Customs procedures were rigorous. A uniformed officer patrolled the train asking perfunctory questions of the compartment as a group. Then a minute later two scruffy youths bounded in from the corridor, flashing identification cards. The passengers were instructed to stand up. Questions were fired in rapid succession and scarcely comprehensible German. One officer took great exception to Gargan's hand being buried in his bag when they entered and ordered him to extract it. When the hand was presented palm down, the Austrian grabbed it and twisted it round. 'Rauchen Sie?' he barked. No, Gargan replied, he didn't smoke. As if there were some connection with the previous question the other youth yanked open the little bin and sifted through the cherry stones. Apparently still dissatisfied, the customs officers invited the passengers to stand in the corridor while they jerked the seats out, found nothing extraordinary and so thrust them back into position.

It was not a pleasant welcome to a new country, whose president one knew to have pursued a mysterious career in World War II. One of the Austrian passengers was reading a newspaper in which the lead story covered Kurt Waldheim's imminent visit to the Vatican City.

Gargan drifted in and out of sleep. At one point when he was awake his open flies told him he had probably been to the toilet in his sleep. He left the compartment to go and check, locking himself in the little cabin at the end of the carriage. The blood on the floor told him what he feared was true and when he dropped his trousers the tissue in the wound confirmed it. He checked the zip-up compartment of his wallet to make sure that his razor blade had been used. Unwrapping the blade he discovered fresh bloodstains.

He needed to make proper use of the toilet. To do so he needed to remove the piece of folded tissue. He soaked it with water from the tap and gave a little tug. It hurt. But it didn't come away. He tugged again and it came unstuck, trailing some glutinous scraps. He bathed the incision delicately using wet tissues, then urinated, cleansing the bowl of blood. Finished, he washed again and slipped in a new piece of tissue to prevent the flesh knitting. Although he would prefer to be whole, he knew it wouldn't be achieved piecemeal. The wound would only be reopened within days. The problem had to be solved at its root and then help sought.

Su found him later when he was back in his compartment and she was prowling the corridors looking for him. She had actually anticipated his boarding the Vienna train because it was the only intercity departure for the next two hours and it was obvious he was eager to leave Zürich and his shadow as soon as possible.

The train had no scheduled stops before Vienna and he

couldn't physically prevent her from occupying the spare seat in his compartment, so she stayed and they talked civilly. They couldn't get very far, however, as long as she persisted in making the claim that Gargan was the father of her unborn child.

Arriving at the Südbahnhof they walked down Prinz Fugen Strasse towards the city centre, past the Turkish embassy, where a uniformed guard brandished a sub-machinegun.

Kärntnerstrasse resembled London's Oxford Street. Turning left and heading north-west they ended up eating fish in a tiny shop off Habsburgergasse. Gargan chose Kabeljau because its name sounded the most interesting. He had no idea what the fish was but it tasted good. Swordfish, perhaps; definitely something exotic.

Su explained how she had known to follow him to Zürich. She had seen the English papers very early in the morning and had taken the first flight to Germany where she bought a German newspaper, which ran additional photographs, including one of the door to which the amateur photographer had followed Gargan and Heike. After a small amount of detective footwork on the right bank of the Rhine, Su located the house. Heike was only too pleased to give her full cooperation.

Apparently, while semi-conscious, Gargan had repeatedly talked about Yugoslavia, saying little other than that it was vital he got there as soon as possible. He didn't say why, just that he had to go there.

Concerned for his safety, Heike followed Gargan when he left her house, losing him on the river crossing, but eventually spotting him again at the station, where he boarded a train to Munich. Together Su and Heike worked out the most likely destination after Munich, given that he was aiming for Yugoslavia, and there were no direct trains there at that time of day. With information and timetable help at Cologne they eliminated Vienna, Venice and Trieste, all good for connections to Yugoslavia, but none of them served from Munich soon after Gargan's arrival there. A train left for Budapest only half an hour after the Cologne train got to Munich, and Budapest would be very handy for Yugoslavia, but Su gambled on Gargan not having a visa for Hungary. The train for Zürich left Munich fifteen minutes after the Cologne train was due to arrive. Plus there was the fact that Su had found a Zürich address in Gargan's address book, but nothing anywhere else in southern-central Europe.

'So I flew to Zürich,' Su finished, 'got down to the railway station just in time and there was no sign of you. I made my way to the address I'd found in your book. And sure enough, you turned up like a drowned rat.'

'And you decided to pretend I'd run out on you after making you pregnant.'

She looked down at her fishbones. 'No, Gargan. It's not a game. The baby is yours.'

'Su. You are either lying or deluded. I'm not going to argue with you.'

They left the fish bar. On his way out Gargan noticed a fish identification chart stuck to the glass door. He found the name Kabeljau above a picture of a cod.

They walked south-east with no apparent purpose, but Gargan was formulating a plan. People marched confidently through the streets, hiding behind sunglasses. Old men wearing trousers that fastened below the knee sat on benches reading pamphlets. Trams looked exactly like trams in Cologne and Zürich, as if they had strayed beyond their termini. After the spacious green of the Burggarten and the clutch of nearby museums, the descent into Mariahilfer Strasse was dismaying.

They walked at the same pace with Gargan half a step in front. Few words were exchanged. From time to time she asked him where he was going in Yugoslavia and could she come with him. His answer remained a shake of the head.

Cheap boutiques and shoe shops desultorily wheeled their shoddy goods out on to the pavement, already congested. Building work was going on behind secretive barriers all over the city. Along Mariahilfer Strasse they were digging up the road to extend the U-bahn system down to the Westbahnhof. Four mysterious towers like oil drums rose up before a church on the left-hand side of the road. One of them bore a sign identifying the nature of the construction work – 'deep excavation'. The chunky green spires of the church thrust resentfully skyward behind, while in front of the towers a statue wrestled good-naturedly with a heavy plastic sack tied around it for protection. The material being translucent, Gargan could see the subtle lines of the figure's morphology.

'Gargan,' she was saying, pulling on his shoulder like a child.

'What?' disengaging himself.

'Can we sit down somewhere and have a coffee or something?'

He looked at the statue. It seemed to acquiesce. 'Come on then,' he said.

The area offered a poor selection of cafés and bars. They ended up in a tacky fast food place with moulded plastic tables and chairs in various bilious shades. Two coffees in paper cups were acquired and Su began.

'Are you still incising?' It was a straight question.

'Yes,' he said, blowing on his coffee to pucker up the skin.

'Do you know why?' she asked.

'No.' He plucked up the skin and dropped it in the ashtray.

'I've been doing some research,' she said. 'Around the world various groups of people practise genital mutilation. In Australia, the Pacific Islands, Africa and the Amazon basin. Occasionally you come across isolated areas of activity in America and Europe also.'

'Yes,' he broke in. 'Like Bethnal Green.'

'I'm sorry?'

'Nothing. Never mind. One place in London I have no wish to visit again in a hurry. Carry on.'

She drew a breath and continued. 'Circumcision of course occurs throughout the world and is widely accepted in most cultures. Less common are certain other practices. Superincision is slitting the foreskin lengthways. The er . . .' At this point she took out a small, grubby notebook. Gargan sipped his coffee with distaste. 'The Marquesans perform the operation without an anaesthetic, which is the case with all traditional mutilations. The foreskin is stretched tightly over a piece of bamboo. Superincision occurs only among Polynesian groups, who believe it promotes cleanliness and reduces the odour from smegma, which is considered repulsive and can be the cause of very serious insults.' She paused to have some of her coffee. 'Shall I go on?' she asked.

'Do,' said Gargan. 'Academically it's interesting.'

She pursed her lips and found her place in the notebook.

'Bleeding the penis without altering its shape is not common, but is still practised by the Wogeo of New Guinea.

'Four societies in the world practise the removal of one testicle. They are found in Africa and Micronesia. The Hottentot believed that monorchy prevented the birth of twins, which was held to bring bad luck.

'Female mutilations are various and widespread. Infibulation. Clitoridectomy, introcision . . . but not relevant to you . . .'

'Whereas you've found something which is, I suppose,' he interrupted sarcastically.

'Yes, I think I have. Subincision. The penis is cut on the underside upwards into the urethra. It's cut from one end to the other. When you've finished you can flatten it out, though that is not thought to be the intention. As a matter of fact, the theorists argue over why subincision is performed. It occurs among Australian Aborigines and some tribes in the Amazon basin. Natives in Brazil subincise to remove the candiru, a tiny fish which swims up the urethra if attracted by a stream of urine when the man is swimming. Once inside they anchor themselves with non-retractable spines and nothing short of surgery will tempt them out.

'One theorist tried to extend this to the Aborigines and claimed that they did it to extract seeds, burrs, splinters and all manner of crawling and burrowing crustaceans and insects. But this wouldn't explain why subincision has become a ceremonial rite.'

At the mention of ceremonial rites Gargan felt she had struck a chord. He sensed vague memories or dreams to do with initiation ceremonies. He said nothing, however, and concealed his interest.

'One writer suggested that Aborigines subincise because of kangaroo penis envy,' Su continued. 'The kangaroo has a two-headed penis and copulates for up to two hours at a time. To be more accurate it's bifid rather than two-headed. The glans is split into two. But it's up to your point of view whether it's divided or duplicated. Anyway, according to this expert, the Aborigines make a connection between the kangaroo's dick and how long it can screw for.

'A more convincing theory is that men wished to resemble women with respect to bleeding. A woman's period was thought to release noxious humours from her system. Since men had no apparent facility for this, they created one. Wounds, once made, could be reopened periodically. The Kwoma men of New Guinea, for example, go to a stream and make a light incision in the glans. The flowing water carries the bad blood out of the tribal territory.'

Su stopped for a mouthful of coffee. 'More?' she asked.

Gargan shrugged, knowing he didn't have to seem keen. She enjoyed showing off.

'There are four stages of initiation for an Aboriginal boy. The first is called ALKIRAKIWUMA and involves painting and throwing the novice in the air. The second is LARTNA. Circumcision. Without Western comforts like anaesthetic and scalpel, this is performed with a stone knife. Next comes the ARILTA, the subincision. The novice is led to the ceremonial ground and made to lie down upon a table formed by two men. Two more men approach. One puts the boy's penis on a stretch, the other makes the incision, effectively opening up the urethra on the underside along the full length of the penis. What's wrong?'

Gargan was frowning. 'Go on,' he said.

'The blood is allowed to flow on to a fire. If the wound is painful – *if* the wound is painful – the boy can put pieces of glowing charcoal on to the fire and urinate on them. The steam – '

' – is said to ease the pain,' Gargan finished her sentence in a hoarse whisper.

'How did you know that?' she asked.

'I know all that stuff,' he said slowly. 'I don't know where from, but I know it. It's so familiar.'

'Well, of course it's familiar.'

'No, I don't mean like that. What I'm doing is not the same. Similar but not the same. No. It's as if I've been told all that before – all that business about the ceremonies, I mean – either that or I've read it somewhere. But I know I haven't.' He scratched his scalp. 'This whole business pisses me off at times.'

'Let me help you, Gargan.' She covered his hand with hers.

'No.' He pulled his hand away sharply. 'I have to sort this out on my own.'

'Are you honestly any nearer to solving it?'

He stared at her, all sorts of answers pressing at his lips, none true and none coming out.

'Obviously not,' she said.

'No. That's not true. I am getting somewhere.'

'To Yugoslavia. Whatever that has to do with anything.'

'You see, Su, you're too nosy. Yes, I am going to Yugoslavia. And I think that will get me somewhere. OK?'

'Who is she?'

'What?' he bluffed, trying to stop the blood rushing to his face.

'Who is she? There's obviously some woman involved. And you think she's gonna make everything all right,' she sneered.

'Su!'

'Wave her magic wand and hey presto! You'll be whole again.'

'Shut up!' he roared as he stood up and 'Fuck!' as he grazed his leg on the edge of the table and lumbered to the door.

The sky had darkened. Clouds thickened in the west. Su was close behind him again. Thirty yards or so. This would make it easier to carry out the plan he'd worked out earlier and now wanted all the more to execute. He accelerated, although he was beginning to sweat as the air grew heavy. He stepped briskly across the tramlines at the junction before the Westbahnhof. Roadsigns pointed left to Budapest and right to Prague. He made sure she could still see him as he entered the station. Across the crowded marble hall he went straight to the escalators leading up to the trains. His luck was in. A suburban train was about to leave. There was just enough time for him to get right to the front and for Su just to make it into the last carriage.

It continued to go his way. She moved up to the front slowly, so that by the time the train got to Weidlingau-Wurzbachtal – only two stops from the Westbahnhof – she had only reached the carriage behind Gargan's. He was tugging on the doors before the train had stopped, giving the appearance of wanting to disembark without her knowledge. In fact, he wanted her to see him and to get off also, but to remain at least fifty yards behind.

He quickly scanned the timetable, then crossed under the line and began striding up the narrow road on the other side. Only eight minutes out of the city and this was the countryside, the Vienna Woods. The road climbed the wooded hills to the clouds which bunched like rotten cauliflower. A few bungalows and smallholdings dotted the roadside. A man wrestled with the bonnet of his car. A gate smacked into its wooden post. Gargan was aware of Su some distance behind. He was trying not to think of what she'd told him and how part of it struck deep resonances somewhere inside him. Better to take things half a step at a time. Lead Su up on to the hills then lose her and get back in time for the next train back to Vienna. It was not elaborate and she was not stupid, but she should at least be down in spirits and might just give up and sit on a log, were she to lose sight of him among the dense trees.

The air was almost singing with electricity as he dived into the wood. It was like entering a church. A velvet-carpeted sanctum where needle- and footfalls were immediately swallowed. The light was purply-green, the air like water. Armies of trees emerged from hiding and slipped quietly behind others as Gargan bounded uphill. From behind a trunk he looked and saw that Su was at least a hundred yards behind. He came into a clearing. It was scarcely any lighter: the cloud layer shifted and swelled. Presently, the gradient levelled out and the gloom sloped away downhill in all directions; otherwise there was nothing to distinguish the summit, modest as it was.

Concealing himself to look for Su, he felt an abrupt shock wave blast through him with incredible force, liquefying his joints. An ear-splitting thundercrack chased the thrusting air and his knees gave way. He looked up and glimpsed the culprits glowering vengefully through the tops of the pines. He became aware of the hairs on his arms standing stiffly erect. Then of his disorientation. He looked left, right, behind, but couldn't see her. He didn't even know any more which direction she'd be coming from. He felt a bastard for putting her through it. Not that acknowledging it made him any less of a bastard. The sweat pricking his forehead, would it cause him to be electrocuted? He rubbed it with a dirty forearm, noticing how his breath was catching. Suddenly the sky was ripped open by a jagged needle, injecting its fierce charge into the wooded hillside.

Never frightened in a storm before, Gargan cowered defenceless. Another rib-squeezing crash spluttered earthwards. His ears and eyes throbbed as if bleeding. A lightning spear shocked the tree-shadows into stark noonlight, printing negatives on the retina, and wrenching open the sky's clotted wounds once more to a bestial explosion of rage and pain.

He ran. Thrashing through dead foliage and stumbling over fallen trunks, he careered downhill. The lightning exposed his folly and the thunderclaps shook his brain loose like an old walnut. The fact that there was no sign of Su indicated he was not going back the same way. He just hoped he was descending towards the railway and not getting hopelessly lost going north.

When he stopped to wipe the sweat from his glasses and his face he realized it wasn't sweat but rain. Even through the trees it was coming down unhindered. He lifted his face up to receive the blessing of cool refreshment. Within minutes he was pleasantly soaked. It washed out some of the tension. He checked his watch and hurried on.

The railway line appeared so unexpectedly he fell over it. No sign of any trains, but there was a station 300 yards to the right. Gargan skipped along on the sleepers and slipped off the tracks just before the tiny station.

It had a different name – Purkersdorf-Sanatorium. It was, if he remembered the map correctly, one stop west from where he'd got off. And three minutes until the train.

All of this proved to be correct. Confident that Su was still lost in the wood he sat panting on the packed train and tried to wring out his shirt while still wearing it. His glasses for once didn't need moistening before polishing. He sat back squelching and returned the affronted gazes of his fellow passengers.

The storm hadn't yet reached the city. But it was coming. Its outriders trooped up Mariahilfer Strasse in Gargan's wake. Militaristic clouds beat their breasts and bellowed overhead. In the streets people fled as if to air raid shelters. But the work on the new line was not complete so they couldn't go underground. They dithered and dashed in the darkness.

The statue in the polythene bag, no longer a passive victim, struggled in alarm for release. It sensed the imminence of battle, the urgency of flight. But a contortion of shadows on the figure's shrouded face evidenced its intention to wreak havoc randomly. The rope around its arms and ankles seemed suddenly frail. Gargan hurried on. He glanced behind but was alone. Had he succeeded in losing his vigilant shadow?

A late newspaper vendor was in danger of losing his hundreds of headlines to the gathering wind. THE POPE HONOURS KURT WALDHEIM AS MAN OF PEACE. EAST GERMANS ARRIVE IN WEST FROM PRAGUE. The man spread his arms wide to save his stall.

Gargan looked at his watch. Eleven o'clock. He still had some ground to cover and the 23.15 train to catch.

Would Rada be there? he wondered as he boarded the train. Would she be there in Subotica? It wasn't far now, it wouldn't be long. She was hoping to make it, was all she'd said.

Slipping In

He stood on the hill growling at the sky. All day there had been strange and distant noises, though no clouds had appeared. Occasionally a veil had been drawn across the sun and a chill had lightly touched his bare brown back, yet he'd been sweating. There had been a tremendous heat coming from somewhere.

The girl was with him but he was not content. Something about her tired him. Walking about with her all day had become as pointless as doing it on his own. And the dreams ... the dreams had shown him the new woman in the territory, the foreigner. Something about her fascinated him. The way her hair and skin were lighter than the people of the land. Not like a mixed-race child, but a white woman darkened by the sun. And those grey eyes with their dancing sparks of yellow.

The girl slumped by his side was heavy with child. But that responsibility in his people's culture carried less significance than the dream and its symbols. The reality of the dream was greater than that of the waking life. It contained messages, signs. The experience was not vicarious but immediate and personal. The appearance of the stranger in the dream was confirmation of the role she would play.

On all this he reflected as huge sections of sky, suddenly gone grey, detached, re-formed and swarmed over his head. Like tribal lands they rucked and rent in confrontation.

He silently thanked the dreaming for allowing him this vision. Sparks juddered between chasmic fissures in the shifting sky. The rumblings had become louder and more frequent. A thin vein of light fell to the earth and for a second illuminated an entirely different landscape. Legions of trees covered the hill and plain; dark, rich, needle-green. In the dull, throbbing afternoon stormlight once more the clouds rolled over again, exploding and unfurling this time a sheet of light. The afforested knoll reappeared and he slipped behind one of its trees, darting quickly away into the new world and leaving the girl behind.

Swallowed by Darkness

Tatters of his dreams fluttered around the compartment, shot through by a diffuse, hovering light. A uniformed man without a face; a faceless woman. An empty railway station. Splashes of red. Aborigines. A black face.

No details remained. They broke up like butterflies' wings in too harsh a light. Now scattering in the air, impossible to catch. Leaving just the vague but certain feeling that these images had peppered his dreams. Even that certainty lost its foundation as consciousness advanced to acknowledge the morning. The light now penetrated all corners, prising open fine cracks in the upholstery and singling out motes of dust buffeted in the turbulence created by arcing flies.

Gargan kept his eyes open until they felt capable of doing the job themselves. He rubbed them. The skin felt tender and vulnerable. Slowly he straightened his legs – he'd fallen asleep sitting up, in an empty compartment, where he could have pulled out the seats and slept supine – and winced as they cracked and popped. He put his head in his hands, scratched it and turned to the window to have a look at Yugoslavia.

Houses. Cars. Trees. People. Bicycles. Lorries. Roads. So what had he expected?

The houses were cuboid and grey, the sky also, a very thin skimmed-milky grey, through which the sun tried to insinuate its light. He looked back at the compartment: it was not as bright as it had seemed upon waking.

The railway crossed over a small road. A woman cycled up out of a tunnel. She produced an umbrella from under her skirts and opened it above her head, while continuing to ride the bicycle. Spots of rain splashed on the train window. Disappointed, Gargan slumped in his seat and hugged his knees. He wondered if inspectors and guards had woken him in the night. He found his passport in his bag and turned the pages. On page twenty-four was an unfamiliar stamp. He checked his ticket. That too had been stamped. Presented with this evidence he began to visualize the officials who had visited him in his sleep. Their faces evaded him and he didn't know if he was remembering or inventing the blue uniforms with red stars.

The passport was getting heavy. It slid out of his grasp and he plunged into the seat. The light dulled to shadows.

The window was dark. A tunnel through the mountains perhaps. He stood up and stared at himself reflected by the darkness. The face looking back was an Aborigine's. The mouth stretched and pulled its lips back in a broad white smile.

He was climbing a mountain alongside a red stream, trying to locate the source of the flow. Rain fell from a cloudless sky, diluting the stream and turning it pink. He hauled himself over the final escarpment and came face to face with a young Aboriginal man kneeling down cutting himself.

A figure came into the compartment. A black face bellowed words in a strange language which reverberated in the small space. He continued until Gargan sat up, rubbing the sleep from his eyes. The face was dark because of the shadow cast by a peaked blue cap, in the centre of which was a blood-red star. The controller repeated his message and Gargan shrugged in dumb incomprehension.

'Sprechen Sie Deutsch?' Gargan asked, certain the man wouldn't speak English.

'Halbe Stunde,' the controller said slowly. 'Dann fahren wir ab.'

'Ja. Danke.'

A half-hour delay. Gargan shook his head and walked out into the corridor. Opening a window, he leant out and breathed in the fresh air. The rain of whenever, several hours ago, it felt like, but probably only twenty minutes or so, had stopped or been left behind. The sun was still pressing at the blocks of cloud. The name of the station, and the town it served, was printed in black letters on an off-white board: LJUBLJANA.

Gripping his bag he stepped off the train. Despite his nomadic childhood, this was his first visit to Yugoslavia. Probably because it was not allied to the Eastern Bloc countries through which his mother had travelled. His mother's disappearance ten years ago was an inconvenience now. The thought had occurred to him before, that maybe she would be able to cast some light on his current problem. However, she had, to all intents and purposes, disappeared off the face of the earth. He remembered the shock of that but virtually nothing else until he began walking tightropes a year or two later. He imagined, if she was still alive, she was most likely whoring again in one of the Eastern European capitals.

The station was drab. He crossed over the tracks, in the absence of bridges and subways, and walked along platform one, past the left luggage office, where voices rose in argument, and turned left through an opening. He found himself in a bar, scarcely more than a counter stuck in a passage. On closer inspection, the dark brown shadows revealed recesses and tall tables to stand at. His mouth felt as if it had been sanded down in the night. A coffee would be useful. A look at the pricelist told him that coffee was called *kafa* and that he didn't have any dinars.

Stepping back on to the platform he saw a sign with a drawing of notes and coins. In the Viennese fish bar he had collected the change after Su had paid with a large note. Neither of them had made any reference to it though he had felt quite ashamed. At the back of his mind he thought he would pay her back some day when it was all over.

He stood at the plastic-topped desk holding the Austrian notes. One of two men sitting working over columns of figures pushed back his canvas chair and came to the desk. He was a large, thickset man with dark eyebrows.

'Pass,' he said without meeting Gargan's eyes. The man flicked through the passport and snapped it down on the desktop. Calculations were made on an old rattling machine and notes counted out in silence. Even when Gargan thanked him in his own language – 'Hvala' – the man remained mute.

At the bar counter Gargan waited alongside customers who kept their heads down but slipped him sidelong glances. Those who arrived after Gargan were served before him. Then he saw they were all fingering little white squares of paper which they gave to the woman with their order. Gargan looked about and saw another, moustached, woman sitting in an alcove set into the wall on his left.

'Kafa,' he said to her and proffered a thousand dinar note. She snatched it and thumped the machine. The drawer flew open and from thick wads she peeled off several notes of different colours. As he thanked her he noticed her moustache twitch. Her fingers rose deftly as if to calm it. The time was 7 a.m.

Kafa was not coffee, after all, but an infusion of treacle and crude oil. He was grateful for the size of the tiny cup. He moved a lump of cream around with a spoon to little effect. When he looked up several pairs of eyes glanced away and heads angled subtly downwards.

The platforms were livelier now, but the aspect of the people was unhappy and decrepit. He was reminded of Euston or Paris Nord. An old woman wreathed in rags counted out a pile of notes the colour of bougainvillaea: one hundred dinars, worth less than ten pence. It bought you more here but you couldn't call her well off. Other derelicts sat around with nothing to count.

Gargan was glad to find his compartment still empty. A last-minute rush, however, just before the train pulled out, brought a large family and their bags up the corridor in search of seats. The man smiled and delivered a volley of unknown words. Gargan beckoned them in.

Between Gargan and the man sat one of the little girls. The sturdy mother sat opposite her husband. Next to her and across from Gargan were the other daughter and a very small boy. The children didn't look away when Gargan met their gaze. The man spoke again in Gargan's direction.

'Engleski,' Gargan declared, pointing at his chest.

'Engleski,' the man nodded. 'Engleski,' he said to his wife, who in turn murmured 'Engleski' to the children.

Gargan watched rugged scarps and luscious forests slip past his window. Upon an instruction from her husband the woman produced parcels of food: pieces of what looked like chicken, a hunk of heavy-looking bread, some fruit. The boy fought the top off a large bottle of orange squash. The man and woman pulled out their seats and lay down, each having the other's feet next to their head. One little girl lay on her mother's breast, the other slumped down next to her father. The little boy steadily emptied the squash bottle. From time to time the woman chuckled throatily and the man grunted. Gargan couldn't see clearly enough in the window reflection what they might be doing. He needed to go to the toilet but decided to wait until Zagreb.

The Petrinjska led straight from the railway station into the centre of town. There was a hat shop selling magnificent Panamas for £3; a woman in a black dress standing out on her first floor ledge to clean the windows with a broad sweep of the cloth; a small shop with a wooden floor and a dusty window displaying toy racing cars and sticking plaster.

He was confident he'd left Su behind in Vienna. Soon he would be in Subotica. For now he could relax.

Republic Square was pastel grey and so clean and polished it shone. The large stone buildings around the sides were shades of pink, blue, yellow. People moved around in groups and singly; they sat on stone benches at the feet of great iron lampposts; they bought newspapers from the VJESNIK kiosk; strolled in and out of doorways and porticoes. A girl in a fluorescent green dress attracted the attentions of a group of young off-duty soldiers.

In the open-air market peasant women wrapped in shawls pressed sprigs of lavender on people as they walked past. Gargan bought a lettuce and a bag of fat red currants for his lunch, which he ate sitting on the edge of a fountain pool in a quiet square opposite St Mark's Cathedral. A stream of men dressed as monks emerged from the cathedral by a side door and gathered in the carpark chatting together in loud, jocular voices. Soon cars skirted the fountain and turned off to the north. Traffic policemen with white shirts and wide, puffed false sleeves stopped the vehicles then waved them on.

He walked round the old part of the city, Gornji Grad, where examples of graffiti caught his eye: MERDE STELLA ROSA SS and BLUE HOOLYGANZ ARMY. He trailed down wide, barren boulevards. Massive, dirty grey apartment buildings hemmed the pavements and sportswear shops in beneath them. He wished he had stayed on the train and gone straight through to Belgrade. Now he had to wait until nearly midnight because if he took the 17.10 or the 18.04 he'd get to Belgrade after eleven in the evening, too late to connect with a Subotica train. But if he took the night train from Zagreb to Belgrade he could sleep on it and be there in the morning.

He felt a little judder in his chest and a thought recurred to him: *what if she's not there?* What was the point of worrying? Even if she was there, as he hoped, he had no idea of the lie of the land, the state of things. He'd told her he was going to the continent. She said if he got far enough east, he should go and see her family. Indeed, she had to go to Europe herself for some reason (*what reason?*) and was hoping to spend some time in Subotica. Gargan was going to arrive at the time when she was most likely to be there.

Would she be encouraging his obvious feelings for her by being there? Or was she just pleased to offer her family's hospitality? What would it be to her to see him in Subotica rather than Panton Street?

How could she help him? If she entertained none of his ambitions for the two of them together, if he was finally forced to accept that she would never be his, would he not be worse off than when he left London? And two and a half inches more deeply split.

What if she did love him as he loved her? If she was coming to meet him to declare that? Then what?

Mission accomplished; and whatever complex or neurosis, insecurity or mental sickness was causing him to do what he was doing would vanish. As if by magic.

He could dream, couldn't he? You had to have a dream. And that was his. They have to come true for someone. Somewhere. Sometime.

Gone would be the need to walk tightropes. No longer would his subconscious mind get the better of his sleeping body.

All of this passed through Gargan's mind like a speech whose orator became increasingly wheedling and ironic as the inanities piled on top of each other.

Basically he was screwed up and he didn't know what the hell he was doing. Rada was his last hope. There was no link, no miracle cure, no rationale that would stand up on its own. He knew what he wanted and he knew what he didn't want. Simple as that.

Republic Square was filling up with Italian tourists. Men in expensive sweaters obliged their large wives to pose for photographs near groups of pretty Zagreb girls. The surface of the square glimmered in the failing light. Soldiers tilted their hats. People walked past in twos. The lights came on and the sky turned a deeper, yet more luminous blue.

The evening darkened rapidly, though remnants of light in the sky above the streetlamps still glowed. Gargan entered a smaller, tree-dotted square where young people sat playing guitars and singing. He felt a sudden yearning to be with them, to be one of them, to lean back and knock his neighbour's leg and know she wouldn't mind. He longed to make throwaway remarks which would be as relevant answered or not, and to share glances and smiles. He wanted to make plans and forget them, go to sleep, wake up and have something to eat, later play and relax some more.

He bought a cold bottle of Coke at the counter of a café and sat drinking in the square as the night came on. For a while it felt right; he almost belonged. Almost.

The streets to the station were empty. White light bathed the platforms, from tall lamps and from the moon. He walked across the tracks a dim shadow, almost completely unconscious of himself. The train was waiting quietly. There appeared to be no other passengers, nor any station officials in attendance. He stepped unseen into one of the rear carriages and was swallowed by darkness.

Just a Drink

There was another party.

Some bizarre streak of optimism told me to take Jenni to the party. I would see; it would be all right. I would wonder what all the doubts had been for.

It was Liz's party. In addition to all her friends and acquaintances she'd invited Charlie, Tom, Jessica, Linda and myself. Her friends included a lot of students and au pairs. The air was full of gesticulations to combat the loud music. These proved inadequate, however, so everybody shouted whatever they had to say, which inevitably was mainly for their own benefit. *voice-filled rooms / with faces, mindless / words filling spaces*

Tom hadn't turned up. Jessica and Linda were bent double over their drinks laughing at somebody's joke. Charlie was engaged in heavy conversation with a full-bearded middle-aged man about a painting on the wall. The dialogue seemed to revolve around was it or wasn't it something or other.

Jenni and I were sitting at the edge of the room. My chair was angled slightly forward of hers. I looked out into the gaps between people, conscious all the time of Jenni just behind me. To turn round and smile or chat would only affirm that everything was all right. Which it wasn't.

I swallowed a mouthful of vodka and examined people's faces as they pretended to struggle to hear what their partners were saying. *senseless sounds falling / on ears deafened by silent years*

Heads nodded rhythmically, noses were stroked, chins rubbed, lips pressed knowledgeably together. *spent learning movements / signifying implied understanding*

There was no one among this crowd I desired to be with in preference to Jenni. Her accurate perception of these partygoers was for me a point in her favour. Not that she needed points. I loved her. But *why*? Because she loved me? Yes. But why did I love her on that particular day? On Friday? Because I loved her on Thursday. So much was assumed. As day passed into night and became a new day, we remained together.

I wanted to know what it would be like to be on my own again.

Jenni's hand appeared on my leg and gave it a brief squeeze. I covered her hand with mine. *assumed agreement / meaning nothing*.

At the theatre the following night I was so distracted during my character preparation – thinking of different possible ways of ending the relationship so as to minimize the hurt to Jenni – that I overdid the heavy breathing.

I lurched on to the stage and the house – quite full; tourists – exploded with laughter. I remember Ed and Dick right at the beginning saying audiences would love me. There was no love in that reception. Just scorn. *Oh my God, look at that jerk!* delivered in a bale of laughter.

'Hey boys,' I gasped, in a manner their looks always told me was far too friendly. 'Mr Lansdale.' Pant. 'Mr Campbell.' I was still breathing deeply and quickly. Dick's lips were moving but I couldn't hear what he was saying above the thumping in my temples. My head began to swim. Black spots appeared before my eyes. I looked out into the audience. The faces blurred in and out of focus. One face seemed to become detached from the other spectators and drift into clearer focus ahead of me. It was that woman again. The one who had cornered me that time. Whom I'd taken for a drink. Just a drink. I hadn't intended to take her home. What was she doing here? What did she want of me? Why did her eyes glitter accusingly in my direction?

My head felt like it was filling with enormous soap bubbles. Realizing I was hyperventilating and about to pass out, I managed to slow my breathing down. Slowly things returned to normal. Lansdale and Campbell, it seemed, had been talking amongst themselves in an attempt to draw the audience's attention away from me. When I came down again, we somehow made our way back into the script. I felt quite reassured to be back on familiar ground: not knowing whether or not I'd been to Vietnam, not quite sure whether I'd smashed up Campbell's car and undecided on whether or not I'd screwed his wife.

When I looked into the audience I could no longer see that face from the past.

After the performance, Ed and Dick were remarkably restrained. Ed said they thought I ought to come in for a couple of rehearsals. I asked why. He said I seemed to have lost the direction of the character; I seemed to be without roots, without a past. I appreciated how important that was? Didn't I? 'Look, Ed. I hyperventilated out there tonight.' 'We're not just talking about tonight. I knew you were hyperventilating. You're lucky you don't do it every night. Matter of fact, Dick and I have a whole routine all worked out in case you die. That right, Dick?' 'Sure,' Dick grinned. 'We just kick you off the stage, asshole. Kick you right off the stage and carry on.'

I was past humouring them. I sighed and set my mouth impatiently.

'I really would like you to come in for a couple of rehearsals,' Ed said. 'We have to get back to the Method. You should be able to tell me everything about yourself at any given time. Your whole past, your experiences, your identity. It should all be up there,' tapping his head, 'as part of your character.'

As far as I was concerned the Method was bullshit. I didn't need a catalogue of details in my head. I *was* Fudakowski.

'Pay me and I'll consider it,' I said.

But it never came to that.

That night's performance, although there was no way of knowing it at the time, was Fudakowski's last.

Smrt

The train worked like a drill bit chiselling into the invisible landscape. For a while it struggled, fighting against a steep gradient. He found himself by the window with his head sticking out. The wind thrust his hair back and his glasses into his eyesockets. A branch line swung in, bringing with it another train. They ran alongside for some time then stopped at an unnamed station. No one got on or off. A few uniformed officials appeared in the shadows of the platform.

He looked into the other train. Its passengers sat white-faced and immobile. The seats were laid out like a tube carriage, so that a whole row of white faces met his stare. Or they would have done if their eyes held any sign of life. There was something bland and dispirited about the faces. Just then their train pulled forward and he saw them now slightly from the side. The acute angle prised up their white masks at the edges. The faces were painted that sickly pallor. Beneath, their skins were clearly black, the bone structure Aboriginal. The train came to an abrupt halt and those ghastly passengers fell forward as one. Heads lolled and snapped uselessly forward, falling on to hollow knocking chests.

His own train was moving again, scraping the rails and crawling uphill. Zagreb was a long way behind, Belgrade even further ahead. The mountains were steep, the track clinging to their scree slopes.

Dawn was dirty; gritty as an enlarged photograph. As if there were a dust storm or clouds of hanging spores. It was in itself thoroughly depressing, yet he had so much to look forward to. Young and in love: what more could he want?

The gradient levelled out. There was enough space for two more sets of rails which ran parallel on the left. He leaned further out and saw a tunnel coming up. The entrance to the tunnel was narrow. The two spare tracks, rusty and overgrown with weeds, ran into the solid stone wall. He saw a small cluster of children sitting on railings close to the embankment wall. As the train sped closer they turned their pale faces. Some had no mouths: the faces were just blanks, the eyes wide and round. In fact, only one boy was equipped with a mouth, which opened as the train approached. The thick wall raced to meet the twin tracks between the boys and the train. A sibilant shriek rose above the squealing of the wheels. It was the boy with the mouth; head swivelling to direct his scream at the right person as the train hurtled towards the tunnel.

The word formed a black cloud, expanding in the mucky morning air like an octopus's squirted ink. A cavernous, resonant roar; also precise, sharp, a short word: SMRT.

He looked to the front, saw the two spare tracks slice into the stone bank, as the tunnel opened its dark throat and sucked in the speeding train.

Smrt. The word reverberated in his head, in the train, the tunnel, all one.

Smrt. Smrt. SMRT.

The Black Tunnel

Belgrade was in chaos.

The panic of evacuation seemed to have gripped the main square in front of the railway station, as if the city had suddenly found itself transported a thousand miles south to the Middle Eastern war zones.

People, cars, trams squirmed through air thick as mud with the scorching heat. He was sweating even before he jumped down to the low platform and was swept along towards the station concourse and buildings, where little was offered by way of protection against the sun.

He stood in a queue for ten minutes to get information about trains to Subotica. No one moved, apart from those at the front jostling and arguing. The open-shirted man behind the glass removed a small metal grille from time to time, leaning forward, to listen to the urgent pleas of the people queuing. He shut the grille and frowned down columns of numbers and times to appease and stall the impatient questioners. Occasionally he enraged the mob by turning and laughing at jokes made by his colleagues in the next office.

Gargan walked away from the queue, left his bag at left-luggage and searched for an alternative source of information. He found a board obviously printed years before which identified trains to Subotica at 1.45 and 4.15. Since he didn't want to queue again he decided to go by these times, and if they were wrong there would be other, later trains.

The streets leading off Balkanska proved to be just as chaotic; people running in all directions, clambering around dusty holes like bomb craters and flimsily erected barriers behind which men dug more holes and filled in old ones.

Shop windows offered less of the instant stimulation he remembered from Western cities, but the same sense of disposability and impermanence. He did a few quick conversions and realized that books, shoes and hardware were not appreciably cheaper than in London.

Eating a potato snack from a street stall he made his way through the gridwork of streets north of Republic Square and wandered into a park, the Kalemegdan Fortress. The trees lining the paths provided welcome shelter from the direct sunlight and the water fountains cooled him down. He held his head under a dribble of water and only when he massaged his scalp did he realise how dirty his hair had become.

Children played around the trees. Old men sat on benches and thin seats talking and playing chess. Park bench intellectuals.

The fortress was host to an assortment of big tanks and guns; Hungarian, Polish, Russian. Their rusted caterpillars threatened no more movement on the grassy slopes of the former battlements. The red paint had flaked off all the old stars. Gargan couldn't help seeing this unmasking as prophetic.

At the north-eastern corner of the park was a gravelly terrace with wooden benches looking out over the confluence of the Danube and the Sava. In the distance to his left was New Belgrade, a nightmare assemblage of concrete tower blocks.

Exhausted after a poor night's sleep and insufficient food, Gargan sat down on one of the benches.

At the foot of the escarpment on which the fortress had been built, and following the curve of the river, ran a line from the main railway station to Belgrade Danube Station, whence it crossed the Danube on a bridge.

There were not many trains. The river itself was obscured from inside the train. He tried to glimpse it between trees and over the low embankment, but either the train was travelling too fast, or he couldn't focus in the poor light, or it simply wasn't there. The rusty secondary track still ran parallel on the left. Ahead, the black disc of the tunnel dilated rapidly in excitement. The solid stone walls rushed forward with it towards the train. The wind lashed his cheeks, stung his eyes. The boys clung with apparent ease to the railings and one turned open-mouthed to the rattling, speeding carriages, screaming the word.

SMRT. SMMRRRRT.

The train, having switched tracks, ploughed straight into the wall, not stopping even after impact. The shock thumped his neck, tendons snapping like perished rubber bands, against the empty window frame. His carriage bucked high in the air as the train concertinaed behind its crushed locomotive and first two carriages. All he could think about was how bloody lucky he was to be five coaches back when suddenly he was lying on his back looking up at the sky, which was clearer and brighter than it had been.

The hard slats of the bench under his shoulder blades were only slightly reassuring.

Smrt. The word worried at him like a mosquito, carrying vague, foreboding threats like disease. The very sound of the word was pernicious and fatalistic.

Feeling drugged he shook his head and checked his watch. 3.46. *3.46!* Time he was somewhere else. He shivered in a film of sweat as he got to his feet. He was soon hot though, and sweating afresh, as he strode through the fortress park looking for a way out. 3.53. The chess-players still played the same moves and identical children ran between the trees. All that had moved was the sun; the light fell differently, more abrasively, through the trees. He hurried beneath them, his face starting to itch.

The streets were full of people going nowhere in particular and in no hurry to get there. Living their lives, travelling from work back home or from home to work, whatever. Was there no one else on their way to a turning point? A meeting which would fulfil hopes and erase troubles. It seemed not. They crossed roads in slow groups which invariably contained off-duty soldiers or military officers carrying briefcases. They seemed to move even more slowly the nearer he got to the railway station, as if the air itself were thickening. They had all the time in the world. The hectic mood of the morning had vanished, in all but Gargan. He wanted that train.

Ten past four. The queue at the left-luggage was stationary.

He craned his neck over shoulders in front. The man at the front was looking straight ahead, unconcerned by the unmanned window on his right. Eventually – 4.12 – the window was opened and a bag pushed through. The Oriental man in front of Gargan was annoyed when his American English proved inadequate for communication. He didn't know how much he had to pay and was reluctant to hand over too much money in case the man short-changed him. Gargan felt sweat trickling into small areas of his back and stomach that had remained dry until then. 'This is ridiculous,' the man in front said at 4.13. Yes, Gargan breathlessly agreed, it was. 'Is this the right change?' the man asked of the vacant stare in the luggage room. 'Yes,' Gargan advised him irritably, 'it's right.' 'Good, good,' he was saying, 'you can't trust these people. These Eastern Bloc people.' *We're not in the fucking Eastern Bloc now please get out of the way and let me get my bag!*

His hand slipped greasily on the rail as he pulled himself on to the train, but he was on. This end the seats were all taken, so he used the corridor to move up to the front. He found two or three single seats left almost hidden by the families crammed into compartments. Feeling as if he deserved it, he decided to sit in first class and pay the extra.

Under cover of darkness, however, in a tunnel they hit just after leaving the station, he sneaked out and back into second class.

Squeezed between two big-bellied Poles, T-shirts rolled up over their paunches, he struggled to relax. Roads and bridges chugged past the window. No one else in the compartment saw the boys climbing on the railings and the black tunnel approaching. No one else was thrown forward headfirst to smash the glass of the window as the boy shouted his word and the train hit the wall and the carriage described a parabola in the twilight. Only three carriages this time had saved him from certain death.

One of the Poles helped him up off the floor. They muttered to each other in tongues neither understood. He backed out of the compartment and pulled down a window for some fresh air. There was no way he could have missed his station, because just beyond Subotica lay Hungary and its border guards, and he had no visa.

In the bathroom he was reassured to see that despite all the train crashes he was in reasonable shape. He was much thinner than he should be, but that was nothing to worry about. Taking down his trousers he confirmed that he had not been cutting himself. In fact, if he was not mistaken, the wound looked as if it might have healed up a fraction. He peed without pain and left the toilet smiling.

In the Convex Mirror

When I arrived at the theatre the next day I found Jessica and Linda sitting down in the bar talking with Monsieur and Madame Poittevin, the proprietors. A boy of about twenty sat against the back wall nursing a black eye. There was no sign of Ed and Dick. I took a seat and listened to the explanation of how our two cowboy producers had swindled us out of 69,000 francs.

The whole production had been a profit-making exercise, a confidence trick right from the start. The printing of programmes, posters and fliers, by far the major 'cost', had been done free by a well-wishing printer who also backed the launch of Ed and Dick's company to the tune of 30,000 francs.

Ticket sales over the three months came to 168,000 francs, of which half went directly to the proprietors. The rest went into two pockets. Real expenses were kept right down: a few costumes, minimal payments to actors and company, hire of the audition theatre: well under 8000 francs. Consequently, Ed and Dick made about 100,000 francs. Personally. Between them.

Monsieur and Madame Poittevin had found out only that day. The printer had been on the telephone tendering for some work he knew Monsieur Poittevin needed to have done unconnected with the current production. The printer had alluded to his patronage of Thunderbird Productions in complete innocence. Monsieur Poittevin picked up on it immediately, indicating surprise. The printer was astounded that the proprietor had not known. Monsieur Poittevin asked about the extent of the patronage. That's when he dropped the receiver.

'In all my years in the theatre,' he told us, 'I have never experienced such a thing.' He was very upset. Although not out of pocket himself his theatre was tainted. 'I am so sorry this has happened,' he said with genuine sympathy.

We looked towards the boy with the bruised face.

Monsieur Poittevin went on to explain. Having collected his thoughts he put his wife fully in the picture and called his son to come over. When Dick arrived alone – Ed was running late on a modelling shoot – Monsieur Poittevin followed him down to the dressing room for a confrontation.

Dick wasted no time. He dodged round Monsieur Poittevin and through the doorway while the proprietor was still delivering his prepared speech. Poittevin junior tried unsuccessfully to bar the exit upstairs and collected a shiner for his efforts.

Going to the police was not a good idea. So far the authorities had turned a blind eye to the foreigners who worked in the theatre without paying tax and often without permits. None of us would have had a leg to stand on. Although Ed and Dick did cheat us out of a lot of money we shouldn't have been working there in the first place.

The only thing we could do, since avenues of constructive action were closed off, was ransack the dressing room. Ed and Dick still had a lot of stuff about the place, naturally, because they thought they had another month to go. And at least another 7000 francs to look forward to.

So we indulged our appetite for revenge in the only petty, pitiable way available to us. We ripped long shreds from their costumes, punched the top out of Campbell's stetson, punctured the toes of Lansdale's boots. There was a framed poster of the show signed by another backer, the former US cultural attaché whose donation had probably been major if the party was anything to go by. We smashed the frame and tore the poster into quarters. The good-luck telegrams and cards we ripped up also. Lipstick and face creams were good for defacing the fashion magazines. Jessica chewed what gum there was and used it to stick together the pages of their acting manuals. Linda funnelled the contents of two ashtrays into the whisky flasks. Emergency medicines, breath-freshener and deodorant mixed well with the Evian water, and the bottle served as a receptacle for those scattered dried flowers which remained from the bouquets.

Of course, we didn't know at the time whether Ed or Dick

would ever dare come back and so cast an eye over our handiwork. As it turned out, they did make a return visit, breaking in the back way while Monsieur and Madame Poittevin were asleep upstairs.

I wish I could have seen their faces.

Still, they didn't do badly. A few mementoes and personal possessions wantonly destroyed. A fairly minor sacrifice for 100,000 francs.

I arranged to meet Jenni in the park. I would have gone to Pontoise but she was coming into Paris anyway. She sounded almost surprised to hear from me, as if she had already assumed what I was preparing to tell her. I suspected I would feel at least a slight tug upon seeing her, but I didn't. We walked round the pond, twice, talking but not really saying anything. I wished I didn't have to do it. I wished I could just *be* on my own.

We took the path which curved up to the bridge. She asked me what the time was. My hopes lifted: did she have a date?

At the top we climbed the steps up to the observation terrace. I walked past the stone bench and leaned on the wall which encircled the terrace. Four pillars rose out of this wall to support the domed stone roof.

I rested on my elbows and looked out across the 19th, over the top corner of the 10th, to the great basilica of the Sacré Coeur crowning the famous hill of the 18th, Montmartre. But my awareness of Jenni just behind me was insuppressible. I turned and leaned back against the wall. Jenni had crossed over to the other side and was looking out to the north-east. I went over and stood by her. She continued to stare into the distance. Recalling the tenderness we had shared I lifted my hand to touch her cheek. She flinched and brushed my hand away then turned to face me.

She appeared armour-plated, her real face hidden away somewhere. All I could see in her eyes was myself. Twice, in fact. I half expected one of my reflections to be smaller because it was behind me, following me.

I looked at those two reflections and wondered just where my bisection began.

I found myself saying that the play had finished before schedule because Ed and Dick had been caught on the make. That Paris had been soured for me as a result. That I thought I ought to leave and go somewhere else and find more work. The obvious place was Berlin. It had lively expatriate communities and an active fringe scene.

But Jenni wasn't stupid. At some point she must have just walked away, because after a time I realized I was talking to myself.

I sat down on the stone bench, feeling nothing.

I scarcely noticed the changing colours in the sky and the drop in temperature.

My cheek was hurting. Someone was pressing my head against the stone. I jerked my eyes round to try and see my aggressor. But he was already walking away from me. My head was heavy. I found it difficult to pull away from the wall. An impression of my face was left there like a fossil. I rubbed at it with the ball of my hand, trying to erase it. The wall darkened, smeared with my blood. The skin on my hand was torn to shreds. But no pain. Looking closer I peered into the wound. Was there something moving in my blood? Something creeping over the exposed flesh? I took a strip of skin between finger and thumb and tore it back like a length of cloth. It didn't hurt.

Somehow, suddenly, the man was behind me again, although he had disappeared in the other direction. He took my hand, catching his nails in the frayed skin, and led me away.

There was a wall on our other side and occasional windows too high up to see through. I couldn't tell if we were inside or outside.

The corridor seemed to curve slightly to the left. So slightly that when I looked in front and behind I could not detect it. We walked on and gradually the curve became more acute like a spiral winding in on itself.

I was in the house. This time it was furnished. In a way which seemed so familiar. It was the house of a rich woman. The interior design, originally conservative, had been subject to eclectic modern additions. Habitat lampshades and fish-eye mirrors clashed in one room.

I walked up close to one of the convex mirrors and peered into it. The person who looked back at me *belonged* in that house. He looked at me like someone in authority about to delegate a dirty job, with a mixture of superiority and condemnation. In the end it was I who was distorted, not the man in the glass. I backed away frightened. He stepped backwards also, confidently, in charge of his destiny. His arrogance angered me. I ran forward, raising a fist. He lashed out at my hand, cutting it with broken glass. When I got to my feet once more the man had gone. There was just me holding a long dagger of silvered glass. I left the room and immediately I was climbing the staircase.

A telephone was ringing behind a door at the end of a corridor as I turned through 180 degrees to climb the next flight of stairs. I hesitated a moment then ignored the telephone and carried on. My hand was numb. I looked down. It was still holding the long thin slice of glass.

My head was hurting. I stopped on the next landing, where there was a small chest of drawers. I pulled open the drawers looking for aspirins. In the bottom drawer a sheet of paper stuffed behind some folded curtains caught my eye. The handwriting was familiar.

Time and almost spaceless
found but already lost
face but not to face
the finite
no way to choose the
infinite
To know briefly
To possess only for a moment
A man known intimately
A certain joy an exquisite
Eclipse
Ecstasy blends with pleasure
makes the pain seem almost
bearable
almost real

Hearts beat lips brush
over and over painting
time into memory.

I thought to myself: how did this get here? Then remembered the morning when I'd watched Jenni with her back to me put something in one of these drawers. There were some lines on the other side but I'd read enough. A sophisticated goodbye. Except that it was me who was making the break. Insulation, maybe, against what she knew was to come. Clever stuff. *Cynical bastard.* Me, not her.

I slipped the poem into a pocket and continued upstairs. My left hand recognized the grain of the banister rail. Blood seeped between the fingers of my other hand, fist clenched around the length of glass.

I began climbing the final flight. The telephone flung hooked notes up the stairs behind me, catching my calf muscles, slowing me down. *Time and almost spaceless.* When I looked down, the steps flattened and I was on a steep slope which my shredded calves would not allow me to grip. I threw myself flat and hauled my body up with one hand on the top step.

Calmly I crossed the short landing. My room was on the left. Hers on the far right. Of course, we shared a bedroom on the next floor down but she was rich so we had more rooms than we needed. I saw my free hand reaching out for the doorhandle. Downstairs the telephone stopped ringing.

Ear-splitting silence. Then a familiar noise from the other side of the door. Splashing. Subsidence. Water dripping from her body as she stands up. Wipes her face. Dries her eyes. Reaches out for the towel. Lifts one leg out. Silently dripping on to the mat. Both legs. Quick rub down. Without pulling the plug out – she never does until later – walking slowly, towelling the ends of her hair, towards the door.

I opened the door and it was as if someone had already begun attacking her. A look of terror appeared on her face and a gash in her side before I had even crossed the threshold. I hefted my weapon and aimed at her side. As my dagger fell there, on her left side, a red line was drawn on her right shoulder. I watched my arm follow to her shoulder while the unseen weapon spilled more blood as it tore open her thigh. In this way I followed each new wound as if to catch up with time or whoever was one step in front of me.

Alex, screaming, retreated as best she could. The only way was back to the bath.

I slumped on to the wet mat on the floor. The glass smashed into thousands of scarlet fragments as it hit the tiled wall.

I wondered what had happened and who had done it. Would I be held responsible? Where was Alex?

I leaned on the edge of the bath trying to get to my feet.

Washed clean by the water now red with most of her blood, my wife's white body floated up to the surface, her eyes staring at me in glittering accusation.

I opened my mouth and screams rang out.

An Echo of Laughter

The sky was graduating darkly towards evening as he touched the platform at Subotica. The air was still and quiet. During the last section of the journey he'd dreamt that Rada was waiting for him at the station. But his train never arrived. She walked over to the information office. His perspective allowed him to watch her coming towards the office, as if he were inside it. But how could he be? How could he be there watching her when his train had failed to arrive? Especially since the information she got was that the train had crashed. Were there any survivors? she asked. Only me. Only me. *Only me!* He woke up shouting.

The Poles had had enough and had already left the compartment. A Hungarian woman on her way back to Budapest after visiting relatives in Belgrade reassured him. 'The dreaming,' she said. 'The dreaming.'

In Subotica he had an address but no map. The station was in fact too small to have an information office. The man at the left-luggage office spoke neither English nor German. It was far from certain that his linguistic capabilities stretched to Serbo-Croat. If they did he was keeping quiet about it, nodding and shaking his head, looking at his feet.

He wandered out of the station. There was an area for vehicles turning; too informal for a square and more than just a wide road or carpark. On the other side under a tree, lights burned at a refreshments stall.

Neither the youth running the stall nor his young customer could understand Gargan. He showed them the scrap of paper torn from a waitress's order pad on which Rada had written her sister's address. The boy took it, pursed his lips, read the address out to the girl, who said something in reply. They looked at Gargan and shrugged. He took back the piece of paper and thanked them.

There were no large-scale street maps affixed to walls like he imagined to be present in all small towns. He walked away from the station. At a main road he looked right and left but saw no clues. He went left, and right when he found a pedestrianized street with cafés and a few shops. Lights were coming on in the buildings and the streets, darkening the blue in the sky.

The buildings were large and stone and plaster were predominant but the feeling was lighter than in Belgrade. The colours were more cheerful: yellows, blues, light greys and a clean, rosewood brown. The cafés dispersed tables and chairs on the pavement, eschewing the formal precision of Paris, inviting greater relaxation.

The end of the street revealed an open square – People's Square – the most beautiful he had seen. It was hexagonal in shape. At one edge was the impressive columned facade of a theatre built in golden-brown stone. On the right of this a yellow library. Then a hard-surface area with scattered trees, telephone booths and padlocked bicycles. Another pavement café, scarcely an empty table. A stretch of pavement leading to a colourful church. Gardens. The first corner of a modest shopping mall. Just off-centre in the square, dozens of people lounged on the rim of an illuminated fountain. Gargan felt a great peace pulling at him, but also a restlessness which stopped him sitting down and staying put. He criss-crossed the square on its diagonals. There was a pungent, smoky smell in the air.

He asked for directions to Partizanska. No one seemed able to help. He began to worry. A shawled old woman lifted her arms in the air and repeated the word 'Policija'. Her gestures were ambiguous: he couldn't tell if she was pointing the way to the police station or if she considered Gargan a threat.

He wandered off the square. The town was obviously larger than he had thought. Large enough to lose him easily in its streets in the space of twenty minutes. Low, bushy trees lined both sides of the narrow roads. Streetlamps hid their bulbs in the foliage so that a level green hue was cast. He turned corners, followed straight roads, inspected streetnames, aware that he was getting nowhere. Slowly.

A large open space gave him opportunity to pause. He felt he was close, like a character in a boardgame who doesn't know he is standing right next to the secret passage. Beneath the distant sky, which still held traces of light, church spires and a war memorial were outlined. Scatters of pigeons were raised out of the shadowed foreground to climb between the spires, where not even the merest thread of a tightrope could be seen. Ivy sprang from the cracks in the crumbling church walls. A small girl in an orange dress skipped up and down the steps of the memorial, laughing to herself. As Gargan moved closer a woman's anxious voice called to the child. She looked round, glanced at Gargan, cocked her head, laughed and ran away.

Owing to the submarine quality of the light, the sky above the low, slightly frayed silhouettes of houses was like cool purple fire. There were telegraph lines and telephone wires, but that was all they were; nothing more. There was no threat. No need – no urge – to climb the poles and walk them. He heard an echo of the little girl's laughter, strangely disembodied now she was out of sight. He turned in the direction of the sound and caught sight of a streetname.

Partizanska.

His heart raced. The sense of peace he had felt was eaten up by excitement. He still didn't know what he'd find when he got there. Rada's sister; maybe the brother-in-law. But would she be there herself? If she was how would she act? Excited? Surprised? Pleased? Indifferent?

He was still worrying when he pressed the buzzer on the wall by the iron gates.

The gate was opened by Rada's sister. She had the same features but her hair was darker. He introduced himself, finding he didn't need to; he was expected. Their linguistic knowledge converged only in the most banal mainstream: they were both well, he'd come a long way, he was tired, he was hungry. She took him inside and he met her husband, Dok, who soon produced a plate of hot meat in a heavily spiced sauce. They gave him coffee, offered to light a fire, showed him a bed where he could sleep. Since there was no sign of her, he waited until morning to ask about Rada.

Rada was not in Subotica. She had been planning to drop by if possible. Apparently it had not been possible.

She was in Berlin.

Dok was watching a news report on the television while Gargan and Rada's sister talked about Berlin. The station was either German or Austrian and Gargan heard the name of the city coming in both ears, from Rada's sister and from the television, and became confused.

She'd been going to Berlin all along, though Gargan hadn't known it. There simply hadn't been time to make the detour to Subotica. She had gone to Berlin to see Karl Neumann, whose name was mentioned in such a way that it was clearly assumed Gargan knew who he was. 'Who's Karl Neumann?' he asked, but the question was either misheard or ignored.

The reporter was saying that thousands of East Germans had escaped to the West via Prague and hundreds of thousands now had found the courage to march through East Germany's cities demanding change. It was unthinkable, the reporter said, but if anything was going to happen it would undoubtedly happen in Berlin.

He couldn't bring himself to swallow his breakfast. Rada's sister watched in concern as he pulled at the bread and worried himself about what to do: ask no more questions, put it all behind him and go home? Or find out exactly who this man was and where Rada was staying in Berlin and for how long?

He knew that cutting short his pursuit wouldn't work. There was no way he could forget her.

He was dimly aware of the sister shyly thrusting breadcrusts towards him.

He had to go to Berlin.

The sister, who no doubt before his withdrawal would have willingly told him who Neumann was and how to find Rada, now needed some persuasion to release any information at all. She retracted into herself, backing away, eyes widening. He regained his composure and did his best to explain he wasn't crazy or dangerous. He'd come a long way to see Rada and didn't want to miss her. It was *important* he see her, he pointed out, omitting to mention that he was in love with her (in case Neumann turned out to be what Gargan feared he would be and the sister's loyalty to Rada ran also to him), that he was desperately depending on seeing her, that his sanity and his possible *unification* were at stake.

All she would tell him was that Rada had known Neumann for years and that she had gone to Berlin in the hope of seeing him. It wasn't certain they would meet up; the reason being, as Gargan finally extracted from the unhappy sister, that Neumann was on the other side of the Wall.

Anticipation

Filtered through the roof of the station and falling sideways into the compartment, that particular light reminded me of another. *Found but already lost*. Was she bitter or resigned?

I was slightly surprised when I realised I was crying. Of the three other people in the compartment none had noticed my tears. I rose from my seat, muttered an apology to the fat woman in the seat by the door and stepped out into the corridor.

I pulled the window down and leaned out. People were still boarding the train. I checked my watch. Five minutes to go. I wiped my eyes and blew my nose. *Hearts beat lips brush*. Someone behind me wrestled an enormous suitcase into my compartment. *Over and over painting/time into memory*. She had ensured that I would never forget her. My throat tightened again. I began seriously to consider getting off and waiting for the next train to Pontoise.

I had predicted this. I had known I would regret what I was doing.

Somehow the fact of prediction made it bearable. It was like having to swallow foul-tasting medicine. I knew I had to do it. Whether it made me better or not, I had to try.

Why though? Why did I prescribe such harsh treatment? After all, it was *my* life. It would be so easy just to get off one train and on to another.

But my plans were interrupted by the announcer's nasal voice – 'Attention à la fermeture automatique des portes!' – and the blue Attention Départ light with its jangling bells. The train began to move.

It was right that I should be on this train. It was what I decided. I had to know what it would be like to be on my own again.

The suggestion of a pattern at work, leaving Paris like I left London, was at odds with the fact that circumstance had brought me to this departure. And *something* was drawing me to Berlin. It wasn't just the attraction of the youth culture and fringe theatres. With hindsight, maybe it was the pull of the future. There was *something*. And the nearer we got, the less sure I became that I would actually be alone when I got there.

The compartment, which was full, seated six. There was the fat woman by the door, whose clothes, if nothing else, looked vaguely German as opposed to French. Next to her was a middle-aged couple. They were well dressed in collars that were only slightly frayed. She was indignant at being squashed into such a confined space with these other people and their voluminous bags. He sought to apologize for her with his wan, humble eyes, which dilated gratefully when they happened to cross with yours.

Sitting across from the fat woman was a student. He was concentrating on a book whose title was in French, but since he was a student it would have been hasty to rule out the possibility that he was German. From his smart casual dress and almond spectacles he could have been either. Next to him was a gentleman with silver hair and tinted glasses. He was reading a Yugoslavian newspaper printed in the Cyrillic alphabet. I must have been looking too closely: every so often the gentleman's head turned two or three degrees to his left, because that was where I was sitting. I always liked to occupy the seat next to the window facing the direction of travel. It gave me access to the little table which on that day, as usual, I had no real use for.

Outside, the evening was turning trees and hedges into silhouettes. My face was dimly reflected in clumps of bushes. The darker bank running alongside the track shrouded my chin with the suggestion of a beard.

I caught my eyes searching for their own reflection. They seemed to lack confidence. My fellow passengers distracted me for a while. They helped me forget why I was there, when in actual fact the truth was that I didn't really know. I seemed to be engaged on a folly. A meaningless mission, the purpose of which was to discover or create its meaning.

I increasingly felt I was being hijacked.

The trees disappeared. Fields sloped away into a compressed sunset.

A discussion was going on in low tones between the two halves of the well dressed couple. She made short sharp remarks while looking straight across the compartment. He turned towards her, murmuring plaintively. The knot of his tie prevented him turning further. The man with the silver hair had folded his newspaper into a rectangle no larger than six inches by four, and was still reading. The student had fallen asleep over his book. Opposite him the fat woman's head was turned away from the compartment towards the window to the corridor. Her black reflected eyes were staring at mine. I looked away. We were passing through a small village. Its streetlamps made it darker than the surrounding countryside. I could see the married couple in the window. He was nodding off while she remained resolutely awake. Were they two halves making a single unit or were they two separate individuals?

I was beginning to feel sick. Just a small knot in my stomach, but growing tighter. I was nervous about Berlin. It was a new place. I didn't quite know what I would find there, nor what I would end up doing. There was a temptation to panic: I didn't know why I'd come this far, nor why I was going further.

But I always get nervous when I'm going somewhere new. I'm OK when I get there. It's just the anticipation that makes me sick.

Sharing a Head

Toothache was toothache, he supposed. But this was something special. It had something about it of the chisel-like prodding of a dentist's probe. Pain like nothing he had experienced before. Not even the incisions hurt quite like this. After all, he bore them in his sleep.

He couldn't remember when the pain had started, nor did he know what might have caused it. Though the problems of getting from Subotica to Austria and eventually on a Berlin-bound train had certainly not helped.

The man sitting diagonally opposite in the corner made him nervous. Not because he kept giving him furtive glances. Quite the opposite: the man was staring straight ahead. Unblinking. Like a dummy. Occasionally, with an awkward flourish, he crossed one leg over the other. The trousers hung uneasily from the knee. There seemed to be little inside them except bone or machinery.

While Gargan, lulled by the motion of the train, began nodding with tiredness, the man continued to stare across the compartment, sitting erect in his seat. Did his head swivel round in a complete circle at one point or was Gargan dreaming? There was something vaguely threatening about the man's virtual inactivity. His face looked like a mask that had been tacked to his head.

There was an offensive, chemical smell in the compartment. Was it the train or the man?

Gargan's eyes snapped open when he heard the word 'smrt', but the man showed no sign of having uttered the word himself. He looked to the window. It was raining. The evening was turning trees and hedges into silhouettes. His face was dimly reflected in clumps of bushes. The darker bank running alongside the track hid the reflection of his beard.

It got steadily darker until before long he was staring into blackness. After some time two pinpricks of white light appeared. Slowly they grew larger like headlamps approaching through the rain. Only when they were right in front of his face was the perspective revealed. He could see the less reflective features of the young man's face. His lips suddenly parted, but not in a smile. The rain trickled in rivulets over an anguished face, the eyes shining with fear.

The Aborigine turned and ran away. He looked back for a moment to make sure Gargan was following. The slope underfoot was slippery due to the rain, and steep. The Aborigine ascended swiftly. Gargan clawed mud to keep up. The rain kept falling. The young man glanced back. Somewhere above, a bird was screaming, regular as a cicada.

He used the Aborigine's footprints to defeat the gradient and to make sure he was going in the right direction, for he had lost sight of him. The hill seemed as if it would never end. The darkness didn't even allow him to see the false summits receding up the hillside as he climbed higher. Suddenly the footprints disappeared. He didn't know which way to turn. All directions offered the same nothingness. Indeed, he realized, he was at the top, or at least a plateau.

He was running on the flat, his way lit by moonlight. Off to his left he saw a small waterhole. Beneath the tree he saw the Aborigine kneeling down. The Aborigine straightened his back and swivelled round. When he saw Gargan he beckoned him to come over.

The Aborigine pointed to the body of a heavily pregnant woman lying by the side of the pool. She was lying on her back, apparently lifeless. The only movement was in her stomach where something struggled. The Aborigine leaned forward and lifted one of the woman's eyelids. He placed his ear above her mouth. Sitting back on his haunches he looked at Gargan, who knelt over and felt for a pulse in the woman's wrist. There was none.

The thing in her belly thrashed about for its life. Gargan looked at the Aborigine and placed his hand on top of the bulge. It immediately convulsed and became more violent in its efforts to escape. Gargan looked up again but the Aborigine had disappeared. He looked around but the darkness had hidden his retreat. The creature squirmed beneath his hands, which he abruptly withdrew.

Suddenly the responsibility was his alone. He was frightened.

But the thing was moving again, more urgently. He couldn't run away. He watched, mesmerised, as the convulsions jerked the woman's body off the ground. Before he knew what he was doing he was down on his knees lifting up the woman's skirt. He saw his hands part her legs and push them further apart.

The baby's head appeared. Since the dead mother couldn't push, Gargan moved round and pressed down on her stomach. Out of the corner of his eye he saw the new body slowly protruding. Finally the stomach imploded. Gargan collapsed on top of the woman. Only an inch from her face he could see the dirt in her pores. He shuddered. Disengaging, he remembered the newborn and reached in his back pocket for his wallet.

As he reached to sever the umbilical cord with his razor blade and determine the sex, he noticed the baby's deformity. He wasn't one baby but two: Siamese twins joined at the neck and sharing a head.

The twins were alive. There was no question of that. Their puling became a ragged scream as Gargan began to slice up between the two perfectly formed bodies into the inverted Y-shaped neck. Gargan himself screamed as he cut deeper. The blade's progress was quick and easy. Was the thing also invertebrate? he wondered as he sliced deeper still. Blood went everywhere. On the floor, the washbasin, the mirror; up the front of his shirt. He continued to cut, oblivious. Another half inch, though, and the pain became quite startling. He came quickly to his senses and threw the razor blade in the sink.

He washed himself down as best he could and left the little cubicle, wincing at every step.

Turning into the compartment he tripped over the student's outstretched feet, waking him up. 'Excuse me,' he said as he negotiated the others' tangled limbs. The silver-haired man had fallen asleep with his head lolling in an uncharacteristically undignified manner against the back of Gargan's seat.

He squeezed through and sat in the corner. He tried to forget what had just happened. Would he find what he wanted in Berlin? The aching tooth, however, wouldn't allow him any depth of contemplation.

I'm finding it hard to keep awake.

At the French/West German border there was the distraction of formalities. The corridors were patrolled by guards made officious by uniforms. Short, clipped orders – 'Pass, Fahrkarte' – relayed in perfect English once they knew you weren't German.

The train flew on deeper into the night and arrived at the border with East Germany, where a fresh selection of abrupt guards was produced.

Having crossed this border the train now has to travel 170 kilometres through East Germany before reaching the island of Western territory which is West Berlin. I have been issued with a DDR transit visa for that distance even though the train does not stop until it reaches West Berlin.

On my knee there is a notepad. I'm puzzling over a word I've written in it – *rai.*

But I can't concentrate because of the motion of the train and the strange unidentifiable smell that permeates it, and the shadows rushing past the window are making me drowsy. Again I feel I'm being taken somewhere I don't want to go or ought not to go.

Three boys, their faces black in the night (no light from the train, most blinds drawn), sit on a railing and watch me as I am led past by a man in a dark suit. The railing is replaced by a wall. We walk along beside it until the man stops by a small window. I feel my head turning against my will to look into the blood-drenched room and suddenly I'm inside looking out. The Yugoslav's silver-haired head is resting on my shoulder. His paper has unfolded in his lap. The words make sense to me: . . . *will possibly necessitate the closure of one quarter of Serbian enterprises* . . . A spot of rain hits the window. The boys are climbing on the railing. More rain. The boys' faces are streaked with red as the rain trickles down the window. One boy's mouth opens like a choirboy's and bellows: 'Smrt.'

I realise I know what the word means. It's Serbo-Croat for death. I twist round to look for the boys but instantly the train thunders into a pitch-black tunnel.

My ears pop and something warm dribbles on to my jaw. I'm pressed back in my seat. There is a terrible grinding. My eyeballs are bulging and even my teeth vibrate in my skull. Everything within my vision turns red. My wife's face appears before my eyes, swimming in blood, her eyes expressing everything I fear most. This is a nightmare, I know, but beyond my control. I am a prisoner in the train, the train within the tunnel. The drilling shakes loose the fillings in my teeth and my mouth fills with grit and blood. I try to recall Rada's face as a distraction. It hovers in front of me insubstantially. Grey eyes flecked with yellow. Gradually I see through them to the old man's face in the opposite seat: old watery grey eyes, yellow-haloed with age. They are wide with terror, which surely I do not inspire, yet they are looking at me. Turning to my right I see the Yugoslav. His face is creased like a mask. A man with only shadows beneath the peak of his cap looks in as he passes down the corridor. The window on my left shakes viciously in its frame. Cracks ripple across its surface and as the train takes a sudden nose dive the glass shatters and melts instantly like red ice spilling on to the floor. The jagged tunnel wall is only an inch from the gaping window, as if the diesel really is drilling into the rock.

The way out is clear. If I just stick my head out of the window I'll suffer no more pain. As I stand up everyone turns to look at me. I even see my own reflection in the mirror above the frayed-collared man's seat. I appear quite calm, if a little red. They don't know what I'm planning to do as I turn to the window and stick my head out. The rushing rock catches my scalp and rips it back like you'd open a can of beer. Before the pain hits me I feel exhilaration.

A dreadful vibration judders through me, shaking my bones. Turning back to the mirror I see that the tunnel wall has filed off the top of my skull leaving my brain virtually intact. I step closer to the mirror, leaning over the old man. I can feel hands persuading me to return to my seat but I'm held by the mirror. The vascular membranes peel back like cellophane wrappers. I gaze at the twin cradles of my personality and I'm unable to prevent my fingers delving in between them in an attempt at separation. Are they two halves making a single unit or are they two separate individuals?

I'm beginning to feel sick. Just a small knot in my stomach, but growing tighter. I'm nervous about Berlin. It's a new place. I don't know quite what I'll find there, nor what I'll end up doing. There is a temptation to panic: I don't know why I've come this far, nor why I'm going further.

But I always get nervous going somewhere new. I'm OK when I get there. It's just the anticipation that makes me sick.

Slowly a signboard slides into view outside the window.

Zoologischer Garten Bahnhof.

The Wall

Where East Meets West

He was relieved when the train pulled into the cavernous Zoo station. The pain from his tooth had not relented but the small, high-ceilinged compartment had oppressed him. Towards the end of the journey he no longer knew who was sitting there with him. The strange smell had got stronger if anything, and he knew what it reminded him of now – formaldehyde. Although eager to get out of the cold echoing station I find myself climbing into compartments on other trains. The reek contaminates them all.

Remembered from within the depths of Zoologischer Garten Bahnhof, the Gare du Nord takes on an air of heady nostalgia. One wishes one was there rather than here. There can't be many places that make you feel like that about the Gare du Nord.

He left the station and crossed to a bar. His throat felt like the bush landscape of his dreams. Coffee helped a little but not much. I pay and walk out. Some initial parallels with Paris dismay me. But the lines of the city are straighter, the shapes more angular. The apartment buildings are often higher, more massive, more foreboding. The people are more solid, more stolid.

Quite apart from these impressions I feel something: a presence. I feel, like I felt in Paris, as if I am being followed.

I don't know what to do first. Whether to look for a cheap hotel or seek out the small theatres, or just wander. Aimlessly I drift up the Kurfürstendamm. It's big and impersonal but that might be just because I've never been here before. It's early. There are not many people about. Yet I feel closely pursued, and, thinking I can shake off whoever is following me, I turn down the first street on the right, Bleibtreustrasse. I hurry under the railway bridges and turn right again into a tiny square. A man passes beyond the shadow of a tree on the other side of the square. He frightened a host of pigeons. They clattered up into the air around him like mechanical things. So close to his ears, their beating amplified the pain in his head. He didn't know whether he ought to find a dentist before looking for Neumann's address.

Tall apartment blocks hemmed him into a narrow alleyway. A telephone line was drawn tightly from one side to the other. For a moment he felt dizzy. A sudden stab of pain in his groin made him flinch and falter.

He soon came across a post office but they had no telephone directories for the Eastern sector. The West refused to recognize East Berlin as the official capital of East Germany. The four powers responsible for West Berlin liked to pretend it didn't exist, as if this reduced its status, whereas it was the Western sector that appeared the anachronism: an exclave in the middle of the Eastern Bloc: a few square miles preserved in political settlement. Like a city, or half a city, in aspic. The smell of formaldehyde made sense.

Without making a conscious decision I find myself drifting towards the U-bahn. On the platform an official stands in a glass booth. He or she waits until the train is full then issues an instruction through loudspeakers – 'Zurückbleiben!' – telling those passengers remaining to stand back. At different stations it is pronounced differently: now it is softly slurred and sounds both alluring and comforting, now staccato and clipped into four distinct syllables.

I look out for my pursuer on platforms and in my carriage, and see you suddenly sitting right next to me. But you're only my reflection in the tunnel-darkened window. Still, if you're who I think you might be, there should be a way to find you down here. Two lines of the U-bahn cross under the Wall and run under East Berlin before returning to the West. Passengers are not allowed to disembark; indeed, the trains do not stop (except at the Friedrichstrasse crossing point) but only slow down as they pass through the former stations before coming back under the Wall. I press my face to the glass and shade my eyes from the light in the train. The disused stations are dimly lit and dusty. Standing by a dull metal pillar is an East German policeman in a green uniform. The door to his little sentry box stands open a few yards away disclosing an off-white bulb. As the train leaves the station you see that the tunnel has been artificially narrowed to hamper aspiring 'escapees' clinging to the side of the carriage. West Berliners on the train ignore the spectacle of the deceased railway stations as if they were no more significant than the disused platforms on the Paris Métro or the London Underground.

Surfacing again I am near the Wall. Right in the centre of a major city – if you take Berlin as one city split into two rather than two separate cities – land has become wasteland. Roads dissolve into mud. Street signs are history. Buildings have been knocked down because their proximity to the Wall threatened someone's illusion of security. A long green tube snakes down the side of a tall isolated building from a hole in the wall: it is a refuse chute for the disembowelment of the building. Acres of land have been reclaimed here, a sign announces, for the Kongresshalle, a new motorway and the state library.

The library was extensive. He walked across the foyer past people reading yesterday's British newspapers whose headlines spoke of hundreds of thousands of demonstrators marching through East Berlin, Leipzig and Halle. He climbed a flight of stairs to a mezzanine floor dotted with globes, a number of which were illuminated and for some reason reassuring. Had he possessed one as a child? He couldn't remember. His favourite was the political map: its pinks and oranges were such a ludicrously cheerful way of showing the range of inefficient, oppressive, self-serving systems created and upheld by power. North Africa looked like a pie chart, divided up with such geometrical precision. Spinning the globe he pored over Europe and found Berlin: a small segment of orange in the East German yellow. Similar anomalies were revealed as he walked round the little world. The small pink circles of Lesotho and Swaziland enclosed within an orange South Africa. A tiny red Hong Kong clinging to enormous ochre China.

He looked for equivalents of Berlin the city. He found Beirut,

Belfast and Nicosia. But Berlin was different. It had been a single whole city before the war. Then it was split and fifteen years later a wall went up, making concrete the already established line of division. It clearly *had been* a case of division, a city bisected. But was it still the case now? Surely not. Split anything up into two parts and if they are both to survive they have to become whole units. But each was still in some way tied to the other. Doubles of each other. The act of bisection became an act of duplication.

The telephone directory, when he finally located it, provided a disappointment. Neumann was a popular name: even its Karls filled a good few column inches. Gargan had nothing to go on; no lead except the name and the city. Depression began to steal over him.

Only walking could distract his thoughts: his mind would produce a constant stream of nonsense. Thoughts as banal as the streets he turned into and out of. As inconsequential as the pedestrian crossings and traffic lights. Less significant than the bridges which carried concurrent streams of trivia over his head. The stench of formaldehyde thickening the air outside a florist and a butcher's shop. Distracted he wandered into an ironmonger's. A man looked up from behind the counter. Gargan looked about quickly, picked up a pair of pliers, dug four marks out of his pocket, and left.

People passed him with blurred moustaches and heavy glasses. He crossed a wide empty street while a little red man and a small group of pedestrians regarded each other patiently from opposite pavements. The bark of a motorcycle horn and an authoritative shout chased him into a side street. Mud-brown buildings with dusty grey windows and no doors shouldered him towards the middle of the road. His toothache throbbed. He heard footsteps. Was the policeman following him? He realized it was only an echo of his own footfalls created by the buildings on either side and the wall at the end of the street.

The Wall.

This was it at last: more than twice his height, graffiti-strewn and hardly believable. From a watchtower on the other side armed guards watched him as he approached the Wall. The graffiti were multi-layered and garish. The people of California, in the name of a young woman from Oakland, demanded religious freedom for East Germans. Three signatories from Düsseldorf warned that the Wall would soon come crashing down.

Gargan turned right into a well-worn dirt track which ran alongside the Wall. Self-portraits jostled with artists' impressions of remembered acquaintances 'imprisoned' beyond the Wall. Brian from North London pledged to wait for Danuta Heinkel of Dunckerstrasse 26 until the Wall came down and she was free to come to London. If he cared so much why didn't he join her in East Berlin? What would he have to give up? What would he really lose? Jim from Melbourne promised Inez of Plauenerstrasse he'd be back. With a bulldozer.

Why couldn't Rada have scrawled Neumann's address on the Wall? And why did his tooth hurt so much?

He looked up to the top of the Wall and was blinded by an arrow of sunlight glinting off the glass booth of a watchtower. The light pierced his lens and sank like a laser into the pupil. Fresh splinters of pain cut into his gums. Holding his head he slumped against the Wall. It felt as if someone was pressing his head against it. He managed to open his eyes to try to see who it was. A figure was walking away from him. His back and his head were nondescript. Gargan's head was heavy. He found it difficult to pull away from the Wall. Was that an impression of his face left in the concrete like a fossil? Or was the Wall a mirror? He looked closer, screwing up his eyes. Not a mirror; a window. A face on the other side returned his gaze. It was a face he'd seen a long, long time ago in a photograph. A picture of himself bereft of his beard and glasses. He rubbed at the face with the ball of his hand, trying to erase it. The wall darkened, smeared with his blood. The skin on his hand was torn to shreds. But there was no pain. Looking closer he peered into the wounds. Was there something moving in his blood? Something creeping over the exposed flesh? He took a strip of skin between finger and thumb and tore it back like a length of cloth. It didn't hurt.

Suddenly I'm being woken up. There's a man towering above me shaking my shoulder. I'm lying on a bench and my cheek's sore where it's been resting on the stone. I have to squint to see the man properly. He's still just a silhouette because of the direct sunlight behind him, but I can see that his suit is bristling with belts, buckles, buttons and straps. You were asleep, he tells me. Sitting up I can see better. His uniform is green and emblazoned with POLIZEI badges. Remembering where I am I become nervous. But he just tells me not to fall asleep again and walks off back towards the Wall, where he must have been patrolling when he caught sight of me.

I remember sitting down because I was tired, but I don't know how long I was asleep. I didn't sleep very well last night in a dirty little hotel I'd found in Schöneberg, waking up with toothache and cramp in my groin. I was also depressed because I was missing Jenni. I'd come across the poem from the drawer with the curtains. On the reverse were the lines I hadn't read when I'd found it.

> Passion weighed on scales of gold
> so light so fine
> Register the phenomenal weight
> of indefinable emotion
> cast of feather's breadth to move
> the world
> Find the scale of hours
> without the mean of time
> no sense but touch leaves
> memory incandescent
> for all time.

An hour and a half later, looking for a complete change, I was at Checkpoint Charlie. I waited three quarters of an hour in an overpoweringly warm room and was eventually issued with a one-day visa. I changed the obligatory twenty-five marks into twenty-five Ostmarks. The customs official reminded me to be back before midnight and then I found myself walking up Friedrichstrasse.

East Berlin is pretty much as I'd imagined it: like West Berlin only less colourful, with smaller cars and fewer of them, hardly any advertising and not too many shops. It didn't take too much imagination.

I wandered around for a while then found this tiny scrap of park squeezed in between a severed railway bridge and a road which skirts the Wall.

My mouth feels dry. The toothache has receded to a background hum and I'm feeling hungry. Walking down Unter den Linden I experience a little pain in my groin which I put down to falling asleep in an awkward position.

As I cross over the River Spree, Marx-Engels-Platz unfolds its elegant open spaces littered with wrought-iron streetlamps. Small knots of men and women pass by deep in conversation. Individuals rush across my path to meet others and walk off in twos, heads bent over illicit magazines. Across Alexanderplatz I come into an area dominated by wide eight-lane roads with tram lines running up the middle and huge apartment blocks planted firmly either side. It seems devoid of life. Drivers sit motionless as dummies in Trabants which hurtle past like dodgem cars. The further out you go the fewer people there are walking the streets. Apartment windows reveal no trace of activity or light. As you approach the Volkspark Friedrichshain a squall of drizzle falls from a cloudless sky. You climb the spiral path to the top and scan the skyline, which doesn't reveal the trace of the West you were looking for – the Mercedes Benz star on top of the Europa Center.

I walk further out in a north-easterly direction up Leninallee where the wind blows harder and colder. Trams heave up the incline; cars throttle by. I turn off, hoping for shelter. The streets are narrow, shadowed by massive apartment buildings. Now and then an old man's voice shouts to children to stop climbing on the window ledge. Another man works under the bonnet of his car. The air is crisp and silent, tense. You slip into a courtyard. There's a dark puddle in the centre unsettled by broken glass. A car is parked in a corner, dumped. The walls are crumbling. The house looks uninhabited but you know it's not. My face peers down at you from a darkened dirty window.

Drifting back south towards the Wall in the vague hope of either seeing some action or getting something to eat, I come across the Ostbahnhof behind a screen of construction work. I kick through rubble to a dark hooded entrance. A sign in the corridor points to a restaurant. Tentatively I push open the swing door with just a finger. A thin black-haired woman dressed in black with a white apron, eyebrows etched in dark archways, sunken shining eyes, comes forward towards me as if on castors and a string. It's too late to back out. Ja, bitte? Table for one, I say, fearing it is an absurd thing to say. She gestures at the many empty tables all covered with starched white cloths. A handful of customers are about to look up and stare at me. Help yourself, the waitress suggests. I sit down. Waiters glide about in black ties, out of place in the ageing, threadbare room. I am sure the menu is lying about its prices. They are too low. I won't have enough money and they will call the police. She comes for my order. I ask for Chicken Fricassee in as confident a voice as seems possible. And a glass of red wine. A family at a table on my right talk genially in Slavic tones. Conversation hovers in clouds around the room. *voice-filled rooms/with faces, mindless/words filling spaces*. A young woman at a table on my left is approached by an awkward individual. She shrugs and he sits down at her table. Will she ever say to him: How lucky we were to find each other even for a moment? I wondered if *anyone* had ever said to him: When I woke up this morning I couldn't believe you weren't there.

My food arrives. The woman on my left smiles at the inquisitiveness of the newcomer. I linger with my wine. From inside my jacket I take out my wallet and count the West German marks which I will need when I cross back over the Wall. The man at the table behind mutters to his wife in German: *Amerikaner!* He proceeds to mumble inaudibly. *senseless sounds falling/on ears deafened by silent years*. The family are talking still. *spent learning movements/signifying implied understanding*. Now the woman is addressing the man at the table on my left. *assumed agreement/meaning nothing*.

I plan something to say to the waitress as she floats down to my table. I drain my wine glass and she smiles kindly at me, almost inviting me to speak: I am not from around here. I say how I try to speak German but fear I am always making mistakes. She confides that her German is far from perfect since she comes from Bulgaria and is staying with her mother in Berlin. I smile and say Auf Wiedersehen.

I go in the toilets and confront two women. Assuming I have made a mistake I turn to go but am beckoned from within. There's one free, one of the women says. I no longer really want to go but feel compelled to, so I lock myself in, take a minute to relieve myself and realize I am terrified to flush and face the two women again. For moments I am paralysed but my hand betrays my paranoia and flushes, drawing a scream from the plumbing. I perform automatically, unlocking the door and proceeding to the washbasins, where a third woman, thin and androgynous, is washing her hands. I wash mine, my mind grappling with the problem of how much to tip the women. I'm shaking my hands dry, wishing there was a hand-dryer, and there upon the wall where the hand-dryer would be is a notice in German and Russian which includes the figure of thirty pfennig. I turn to face one of the women who is proffering a paper towel with Mitropa printed on it in red. I mutter my thanks, drying my hands, throw the towel in the bin and place three coins in her hand.

The daylight has failed considerably and I feel completely disorientated. Close by the Wall at Spittelmarkt I enter and climb to the top of a tall apartment block to get a panoramic view of the West. From the top, giddy from the speed of my ascent up twenty-two flights, I see clearly the two separate Walls enclosing the strip of East German territory whose barbed wire threatens to swarm over the concrete watchtowers like poison ivy. Beyond the Wall lies a desultory neighbourhood of West Berlin. Trapped between a main road and the Wall are a few rundown businesses, some old housing and a clutch of cheap hotels. On the top floor of the nearest hotel somebody tears the curtains apart and looks out. His mouth is wide open, either yawning or in pain. I look away before he sees me.

There is one block of apartments almost as tall as the one I've climbed. Halfway down I see a head turn at a window with a swish of fair hair which makes me think of Jenni. I suddenly wish I was with her on the other side of the Wall. But how then would I explore the Eastern city? If only I could be here and there at the same time. Would that be the answer?

It was an unpleasant hotel but marginally cleaner than the one in Schöneberg, even with the previous guest's dirty plate and cutlery sitting on the table. He'd found it by chance after straying from the Wall.

Shortly before dawn he sat up abruptly in bed. The wind sucked the edge of the off-white lace curtain through the open window. He got out of bed and walked across to the chair which stood beneath the window. He fished into the bulkiest pocket of his jacket and withdrew the pliers. The only mirror was on the inside of the wardrobe door, which swung open rustily. He pulled it towards him an inch or two to catch the dim light from the window, then opened his mouth to expose his teeth. He put the jaws of the pliers into his mouth. They were heavy and he accidentally chipped a front tooth. He clamped the handles together tightly. The grip ground and slipped on the tooth, causing his whole skull to vibrate. He began to pull downwards but without any obvious result, so switched to a position of leverage and the tooth squeaked in response. Opening even wider he swung his arm down in an arc and the jaws crunched together smashing the tooth. He looked in the mirror. There was enough of the tooth left to get the pliers around. He got a hold on the remaining enamel surface and tugged. The base of the tooth splintered and bled. The nerve now exposed, he pinched it hard and twisted. His body shuddered involuntarily as it slipped out with all the ease of barbed wire.

The job wasn't complete. The tooth having been fragmented, much of the root was still embedded in the gum. The pliers were no use. He dropped them and went towards his jacket to look for the wallet which held the razor blade. But his eyes alighted on the plate on the table.

The fork looked useful.

He returned to the mirror, tilted his head back and dug the fork up into the gum. Slivers of pain shot through his brain like bolts of lightning. Part of the root, loosened, fell from the wound. Another stab of pain almost halted the proceedings.

Instead of entrenching the remaining fragments by pushing them up beyond reach, he pulled his lip up higher and attacked from the front. The long thin tines sank a quarter of an inch into the gum before the pain became too great and jolted him from his trance.

He saw himself in the mirror, the fork sticking into his mouth, and shrieked in shock and agony. His hands scraped through his hair, nails raking his scalp. The fork was elbowed to the floor. When his eyes opened again he looked with horror at the gash in his mouth, the blood everywhere.

He ran across the room, swept the curtain aside and thrust his head out of the window. His mouth open wide screaming silently, spilling blood on to the hotel wall and the pavement, he stared blindly over the Wall through tears of pain.

He walked beside the Wall, his head drumming like an egg being boiled. The pain had not eased since morning. Instead it changed: one minute it spiralled like a drill, the next thumped like a rubber mallet. The watchtowers slid into view regularly behind the Wall, like knots on rope; barbs on wire. Slicing through him, cutting him in two. Duplicating him.

The foray into East Berlin had been unsuccessful. He'd gone to a couple of addresses inhabited by Karl Neumanns and came across no traces of Rada. As he'd roamed he'd tried to come to terms with the failure of his mission. He hadn't much liked East Berlin. The city itself was fine but he had been convinced at certain points that he was being followed. He couldn't believe he was falling for the Cold War nonsense. In any case, why would anybody follow him?

He felt as if he were walking the wire before he actually got up on the Wall; and he was up on the Wall before he knew it.

Thirteen feet high, he didn't quite know how he'd got there, but he had. He glanced back and saw a small crowd of people urging him on. Had they helped him up? They looked like ordinary Berliners: a middle-aged couple, a fat woman, a student, an elderly man with grey hair, a thin man in a dark suit, a young man with glasses and a beard. They were joined by others who streamed towards the Wall from side streets.

He walked at some speed. Easier than any wire, the top of the Wall was rounded, like a rope or wire but at least twelve inches in diameter. It had been walked many times before in different versions of the same protest.

The crowd on his right had begun to follow him and call out messages of support. He was also drawing attention from the approaching watchtower on his left and each half of himself stiffened in acknowledgement. When had he cut himself so deeply? He suddenly resented the admiration on his right and turned his eyes towards the glass booth on the watchtower. The windows had been slid open so that the muzzles of a couple of automatic rifles could be pointed unambiguously in his direction. I'm one of you, part of him wanted to tell them. You don't need to do that. I'm not threatening you.

Gargan wondered which side of his wire Rada was on and did it make any difference? He no longer knew exactly what he felt for her. He'd been in love with her a week ago, two days ago, an hour ago, so he supposed he still was now. But her trump card in his reunification had never even been played. Maybe he didn't need her any more. But if not her what did he need? Something, certainly.

Beyond the watchtower the people of the Eastern sector had seen him. They flooded out of nearby apartment blocks and factories and ran to the Wall, ignoring the orders of police and border guards and chanting, 'The Wall must go. The Wall must go.' As those on his right took up the same chant, the cries of East and West rose as one voice above the Wall itself.

But, as he narrowed the gap between himself and the watchtower, the rifles did the same.

There was no point now staying in Berlin any longer.

Angry voices shouted something through a megaphone which he couldn't understand.

He supposed he might as well return to London. At least he had the place in Vauxhall Grove; he wouldn't have to sleep on any more trains. Provided nobody had squatted the house in his absence.

One of the guns must have gone off because suddenly he was falling. Had he jumped? He didn't know. He hadn't been shot but he was falling. Which side? He didn't even know on which side.

He didn't need to know.

Initiation Ceremony

It was true in a sense, I didn't need to know. I was on both sides. I was here and there. That's what it felt like being in Berlin.

Going there altered my self-perception. It no longer made sense to refer to myself exclusively in the first person. With hindsight, I became aware of you as soon as I stepped down on to the platform at Zoologischer Garten, as surely as if you had come to meet me off the train. But it was I who had come to meet you.

You seemed to offer a solution to the problem which drove me out of Paris. My happiness with Jenni was not enough. I wanted at the same time not to be in love with her. So it seemed like a good idea that you should love a woman in the East while I remained unattached in the West. Thus I would experience two worlds simultaneously: one with love, one without. We would be here and there at the same time and so would never be dissatisfied, would never seek to find something better, or different, than that which we already had.

I am you and you are I. Either you never existed before I went to Berlin or you were always there, waiting for me to come and identify you, as myself. I was warned a few times in Paris, but I never quite understood what was happening until I got to the city where East is split from West by a thirteen-foot-high concrete wall. It was like a mirror in which I saw myself reflected and you were my reflection. The image changes like the state of mind and the ideology: it is distorted on one side to the viewer on the other. You are no more my reflection than I am yours.

In theory you should never leave Berlin but always await my return there. So why do I have this impression, as my train makes its way across The Netherlands towards the Channel ports, that you are still here with me in this otherwise empty compartment?

As soon as he reached London he went straight to Vauxhall Grove, which required little more than a crossing of the river. He used Vauxhall Bridge but kept glancing to his left trying to see over Lambeth and Westminster Bridges to get a look at Hungerford.

Returning home affected him with nervous excitement. As he turned the corner and saw the streetname he felt his face redden with anticipation. The same streetlamp marched across in front of the same dingy second floor windows as he narrowed the angle of parallax. The orange Reliant Regal Supervan III was still parked outside number sixteen The tax disc and dust indicated the car had not been driven for months. He suddenly panicked: the keys to the house were in Yugoslavia or Austria. Or at the bottom of the Rhine.

They were in the right-hand pocket of his jacket.

The only trouble was they didn't fit the locks.

The locks had been changed. Who'd done this? Squatters? He hammered on the door. He grasped the letter box and shook the door in its frame. He bent down and looked in through the letter box. The hallway looked bare and dusty, just as he'd left it. There was just one thing wrong: a rickety wooden chair from the back room slewed on its side at the foot of the stairs.

Straightening up he saw a small envelope pinned to the wooden door-surround near the bell. Dirty and rain-streaked, it had obviously been there some time, a week or two, but it bore his name. He snatched at it but the drawing pin held. He dug his nails under the head of the pin and tugged. Rust scratched the raw skin beneath his nails. 'Shit!' he shouted as one of his nails broke. He sucked his finger and tried to calm his nerves. The envelope came away easily when he gripped both ends and levered the pin out. He read the letter inside.

> Hope you enjoyed the rest of your trip. I changed the locks on your door and I've got the keys. If you can

remember where I live you're welcome to come and get them. – Su.

He changed at Oxford Circus from the Victoria Line to the Bakerloo. He liked the Bakerloo. It reminded him of the Northern Line but without the delays. Some of the rolling stock was ex-Northern Line: a short stretch of black line punctuated by Tufnell Park, Archway and Highgate appeared where the Bakerloo map had been torn away. Since it was 5 p.m this train would take him all the way to Kensal Green; outside peak times they went no further than Queen's Park. He knew that because she'd told him.

It was no good: the distractions of the Bakerloo Line failed to dissipate his anger.

The uniform terraces trailed past him, the street seeming almost to rise in front of him and fall in his wake. His mouth was hurting again.

He rang the bell and waited. Hearing movement above, he stepped back and looked up, but she was already disappearing back inside. He jabbed his thumb on the bell once more. He heard her coming down the stairs and a shape appeared in the pebbly glass in the door. He reached boiling point as she opened the door. Which of his rehearsed lines was most fitting?

'Come up,' she said, too lightly.

She trotted up the stairs while he pushed the door behind him to close it. But it caught on the doormat and he had to go back to close it properly.

He got to the top of the stairs, a little out of breath from breathing too deeply in anger. The door to the flat was open. He closed it quietly and precisely and walked up the hallway. He looked in the first two rooms, forgetting they were the bathroom and one of the bedrooms. She was in the kitchen pouring water from the kettle into two large mugs. 'Tea?' she said, still pouring, without looking up. She passed him in the doorway and crossed to the living room.

He couldn't believe her offhand assuredness; it was staggering. This woman had chased him round Europe, lost his trail, come home and locked him out of his own house. Now here she was making him tea as if they were old acquaintances. As she sat down she said, 'How are your teeth?'

'What?'

'Your teeth. Are they all right? Have they been bothering you?'

'Why do . . .' he choked, high-pitched. He cleared his throat. 'Why do you ask?'

'It's the only thing you still haven't done.'

'What are you talking about?'

'The ceremonial rites practised by Aborigines in the course of a boy's initiation. You've mutilated yourself. You've performed subincision. And some. The only thing you've missed out – apart from being painted and thrown up and down, which is generally considered optional – the only thing you've missed is ritual dental mutilation. The removal of a tooth.'

Gargan's tongue flicked into the hole in his gum. He twinged.

'You know your stuff, don't you?' he said ruefully, beginning to feel a little uncomfortable as she stared at him levelly. He curled his lip and exposed the swollen gum wound. She nodded to herself.

'Well, aren't you going to tell me why?' he inquired sarcastically.

'Certainly,' she answered jauntily after a moment's pause. 'You're insane.' She was antagonizing him. 'That's melodramatic,' she moderated. 'You're suffering from a delusion. A very convenient, if at times discomforting delusion. Australian Aboriginal belief also provides the individual with a spirit-double, known as rai. The rai is associated with the placenta. But whereas the placenta is buried at birth, the rai is not. It grows at the same rate as the child and eventually enters adulthood.'

Su's voice steadily amplified and squashed him further down into his chair. Her chair seemed to have moved closer and now loomed over him. He tried to see round it. The windows had retreated and were getting smaller and darker as he watched.

'The rai – '

Rai. That word! He rubbed his eyes and ground his knuckles into his temples.

' – can travel independently of the individual or stay in the native land if the individual goes abroad. How convenient it must have seemed,' she continued, booming, 'to offload your paternity on to your double, thereby convincing yourself it was not your child I was pregnant with.'

She was enormous now, all around him, her voice impregnating his pores. The baby: where was it? Born? Miscarried? Aborted?

'If only,' she was saying as she swept past him leaving the room, 'that's all it was. If only it was all just in order to evade your parental responsibilities.'

Alone in the room he felt himself shrink back into the corner. The windows snapped back into perspective. What did she mean? *If only* that's all it was.

He leaned round the back of the chair and tried to see into the room where she'd gone. The door was only half open. She passed within his field of vision twice and vanished into the part of the room he couldn't see. He heard her murmuring to herself. Then there was a jangling, a piece of jewellery or something, and she appeared in the doorway, the jangling louder. She'd put on a long set of beads and a chain necklace. In front of his face she dangled her keys to his house, which struck each other and chimed.

'Come on,' she said. 'Let's go.'

He allowed her to drag him out of the chair and to the door. In her free hand she picked up a school exercise book from the bookshelf in the hallway. There was a Mini 1000 parked across the street. She produced keys and bundled him into the back. The engine wheezed into life and then shrieked in protest when she slammed into first and lurched into the middle of the road.

She took corners without decelerating. He was tossed from one side to the other with no cushioning to protect either himself or the car. Her face in the rearview mirror was a mask of concentration, but not, it seemed, on the driving. She cut up two cyclists riding side by side. One of them fell off and the other gave her the finger, glaring viciously at Gargan.

'I did some research,' she said. 'About your tightrope walking. I went to the library. Looked through old newspapers. I wanted to find the report on your first walk.' She flicked the indicator, traversed three lanes of traffic coming up behind and veered into Whitehall. 'Don't know why I came this way,' she said. 'On the same page in *The Guardian* and the *Telegraph* . . . page before in the *Telegraph* . . . I found something much more interesting. Here . . .' She picked up the exercise book from the passenger seat and tossed it into the back. 'Have a look. See what you did. What you've been running from.'

Gargan opened the book. Photocopies of newspaper cuttings were pasted on to the first few pages. Thereafter the pages were blank. He flipped back to the front and tried to read.

The speedometer needle danced between fifty and fifty-five as the little car bounced over Westminster Bridge. He looked down again. There was a brief paragraph telling of his walk in the City and giving details of the small accident which followed. The tightrope walker was not named because he had fled before the police arrived on the scene. Su took the roundabout at forty-five and twisted the car into Lambeth Palace Road, throwing him across the seat. Beneath the small paragraph was an article about a man who was accused of killing his wealthy wife and who walked out of court when the evidence against him collapsed under scrutiny. There was a grainy photograph of the acquitted man. He looked like a younger version of the man in Su's framed photograph. But as he looked closer he felt more uncomfortable. He felt something like a hood tightening over his head.

Despite the Mini's grip, the nearside tyres left the road as Su swung into Vauxhall Grove. She slotted the car into an impossible gap behind the Reliant, nudging it lightly as she straightened up.

He wished he'd never met this woman.

Since he'd started walking the wire, though, with her following him everywhere like his conscience, it was inevitable they should meet.

On the next page was a feature about the murdered woman. Her name was Alexia Pryce, heiress to a considerable fortune. A large part of her fortune went to her alleged killer, later acquitted and for a short time hospitalized.

The drawstring on the hood was pulled tighter.

Alexia Pryce – Alex – was the name of the receptionist at the restaurant where he used to work.

Gargan buckled as the driver's seat on which he was resting his forehead was jerked forward. Su dragged him out of the car. He looked up at the house he considered his own. Lights burned in the windows, red, yellow and blue.

Su unlocked the front door and he stumbled into the hall. Several different records and tapes were playing in different parts of the house. Standing in the hallway he distinguished nothing from the discord. The chair he had seen earlier through the letter box had been moved from the bottom of the stairs. To the top. Where someone was sitting on it. He focused immediately on one of the chair's legs which should have been resting on the top step but was not. He saw what was going to happen and rushed forward instinctively, shouting, 'Watch out!' But the bundle of man and chair overbalanced and toppled forward. Su pulled Gargan back as the man on the chair came tumbling downstairs. A chair leg lodged between two banister rails and the man's head bounced off the unpapered wall. Gargan was sure the face was grinning. The man somersaulted the remaining stairs and the chair landed on its side on the floor. The man sprawled and began laughing before he got his breath back, spluttering.

Gargan saw now why the man had not used his arms to protect himself. His wrists were tied behind his back with piano wire. Reflex reactions had already drawn a thin red bracelet around each wrist. Gargan turned to Su.

'He does it all the time,' she explained.

Gargan didn't know what to do. He wanted to sit down and read the newspaper cuttings and he wanted to look round the house and see what was going on. The cacophony swelled in his eardrums like a bruise. Who was this man who was now laughing uncontrollably as he worked his wrists around within his wire restraints? Gargan watched in appalled confusion as blood spotted the floorboards. His own head had begun to ache.

As Su pulled him upstairs Gargan looked back at the man in the hall. What frightened him most was that he could see wary intelligence in the man's eyes.

Up on the first landing the situation became clearer and the conditions more oppressive. In each of the rooms which opened off the landing there seemed to be a different party going on. Gargan feared, the music now inside his head and pounding to get out, that the guests would turn out to be all of a certain type. He edged towards the room that had been his bedroom.

People were sitting around the edge of the room drinking. A man and two women sat on Gargan's bed. They were naked. The man was threading a needle through one of the women's nipples. She watched his fingers at work as she brushed her own over the stubble in her groin. The other woman toyed with a brass padlock which pulled tight the man's foreskin over his glans. Round her neck a key dangled on a chain.

Several people were smoking cigarettes. He wanted to tell them he didn't really like people smoking in his bedroom.

In the far corner he caught sight of the tattooed woman he'd seen in Bethnal Green. The music throbbed and ground like machinery. The woman's eyes glittered in his direction. He panicked, glanced about. She was staring. She recognized him. He sidestepped to the door. Not everyone had noticed him; the music was too loud. She was getting up, leaning on another woman's shoulder. Not a woman. The hermaphrodite turned and rose in a single motion. The hermaphrodite and the tattooed woman obviously commanded a degree of respect from the rest of the room's occupants. Even the record player was turned down. Now they began to cross the room. Others turned and watched. Some began to get up. Gargan ran.

Standing on the landing with his back to the door he caught his breath.

It was strangely quiet on the landing. They must have decided not to pursue him. He felt a presence in the vicinity.

There was someone standing at the top of the next flight of stairs watching him.

Without turning his head Gargan could only half see a dark form and behind it a closed door, the door to the top room. He could no longer hear any noise from the rooms on this and the floor below. His awareness of the other person was total and exclusive. There seemed to be some kind of channel between them and a mutual assumption of inevitability.

In the instant before the door across from him opened to reveal Su, Gargan glanced up the stairs and saw clearly the young Aborigine who was standing there.

The rai smiled and his face broke into a light clatter of laughter. Gargan recognized the face from his dreams and the hypnosis. JB had been right. But now he felt no fear.

Gargan looked at Su, then back at the rai. But he'd gone. The door behind him had not opened: the young man had simply vanished.

Behind Su stood a number of people of familiar appearance. Some of them he'd seen before in Bethnal Green. He recognized the man with the rings chain-linked through foreskin and nipples, and the pensioner with the shaved head and antichrist earring. He'd already encountered the tattooed woman and the hermaphrodite. Joining the back of Su's little group he saw the nose-ring and ponytail of Radcliffe.

Somehow she'd found them and offered them a better venue than they'd had in Bethnal Green. Maybe she'd invited them to move in. Gargan dimly remembered mentioning Bethnal Green during their talk in Vienna. She must have found his copy of *Loot* with the piercers' ad underlined when she'd helped herself to his address book.

They moved in closer forming a loose ring around Gargan. What did they want? They'd got his house.

Su had worked her way to the outer edge of the group.

Subtly they moved as one back towards the room they and Su had come from. Gargan had no choice but to go with them.

By now there were as many as ten or fifteen people around him. They pressed closer. Their sweat filled his nostrils. Their mutilations were such as he had already seen but none the less shocking for that: previous exposure and personal experience had not numbed him. There were some things he hadn't seen, like the man with the artificial second urethra pierced on the upper side of the stem of his penis; and the eunuch, who to a large degree stood separate from the other men, carrying his preserved genitals in a pickling jar like any ambitious young palace servant in Imperial China.

The group tightened around him like a tourniquet. Individuals began to touch him, fingers trailing over his clothes. He craned his neck and could just make out Su at the edge of the room. She shrugged and curled her lip down at the corners of her mouth.

He offered only token resistance when they undressed him. There seemed little point in opposing so many of them, unpredictable as their behaviour was. They moved closer to the centre of the room. If they were not careful they would trip over his practice wire if it was still there.

A man with two scars on his chest where his nipples had once been came right up to Gargan, bent down and unbuckled his belt. He removed Gargan's trousers and pants.

With great regret Gargan watched his penis become erect. They all looked at it, admiring the neat divide between the two halves. It shocked him to see it cut so far down – almost to the root. The bisection was clean; the interfaces had healed up without any unpleasant contusions. They touched it. He was unable to prevent its jerky reaction. They pulled the twin heads away from each other. His brain seemed to dissolve into gas. They tugged. He stumbled over something – his wire. Powerless, he submitted as they gently pressed his body down on to the wire, a foot and a half off the ground. They guided him down. He straddled the wire, his back towards the floor, one leg and one arm on each side, in the crab position. He tried to hold his head up to see what would happen. They seemed very tall and straight now like trees. The wire bisected his body. The last vestige of a defunct reality held the right half of his penis closer to the wire than the left by maybe an inch. The gaseous hemispheres of his brain strained at the vascular membranes which held them together. His eyes tensed to resist the pressure from within which threatened to squeeze them out of their orbits.

Something was being pushed through the crowd to the front. Its tiny wheels squealed and the weight above them produced a drumming on the boards. It was a trolley carrying a selection of surgical instruments and a small autoclave for sterilizing them.

Two women bent over him. He shuddered helplessly in expectation. The women – both tattooed all over – wielded stainless steel piercing guns. He felt a sharp prick in both sides but no initial pain. Only dimly was he aware of figures rushing around him and pads being clamped to the parts pierced. After some time the pressure was removed and something inserted. He managed to lift his head far enough to see blood still trickling from the holes where two rings were now in place. The women were dabbing at splashes of blood with pads soaked in a tawny solution which came from a bottle on the trolley's lower level. He let his head fall back again. More tinkering went on; it felt as if something was being attached to the rings, and then two steady forces were applied, pulling away from each other on both sides. The back of his head rested on the wire. He tried not to think about the pain in his arms and legs because he knew he had to hold the position. Time passed; some people went away. The wire cut into the back of his scalp like a razor. The light which hung under the ceiling dimmed and its influence shrank from the corners to occupy just a small area above his head, until this too disappeared.

He barely registered the door opening and an ochreous stain of light falling across his face. Someone had come in. The wire felt as if it had become part of him; he could almost hear skin tearing as he raised his head. Su was releasing one of the two chains, which by attachment to the inserted rings were slowly pulling him further apart as he sank further down. His muscles had atrophied: she had to lift him up bodily and he needed her support to remain on his feet.

Apart from the two of them the room appeared to be empty. The chains that had held him were attached to hooks screwed into the walls. Blood stained the floorboards. His tightrope practice room had been converted into a ceremonial initiation site.

Su led him out of the room. Tired and unhappy, he didn't protest. Somewhere down below a guitar was being tormented. She took him to the staircase. Opening the door at the top, she went in, leaving him on the threshold peering into the darkness.

He didn't know how long he stood there but eventually the

light from the hall below and from the gaps in the weave of the skylight curtain penetrated far enough roughly to outline the contents of the room.

Su was standing next to what appeared to be a cot. Gargan noticed another, younger woman in the shadows who appeared to have been watching over the cot, like a nanny. Now that Su and Gargan were in the room she quietly left. Su bent down over the cot murmuring quietly. Only now did he hear the mewling cries above the music playing downstairs. Su continued but the whining did not relent. She reached long arms into the cot and lifted out a large, dark, unwieldy mass. Gargan watched as she hefted the shape and hitched it up into the crook of her arm, for all the world like a proud parent.

The cries continued.

Gargan took a step forward, feeling nauseous with sudden fear.

Su swung from side to side, back and again, her offspring sitting on her hip.

As she swung once more into the thick grey light shed by the curtained window, he saw clearly enough the baby's two heads, looking in different directions but unambiguously attached at the neck.

It was only when he saw his own arms stretching out to take his child that he became conscious once more of the gassy lightness in his head.

Over

I slept badly last night. Very badly.

I never sleepwalk. But the fact that last night I did is an indication of how badly I slept.

The dreams were disturbing enough, but positively comforting compared to what happened next.

In my sleep I left my bed in the grimiest corner of Vauxhall and walked east, presumably along the main drag through Camberwell and Peckham. I ended up in Nunhead face down in an upturned grave. There was soil in my mouth, particles of grit between my teeth and under my eyelids. The roads had cut my feet quite badly.

Upon waking I recoiled, digging my feet in even further. There was a gravestone at the head of my bed bearing the name Alexia Pryce. I shivered and began to tremble: it was cold anyway and I had gone to bed as always undressed. By some stroke of misfortune I had not been stopped by the police on the way to Nunhead.

I was frightened. Why was Alex's grave partially dug over and who had pushed me into it? Or had I tripped over the debris in the path and fallen in?

It wasn't until later that I noticed my fingers, how they were ingrained with dirt; wedges of earth under my nails.

I struggled to my feet, thankful at least that Alex's coffin had not broken the surface. Placing my feet as carefully as the trembling would allow I set off in one of the two directions offered by the gravel path. From the thin light I guessed it was still very early in the morning: safe enough to walk naked around a cemetery. As if it mattered.

The path went on past grave after grave, most of them overgrown, their inscriptions almost illegible. I had the impression the path was curving very gently to the left, but when I looked behind all I could see was a dewy curtain of mist drawn across the track. I just kept walking. Although the sun was presumably getting higher I had not yet seen it and the mist seemed to be thickening. It wrapped itself around my naked body like a moist blanket and made everything eerily quiet.

I walked and walked and reached no intersection. The mist closed me in; I was afraid I might never get out. It seemed to fall in step behind me. I glanced over my shoulder. What was the black shadow I glimpsed? A tree or an optical trick? It didn't feel like either. It felt as if I was being followed again.

The path merged with another and I became convinced all I was doing was describing a large circle. Maybe I was on a spiral which would deliver me to the streets which surely still existed somewhere beyond the mists. I had no idea of distance covered or time passed. The shadow remained at my back. The high gravestones lining the path imprisoned me like walls. Maybe I was spiralling inwards and would have all this ground to recover. I was still conscious of being followed. Suddenly there was a gap in the wall on my right like a window. When I looked closer I saw it was another upturned grave. Of course, I knew it was the same one. *Who was behind me?* I was back where I'd started. I became aware of the soil crumbling away beneath my toes. *He was pushing me in.* I wheeled round, grabbed his arm and twisted it. What I could see of his face through the mist and beneath his beard was contorted with pain.

I felt a certain confederacy with this man. Here we both were in a remote cemetery at dawn. He'd followed me back to the grave which presumably he had desecrated. Now was trying to push me in again, to complete the transfer of his guilt to me.

I didn't want his guilt. I never had. But he didn't want mine either.

He tried to free his arm and kick my feet from under me at the same time. I doubled the twist on his forearm. He struggled but I had him. I bent a little at the knee, gained the leverage required and flicked his wrist. He toppled over in front of me and I bundled him easily into the grave. Although it had not been my intention, he struck his head on the stone and lay still.

My hands were shaking in shock. The fighting over, I felt the cold again, my whole body trembling.

I had some difficulty undressing him, but it was the only way I was going to get warm and stay warm. I took everything with the exception of his pants, leaving them not because I disliked the idea of wearing them, but in order to allow him a little dignity. Alive or dead, guilty or not guilty, he deserved at least that. For some time I sat with him, but he did not stir, so I started to push the dirt in on top of him. As I worked I had a strong feeling I was burying more than just this poor stranger.

Once more I tackled the curving path. I soon warmed up; the clothes felt comfortable on me, a perfect fit. I pushed my hands into the jacket pockets and found only a business card for a restaurant in the West End. At the point where my path merged with another I took the other. The mist had lifted somewhat; a milky light hung over the headstones and monuments. The path seemed to go nowhere but I had to keep walking. The place would normally have depressed me: so many people but all of them dead and mostly forgotten, so overgrown were the graves, so fertile the earth.

I came to a small circular area, a conjunction of paths. I chose the path which sloped very slightly downhill. Before long I was approaching the exit gates. Two Rottweilers snarled at me from behind the fence of their enclosure. I turned right out of the gates and walked until I found a taxi. The driver gave me a quizzical look. I straightened my hair and showed him the business card before climbing in. He watched me cautiously in his rearview mirror. It didn't matter what he thought. Eventually he pulled away from the kerb.

We drove through several different areas, all of which looked the same. The roads were busy and there was no trace here of the mist. Leaning my head back I closed my eyes and didn't open them again until the taxi's brakes jolted me awake.

'Where are we?' I asked, dazed from sleep.

'It's just down there,' the driver said. 'I can't turn in.'

I paid him with money from one of the trouser pockets. Without waiting for change I walked into the crowds. It was not warm but I was hot. Tourists went this way and that in droves.

Office girls and computer salesmen jostled for sandwich lunches. Sharp winter sunlight glinted off a mirrored shop sign into my eyes. Dust rose from the ground in swirls. Voices babbled in strange accents and tongues. A handbag clipped my elbow catching the humerus, making me wince and curse. I was hungry and thirsty. Buses rattled past. In Haymarket I got caught up in a stream of girls trailing fly-repellent perfume. I sidestepped past a newspaper kiosk where the first headline to catch my eye read COMMUNISTS OPEN BERLIN WALL, and slipped into Panton Street. The restaurant was on the left.

The waitress looked at me strangely. Her striking eyes widened; large grey irises flecked with yellow. She asked me where I had been. I straightened my dishevelled hair again, brushed some dust off the arms of my jacket.

The restaurant was not overcrowded. Many tables were shared but I had one to myself for the time being.

I could feel the waitress watching me as I devoured my main course. She was leaning against the cappuccino counter, head turned in my direction. I was feeling better and better all the time, despite becoming slightly hot and itchy in my new clothes as a result of the waitress's attentions. I shrugged the jacket off and laid it on the bench seat next to me. I noticed a folded piece of blue paper sticking out of the inside pocket. Drawing the paper out and unfolding it I set eyes on familiar handwriting. It was laid out in verse.

> Quiet, safe, out of sight
> a place to hide day and night
> serene, secure but never quite
> The time goes on without –
> within
> it's so difficult to begin
> to live outside on skin and bone
> no way to live – except alone.

I felt a stab of tenderness and regret. Even without the handwriting I would have known it was hers. It hurt in the way that Jenni's verse always hurt.

In that moment I wanted desperately to be with her. If only the time didn't go on, without and within.

But in fact there could be nothing worse than being here and there at the same time, loving and not loving at the same time. The desire to know something better or just different is an insoluble part of my condition, the part that drives me on to the next day. The torment and frustration are inevitable and the result of removing them would be no less destructive than if I were to tear the protective membranes from between the twin hemispheres of my brain.

Better not to wish to be there but to remember.

The illusion of duplication conjured in Berlin is dissolving into nothing and losing any truth or relevance I may once have imagined it had. *no way to live – except alone.*

The waitress comes to remove my plate. She looks at me closely. It was lovely, I tell her, but I let it go cold. She smiles and laughs. I can't help looking into her eyes.

She smiles again and asks me a question.

'Something else for you?'

READ MORE IN PENGUIN

PENGUIN AUDIOBOOKS

Virtual Light by William Gibson, read by Peter Weller
Having It All by Maeve Haran, read by Belinda Lang
Scenes from the Sex War by Maeve Haran, read by Belinda Lang
Thunderpoint by Jack Higgins, read by Roger Moore
The Iliad by Homer, read by Derek Jacobi
More Please by Barry Humphries, read by the author
Four Past Midnight: The Sun Dog by Stephen King, read by Tim Sample
Nightmares and Dreamscapes by Stephen King, read by Whoopi Goldberg, Rob Lowe, Stephen King et al
Two Past Midnight: Secret Window, Secret Garden by Stephen King, read by James Woods
Shadow over Babylon by David Mason, read by Bob Peck
Hotel Pastis by Peter Mayle, read by Tim Pigott-Smith
Waiting to Exhale by Terry McMillan, read by the author
Murderers and Other Friends by John Mortimer, read by the author
Under the Hammer by John Mortimer, read by Tim Pigott-Smith
Bitter Medicine by Sara Paretsky, read by Christine Lahti
Guardian Angel by Sara Paretsky, read by Jane Kaczmarek
History: The Home Movie by Craig Raine, read by the author
First Offence by Nancy Taylor Rosenberg, read by Lindsay Crouse
Frankenstein by Mary Shelley, read by Richard Pasco
I Shudder at Your Touch by Michele Slung, read by Stephen King et al
The Devil's Juggler by Murray Smith, read by Kenneth Cranham
Kidnapped by Robert Louis Stevenson, read by Robbie Coltrane
The Secret History by Donna Tartt, read by Robert Sean Leonard
Bad Girls, Good Women by Rosie Thomas, read by Jenny Agutter
Asta's Book by Barbara Vine, read by Jane Lapotaire
A Dark-Adapted Eye by Barbara Vine, read by Sophie Ward
No Night is Too Long by Barbara Vine, read by Alan Cumming

READ MORE IN PENGUIN

A CHOICE OF FICTION

The Lying Days Nadine Gordimer

Raised in the conservative mining town of Atherton, South Africa, Helen Shaw, seventeen, longs to escape from the sterile environment that has shaped her parents' rigid attitudes and threatens to corrode her own fragile values. At last, finding the courage and maturity to stand alone, she leaves behind the 'lying days' of her youth.

The Eye in the Door Pat Barker

'Barker weaves fact and fiction to spellbinding effect, conjuring up the vastness of the First World War through its chilling impact on the minds of the men who endured it . . . a startlingly original work of fiction . . . it extends the boundaries not only of the anti-war novel, but of fiction generally' – *Sunday Telegraph*

Strange Pilgrims Gabriel García Márquez

The twelve stories in this collection by the Nobel prizewinner chronicle the surreal, haunting 'journeys' of Latin Americans in Europe. 'Márquez's genius is for the physical. Characters urinate, devour songbird stew; old people remember their youthful lovemaking . . . It is this spirit of generous desire that fills his work' – *The Times*

Millroy the Magician Paul Theroux

A magician of baffling talents, a vegetarian and a health fanatic with a mission to change the food habits of America, Millroy has the power to heal, and to hypnotize. 'Fresh and unexpected . . . this very accomplished, confident book is among his best' – *Guardian*

The House of Doctor Dee Peter Ackroyd

When Matthew Palmer inherits an old house in Clerkenwell he feels himself to have become a part of its past. Compelled to probe its mysteries, he discovers to his horror and curiosity that the previous owner was a practitioner of black magic. 'A good old-fashioned spine-chiller of a ghost story . . . which will also be taken as a serious modern novel' – *The Times*

READ MORE IN PENGUIN

A CHOICE OF FICTION

A Border Station Shane Connaughton

The story of a young boy's growth to maturity; the love-hate relationship with his father, a frustrated Garda sergeant in the virtually crime-free village of Butlershill, and the adoration of his tender, doting mother are the focuses of his daily life, highlighted in a series of poignant – at times terrifying – but always acutely absorbing discoveries.

A Home at the End of the World Michael Cunningham

'A superb and major novel, ambitious in its scope, its historical largeness, and at the same time intensely, almost painfully intimate. The story of Jonathan, Clare, Bobby and Alice is also the story of the seventies and eighties in America' – David Leavitt

I am the Clay Chaim Potok

'Excellent . . . Potok is a poet and a visionary who writes with breath-taking ease about the limits of human experience, of death, of the superstitious and spirit worlds of the peasants and of courage born from suffering'– *The Times*

Something to Remember Me By Saul Bellow

Dedicated to Bellow's children and grandchildren, *Something to Remember Me By* tells the wonderfully tender and funny story of a young man's sexual initiation and sexual guilt, one bleak Chicago winter's day in 1933. That story, narrated like a memoir, is collected here with Bellow's acclaimed novellas, *The Bellarosa Connection* and *A Theft*.

The Cockatoos Patrick White

'To read Patrick White . . . is to touch a source of power, to move through areas made new and fresh, to see men and women with a sharpened gaze' – *Daily Telegraph*. These six short novels and stories achieve the majesty and passion of Patrick White's great novels, probing beneath the surface of events to explore the mysteries of human nature.